I0535840

THE UNIQUE MAGAZINE
Fall 1991

ISSN 0898-5073
Cover by Bob Eggleton

Weird Tales® is published 4 times a year by Terminus Publishing Co., Inc., PO Box 13418, Philadelphia PA 19101-3418 (4426 Larchwood Ave., Philadelphia PA 19101-3916). 2nd Class Postage paid at Philadelphia PA & additional mailing offices. Single copies, $4.95. Subscriptions: 4 issues (one year) $16.00 in U.S.A. & possessions; $20.00 in Canada & Mexico, $22.00 elsewhere, in U.S. funds. Publisher is not responsible for loss of manuscripts, although publisher will take reasonable care of them. Postmaster: send address changes to *Weird Tales®*, PO Box 13418, Philadelphia PA 19101-3418. Copyright © 1991 by Terminus Publishing Co., Inc.; all rights reserved; reproduction prohibited without prior permission. Typeset, printed, & bound in the United States of America.
Weird Tales® is a registered trademark owned by Weird Tales, Limited.

THE EYRIE

We begin this issue with our humble apologies to artist Bob Eggleton. We previously announced that he was to illustrate this issue in its entirety. As you can see, other artists' work appears in this issue as well as his. The cover is a reprint, from a Dark Harvest edition of a Ray Garton novel, which went out of print so fast that many of you may not have seen the fine painting Bob did for the dustjacket.

But the issue has the look of last-minute improvisation. We breathed a sigh of relief at how it turned out, but we must explain that there was *indeed* a mishap, and it was not in any way Bob Eggleton's fault. *He* is completely reliable. We editors, sometimes, are not.

This is what happened: through an oversight, we gave Bob a deadline which was two months *later* than when this issue had to go to press. At times like these, we editors get grayer under the tentacles:

"Er, Bob," we found ourself saying, "there's been bit of a slip-up. You know that artwork we said we needed from you in July?"

"Yes?"

"Well, we need it in *May*."

There was no screaming at this point, at least not from Bob's end of the line.

Many book publishers, he graciously explained, move a book up several months and spring this sort of surprise on the artist without so much as a "Sorry about that." But an artist as good and as popular Bob Eggleton is in constant demand and his working time is tightly scheduled. He wasn't able to drop everything, rush out a cover painting and illustrations for every story in this issue, and still produce work up to his usual high standards.

For a minute, we thought about flipping the contents of issues 302 and 303, but only for a minute; that issue is intentionally a multi-artist issue, and if it's hard enough to get one artist to move his deadline up two or three months, imagine trying to do that with *several*.

So, a compromise was worked out, and this issue is the result. By way of further apologies, we're going to let Bob Eggleton have a whole issue to himself in the future, probably the F. Paul Wilson issue, number 305.

And, as long as we have our sackcloth and ashes on, let us also apologize to Bob Walters, whose name, most conspicuously, did not appear on the cover of issue #301, which he illustrated so handsomely.

We've been crediting featured artists on the cover since issue #293 and intend to do so in the future. We can only express regrets at the omission.

While we're on the subject, a few words about artwork. There was a time when all fiction, in books and magazines alike, was illustrated. But the practice has diminished, all but vanished in novels for adults, and become relatively rare in magazines, outside of the science-fiction and fantasy field.

We like illustrations. They enhance the reading experience. They make the overall package more attractive. For *Weird Tales*®, we hit on the not-quite-original idea of entire issues, each illustrated by a single artist. For the chosen artist, it is a chance to present a showcase of his or her work, which allows a wider range of styles and techniques than might otherwise be possible. We're convinced that for such an opportunity, many famous artists would be willing to make their special issues very special indeed. Yet we thought a multi-artist issue could be no less good; issue 298 pleased us highly, and we decided to do it again with issue 303. And we're doing it with this issue, though not by design: you know, the best laid plans of mice and men . . .

We occasionally receive inquiries from artists. How does one get to illustrate for *Weird Tales*®? Obviously, if three issues out of four are illustrated by a single, usually quite famous artist, *Weird Tales*® is not a large market for new artists. But we can use one or two new artists in the multi-artist issues. That's something. We point to Jason Van Hollander as, essentially, a *Weird Tales*® discovery. He had done a small amount of work for Arkham House, but had been inactive for several years before he turned up in Darrell Schweitzer's writing class. We're also happy to bring Denis Tiani in front of the public eye again. He was one of our favorites from the small-press and lim-

Publisher:
George H. Scithers

Editor:
Darrell Schweitzer

Managing Editor:
Carol Adams

Assistant Editors:
Leslie Smith, Dainis Bisenieks, Diane Weinstein, Michael W. Betancourt, & Don Keller

Circulation Manager:
Richard Kabakjian

Computer Consultant:
David J. Williams III

Of Counsel:
Yale F. Edeiken

Typesetter:
Campus Copy Center

Printer & Soft-Cover Binder:
Malloy Lithographing, Inc.

Hard-Cover Binder
Hoster Bindery, Inc.

Mailing:
Unit Packaging Corporation

Manuscript Submissions:

Yes; we read unsolicited submissions — **if** they are in standard manuscript format. Editors survive only by insisting on a few Rules: each submission must include a return envelope with your address and enough postage to bring the manuscript back to you. If it's cheaper to have us discard the manuscript if not bought, tell us so, but include a business-letter-size envelope with your address and postage so we may send you our comments. Affix postage to envelope; don't send loose stamps.

Proper manuscript format is discussed in many reference works. Some of us have even written one: *On Writing Science Fiction: the Editors Strike Back!* by Scithers, Schweitzer, & Ford; $19.50 in hardcovers, from Owlswick Press, P.O. Box 8243, Philadelphia PA 19101-8243. Another excellent work from the same publisher is Barry B. Longyear's *Science-Fiction Writer's Workshop*: $9.50 in trade paperback. These prices include shipping and handling; in Pennsylvania, please include 6% sales tax.

We cannot be responsible for manuscripts in transit or in our hands; you **must** keep a copy of every manuscript you send out, and you **must** put your name and address on the first page of every manuscript. Please: no padded envelopes, folders, or binders; and no registered or certified mail.

ited-edition book scene in the early '70s, particularly for his work in Harry Morris's excellent *Nyctalops*. Then he popped out of the woodwork after some years' absence. We published him in issue 298, and will do so in 303. (*Nyctalops*, incidentally, has also popped out of the woodwork for one last issue, after eight years. It's a wonderful Lovecraftian/surrealist/horror publication, notable for showcasing Tiani and discovering J.K. Potter and the forthcoming *Weird Tales*® feature author Thomas Ligotti. Send $10.00 to Harry O. Morris, Jr. 502 Elm St. S.E., Albuquerque NM 87102 for the final issue.)

New artists should send us portfolios of black-and-white and color work (slides will do, but we prefer color prints) which are either disposable or accompanied by adequate return postage and packing. We'll look. If you're the next Hannes Bok or Virgil Finlay, we want to know about it.

What are we looking for? Imagination. Technical excellence. Something we haven't seen before. Illustration, 99% of the time, is *representational,* but not necessarily realistic. Nevertheless, realistic art, like rhymed poetry, must *succeed* if the attempt is made at all. If you're trying to do realistic human figures, you need to know proportions, and where the muscles go. Do your research. A story set in Byzantium of the 12th century can't have the characters in Periclean costumes. However, we hasten to add, the Howard Pyle / N.C. Wyeth school of illustration is only *one* possibility. We also think of Sidney Sime, Harry Clarke, Salvador Dali, Leo and Diane Dillon, and Richard Powers, all of whom must be accounted superb illustrators, none of whom are strictly "realistic."

One quick announcement: we regret that John Betancourt will no longer be reviewing for *Weird Tales*®. He will be replaced by alternating columns written by Alan Rodgers and Gahan Wilson. John still reviews for *Amazing Stories,* so fans of his criticism need not lose heart. Fans of his fiction (and there seem to be many, since his "Tap Dancing" in issue 300 did respectably on the reader voting and is doing quite well on preliminary Nebula-award recommendations) will be glad to know we have another Betancourt story in inventory. But otherwise, John, who was one of our founders, is no longer affiliated with this magazine because of the press of his other commitments.

Reader **Andrea B.M. Wood** digs up the undead:

. . . on vampire stories, I am enormously pleased to see an endorsement of folklore over Hollywood. Vampires are a good example because there are literally dozens of different kinds, each worthy, perhaps, of dozens of stories. The "Dracula-variety" is, quite obviously, attractive to writers and readers alike, but if a writer remembers the folklore definition of a vampire as a re-animated corpse, not merely an urbane gentleman with unusual dietary habits, whole new vistas of horror are opened.

Indeed, this has been something of a sore point with us — conjuring up images of fangs in the neck and stakes through the heart. We'd like to drive a stake through the next few trite rehashes of the "standard Hollywood vampire." There are lots of good books on vampire folklore. Two that we recommend are *The Vampire: His Kith and Kin* and *The Vampire in Europe,* both by Montague Summers.

Speaking of stakes, some centuries ago **Greg Koster** might well have found himself in uncomfortable proximity to a somewhat larger pointed stick:

I know it is heretical to say so, but I think the Lovecraft veneration, in general, has gone far enough. Granted that HPL is a seminal author, it doesn't say much for the field if he is the only one we can point to as seminal. You yourselves are saying something similar when you ask for fresh tales, not elaborations of the Cthulhu Mythos, but something that is as innovative today as the Mythos was in Lovecraft's time.

Having gone this far, and being doomed anyway, let me continue by saying that for all Lovecraft's merits, he has always inspired doubts in me. For example, every time I read "The Whisperer in Darkness," I have two simultaneous reactions: a) The narrator is acting idiotically, and the reason he is doing so is because if he acted sensibly, there wouldn't be any story. And, b) Idiotic actions or not, this sure is interesting.

This is surely an unusual reaction. I can't explain it. I do know that when I read, say, William Hope Hodgson's novels, I have the second reaction, without also having the first. To my way of thinking, this makes Hodgson a better writer. And to say that Lovecraft was "ultimately wise," as the toast given to him at NECon X does, seems grossly excessive. Why this urge to blow HPL up to ten times live size? That will only invite a reaction of "Oh yeah?"

As we see it, the problem with Lovecraft's characters is that, quite realistically, they don't know they're living in a fantasy story. They must first exhaust every logical, non-supernatural explanation for what is going on, even though we, the readers, know perfectly well that There Really Are Such Things. Ye Editor, Darrell Schweitzer, addressed this point in "Character Gullibility in Weird Fiction, or, Isn't Yuggoth Somewhere in Upstate New York?" in *Discovering H.P. Lovecraft* (Starmont House, 1987).

As for Lovecraft's wisdom, you're not in a position to decide until you've really gotten to know him, not just through his fiction, but through his voluminous letters (which constitute the bulk of his total output) and his essays. Are there other seminal writers? Sure: Poe, Dunsany, Bradbury, Richard Matheson, Stephen King. But maybe the importance of Lovecraft is surely demonstrated by the fact that as far back as fifty years ago, people were having this same argument. It hasn't stopped. In another fifty years it won't either.

John Bracy pokes his finger into an already open can of worms:

I couldn't help but notice that The Eyrie has recently been infiltrated by readers who contend that profanity is some sort of exercise in offensive redundancy. Hmm . . . It seems to me that this so-called "smut" is an ingredient of language — or at least a condition of the human internal dialogue — and I myself like the idea of realistic weird fiction. Profanity must serve some gut-level purpose. It wouldn't endure if it didn't. Consider life on the battlefield. I'm sure that troops experiment with all sorts of verbal metaphors regarding conditions in general. I suppose there might be one super-human individual among them

Special Edition Chapbooks

FOOTSTEPS PRESS

Raising Goosebumps for Fun & Profit by T.E.D. Klein, signed & numbered, $13.95
Slow by Ramsey Campbell, introduction by T.E.D. Klein, $6.00
The Dragon by Ray Bradbury, signed & numbered, $20.00
Pelts by F. Paul Wilson, signed & numbered, $15.00
Through Channels by Richard Matheson, signed & numbered, $15.00
. . . mention *Weird Tales*® & get $1.00 off the cover price . . .

send all orders to: **Footsteps Press Bill Munster, Publisher Post Office Box 75 Roundtop NY 12473**

P.O. Box 322, Circleville NY 10909
(914) 361-1190
MONTHLY CATALOGS ISSUED: Science fiction/
Fantasy/Horror/Detective fiction. Many new re-
leases, including hard-to-find imports, plus large
out-of-print stock. $1 brings 3 sample issues.
Nicolas J. Certo, Box 322-W, Circleville, NY 10919

Fantasy, Horror, & Science Fiction Books
for sale. Send $1.00 for a sample catalog
listing hundreds of titles (first editions,
signed limited editions, etc.)

Other Worlds Bookstore, 1281 North
Main Street, Providence RI 02904

I've been selling reasonably priced
science fiction, fantasy, horror, and
mystery paperbacks, hardcovers,
and magazines since 1967. With over
125,000 items in stock, I am bound to
have something you're looking for. I
issue ten huge catalogs each year.
Write for your free sample.

PANDORA'S BOOKS
BOX WT–54
NECHE, ND 58265

who's in complete control. A tank-driver,
maybe. Imagine that: The rockets are
whizzing past overhead as this guy yells
back to his gunner, "Please, no unwhole-
some talk. After all, you don't see it in
Weird Tales® — now go ahead and blast
anything that moves . . ."

We somehow don't think the gunner
will reply, "Gosh-darn it! We'll kill the
no-good nasty people!"

Henry Wessells comments on issue
#299:

*I am moved moved to write a somewhat
belated letter of congratulations for the
first unreservedly excellent issue of Weird
Tales® that I have seen. The quality of the
fiction in issue #299 was for the first time
worth all the fuss; the Jonathan Carroll*

*pieces, and the superb story by Ian Wat-
son, "Stalin's Teardrops," repaid and
continues to repay the pages of less note-
worthy fiction I have waded through in
previous numbers. I cannot praise Ian
Watson's skill enough: the space he cre-
ates and distorts in that short piece is
surely unique. To move from a decaying
bureaucratic order into the strangely pris-
tine world is no simple accomplishment.*

*Okay, enough for simple praise. I think
that there is a noticeable difference in the
"energy of attention" present in writings
by Watson, Carroll, and Sheckley, and in
works by other writers you publish. I don't
think my objection is based on subject or
stylistic concerns. I am all too happy to
read anything, no matter how grisly, if in
the gaps between the words where real
meaning emerges, I can sense the integ-
rity and intellect at work. Take the work
of Patrick McGrath, for example: his
portraits of depraved and monstrous in-
dividuals are always rendered with a
moral capacity far greater than any of the
characters themselves possess (quite a
trick for first-person narrative to reveal
that strength). I think Harlan Ellison
also has this quality at times.*

Robert Bloch responds to issue 300:

*To say that I'm delighted is an under-
statement. I read it with the eyes of a
teen-age boy, incredulous to find that,
after a lifetime's years, I'm a part of the
magazine's history.*

*Believe me, I appreciate all the time
and effort. You did wonders!*

The Most Popular Story: Voting
was a bit stronger this time, which is
appreciated. The winner for issue 300 is
"Wager of Dreams" by Michael Rutherford, closely followed by "Rumors of
Greatness" by Nina Kiriki Hoffman.
Third place is a tie between Robert
Bloch's "Beetles" (the story, not the
screenplay) and "Turn, Turn, Turn," by
the perennial favorite, Nancy Springer.

Ω

DARK BEDFELLOWS:
The Horrors in My Life

by William F. Nolan
art by William F. Nolan

Early June, 1943. Kansas City, Missouri. A lazy summer afternoon, hot and muggy. I'm fifteen, and school is out until fall (a million years away!). The day is wide open: I can ride my bicycle (The Green Bullet) down to Gillham Plaza and go roller skating, or walk up to the ice cream shop on Troost for a strawberry malted, or stop by Rae's Drugstore for the latest superhero comic (I had a great collection of *Batman*), or take in a movie at the Apollo. . . .

Or I can head for a bookshop.

I do that. I walk into Cramer's to check out what's new. I love to read. I've got enough change in my pocket to buy a Tower book. They cost just fifty cents. Published in hardcover. The country's at war, so they use cheap paper; it quickly yellows at the edges like old parchment.

A title jumps out at me: *Tales of Terror.* Boris Karloff is scowling under dark brows from the front jacket. Which also features a shadowy hand below the title. And, by golly, Boris himself is the editor!

In those days he was my favorite actor. I had vivid memories of seeing the Karloff film, *The Man They Could Not Hang,* in 1939 at the Apollo (just a block and a half from my house) and walking home in a cold sweat, convinced that I would encounter Karloff's shambling, broken-necked figure moving inexorably toward me along the damp night sidewalk. But I figured he couldn't sneak up on me if I walked down the middle of Forest Avenue, avoiding all contact with the tree-shadowed walks. And it worked! I got home safely.

Anyway, here I am in Cramer's in 1943. I pick up *Tales of Terror* and read the subtitle: *The world's most terrifying stories presented by the outstanding living exponent of horror.*

Copyright © 1991 by William F. Nolan

Wow!

Then I look over the contents page. "The Waxwork" . . . "Clay-Shuttered Doors" . . . "The Damned Thing" . . . "The Hound" . . . "The Tell-Tale Heart" . . . "The Beast With Five Fingers" . . . "The Willows" . . .

The titles alone are enough to give any kid the shivers. This one *has* to be a winner.

I dig out my fifty cents and buy *Tales of Terror.* At home, in my "hideout" under the back porch, I hunker down and begin reading. Here's Poe and Bram Stoker and R.H. Benson and Joseph Conrad and William Faulkner and Hugh Walpole and Ambrose Bierce and Algernon Blackwood. I'd lucked out. Ole Boris had plunged me, headfirst, into the wide sea of printed horror.

In 1944 I bought a copy of *Great Tales of Terror and the Supernatural* — discovering Wilkie Collins and H.G. Wells and Conrad Aiken and John Collier and J. Sheridan Le Fanu and M.R. James and Arthur Machen and A.E. Coppard and H.P. Lovecraft . . .

Life's never been the same since.

I began reading horror as avidly as I watched it on the screen — and the first genre magazine I went for on the stands was *Weird Tales*. It was here, in 1944, that

I first encountered the wondrous work of Ray Bradbury (with "The Jar") and I was soon eagerly racing The Green Bullet to the drugstore each month for the latest issue.

By the time I graduated from Lillis High in Kansas City I'd written a half-dozen horror tales of my own (all terrible rather than terrifying) and thought of myself as an *aficionado*.

Years passed (as years tend to do) and I explored many other literary passions from Westerns to science fiction, but the spectral world of horror always hovered nearby — and I continued to savor its dark delights in films, television, books, and magazines.

As a fulltime professional writer (from 1956), I worked in many genres, including horror, but it was not until I wrote "The Party" for *Playboy* in 1967 (the year my first novel, *Logan's Run,* was published) that I felt I had made any real impact in the field. Then came "He Kilt It With a Stick" (1968) and "Coincidence" (1973). It took the writing of "Dead Call" for Kirby McCauley's *Frights* (in 1976) to make me realize just how much sheer *fun* it was to create horror on a printed page.

A bit earlier, in 1973, I had linked up with producer/director Dan Curtis (of *Dark Shadows*) to script three major horror projects for television: *The Norliss Tapes* (1973), *The Turn of the Screw* (1974), and *Trilogy of Terror* (1975). And the following year, as a team, we entered the motion picture arena to adapt Robert Marasco's classic, *Burnt Offerings.*

More recently, since I'm on the subject of scripted horror, I wrote *Terror at London Bridge* for NBC (in which I brought Jack the Ripper into the 1980s), and I have worked on several other horror projects, including an adaptation of Peter Straub's *Floating Dragon,* which have yet to reach the screen.

But, from the mid-1970s, it was

printed horror that attracted me most as a writer. I set myself a personal goal. Beginning in 1979, while continuing to write in a variety of other fields, I determined to see at least one distinctive horror tale of mine published each year.

This resulted in "Saturday's Shadow" (1979), "The Partnership" (1980), "The Train" and "The Pool" (1981), "Fair Trade" (1982), "Something Nasty" (1983), "Trust Not a Man" (1984), "Ceremony" (1985), "The Halloween Man" and "The Final Stone" (1986), "The Yard" and "My Name is Dolly" (1987), "The Cure" (1988), "Stoner" and "On 42nd St." (1989), "Gobble, Gobble!" (1990), and "Blood Sky" (1991). I was gratified to see these stories published in the prestigious *Masques, Whispers,* and *Shadows* series, and in a variety of top anthologies.

Since I was working in so many other fields my emergence as a horror writer was necessarily gradual, but I felt that I was making solid progress. Each year, more and more readers were discovering my work.

My first all-horror collection was published in 1984, *Things Beyond Midnight* (Scream/Press), but it took me several more years to tackle horror in the novel format. When I finally wrote *Helltracks* (for Avon), I'd had eight other non-horror novels published (three in the *Logan's Run* series), but no one of them had given me more personal satisfaction. In 1990 I edited my first anthology in the genre, *Urban Horrors* — and another collection of my shock-terror tales,

Nightshapes, is due from Avon. I'm also the author of *How To Write Horror Fiction,* for Writer's Digest Books.

As a professional, am I now planning to devote my full writing efforts to this genre? I've been seriously considering it. Having written science fiction and fantasy, crime-suspense and hardboilers, show business biographies and Westerns, auto racing volumes (eight of these!) and sports stories — as well as verse, book reviews, critical essays, and Mickey Mouse adventures for Walt Disney, horror remains my favorite literary bedfellow.

Demons . . . ghosts . . . vampires . . . zombies . . . ghouls . . . mummies . . . witches . . . werewolves . . .

What a grand bunch!

Ω

Want to Dress WEIRD?

The attractive *WEIRD TALES*® T-shirt features the magazine's famous logo on a red shirt. 50% cotton, 50% polyester.
Available in medium, large and extra-large.

Send $10 to:
Terminus Publishing Co. Inc., PO Box 13418, Philadelphia PA 19101-3418

BROXA
by William F. Nolan
art by Keith Minnion

Night. A victim . . .

She lay sprawled back against the cold stone, naked, her chilled flesh quivering, eyes wide, nostrils distended, her breath chopped and ragged. She pulled the fetid air into her gasping mouth, expelling it in broken, bubbling sounds.

She was an animal brought to slaughter; her young flesh would be torn and devoured — muscle, joint, tendon — chewed to raw bone, and the flowing product of her veins would slake a dark thirst.

She was alone. Trapped. Vulnerable. Beyond help, beyond hope.

Then she heard them coming for her. And screamed.

I raised my head at the sound. The gull's sharp cry had broken through my meditation. A screaming wedge of birds wheeled above me, then winged off across the darkening water.

I stood up, brushing sand from my pants. Time to head home. I shook out my blanket, began folding it.

A mild breeze was flowing inland from the Pacific, making the waves restless, and the sun, like a magician's gold coin, had vanished below the wide horizon of water. The sand still retained the heat of the day (it was August), and was warm against my bare feet as I trudged back to my parked car.

The little red CRX Honda waited for me like a faithful dog at the edge of the Coast Highway. In our totally mobile society of Southern California, cars are much more than transportation; they're a way of life.

I live off Malibu Canyon, on Las Virgenes, at road's end near the Cottontail Ranch, so it didn't take me long to drive home. The phone was ringing when I unlocked the front door. I picked it up. "Yo."

"David?" Kelly Rourke's velvet voice, tinged with annoyance.

"Who else would it be?"

"Why can't you just say hello like ordinary people?"

"I'm not ordinary people. You should know that by now."

Kelly is by way of being my girl. Nothing heavy. No engagement or wedding plans. But we seem to be drifting into a relationship that might or might not lead somewhere. Neither of us is in a hurry.

"Anything on for tonight?" she asked me.

"It's Tuesday," I said. "We're not supposed to get together till Friday."

"You didn't answer the question."

"I planned to slave over a hot word processor," I told her. "The final draft of *We're All Psychic* is a month overdue. And I was late with the last book."

"It can wait another day. I just got invited to a press preview in Westwood for *Demons By Darkness* and I need a hand to squeeze in the gross-out scenes."

I groaned. "You know how much I hate horror movies. They're stupid."

"This one's a DeMarco. He makes only one film a year, and they're all smash."

"De-who?"

"Alexander DeMarco. C'mon, even *you* —"

"The Sultan of Slice 'n' Dice. Yeah, I know. Stephen King's favorite actor."

"Precisely. And when DeMarco makes a fright flick it's big news. I'm getting an exclusive on this from the *Times*. Their regular reviewer is out with a flu bug. C'mon, David, give it a shot. Might turn out to be a classic."

"Okay, okay — but fair warning, lady. I haven't liked a horror movie since Janet Leigh took her shower in *Psycho*."

"Kincaid, you're turning into a damn curmudgeon."

She never calls me Kincaid unless she's pissed.

Demons By Darkness was no classic.

Copyright © 1991 by William F. Nolan

In fact, aside from some neat special effects and a bravura performance from DeMarco, it was mostly big budget nonsense. But I had to hand it to DeMarco; when he was on the screen you couldn't take your eyes off him. And despite a plethora of exploding vampires and dancing demons, he made the film come to life. The silly plot didn't matter. All that mattered was Alex DeMarco.

In the lobby of the Village Theater, while I waited by the door, Kelly buttonholed the film's producer, Lucas Appleton, for some quotes. I didn't pay much attention to what they were saying to each other until Appleton walked over to me. A big, florid-faced man in Bugle Boy jeans, Reeboks, and a $400 Italian silk shirt from Rodeo Drive. And I'd be willing to bet the gold chain around his thick neck probably cost three times what the shirt did. He was wearing mirrored glasses, so I couldn't see his eyes, but I had the feeling he was sizing me up.

"So you're David Kincaid," he said, without shaking hands. "Kelly here tells me you're an investigator."

"Of sorts," I said. "I work in the paranormal field. Teach, write, hold seminars, conduct consultations . . . that kind of thing. Investigation is part of it."

He handed me his card. "You'll do. Be at my office at ten tomorrow morning."

And he walked off.

I stared at the card, then at Kelly. "What the hell was *that* all about?"

"He's a very abrupt man," she said. "But he obviously wants to hire you."

"For what?"

"How should I know? Go see him and find out."

I did. Mainly out of curiosity — to discover what one of the film industry's top producers wanted from me. Maybe he had a crazed poltergeist haunting his kitchen.

Murdock Studios was in Burbank, cheek by jowl to Warners. The valley smog was taking a coffee break, so you could breathe without wearing a gas mask; it can get pretty murky in Burbank.

The gate guard looked like Sylvester Stallone. Tall and chunky. He gave me a hard look and checked my name against his clipboard. Then he smiled. "Righto, Mr. Kincaid. It's that big green building on the right, just past the water tower. Mr. Appleton's on the second floor."

"Which office?"

"It's *all* Appleton Productions," he said.

Which figured. When you swing the weight Lucas Appleton does in this town you don't get offices, you get *floors*.

"Mr. Appleton is in Projection Room C," a pert blonde at the reception desk told me. "He's expecting you."

I checked my watch. Three to ten. At least I was on time. I walked down a hall flanked with framed photos of Appleton's stars, the major talents he'd worked with through the years, and stopped in front of Alex DeMarco. He was standing at the door of a fake castle (cobwebs courtesy of the production department), a blood-stained ax in his hand, scowling at the camera, head lowered to accent his dark eyes. They were menacing and intense, reminding me of another horror great, Boris Karloff. When I was a kid at the movies, whenever old Boris leveled those piercing eyes at me, I'd cringe in the seat. DeMarco had The Look.

I continued on to Projection Room C at the far end of the hall. Easing open the door, I stepped inside. A film was being screened, but I couldn't see a damn thing in the darkness.

"Come ahead, Kincaid," a voice directed. "I'm three rows down."

I moved forward, fumbling like a blind man. As my eyes began adjusting to the reflected light from the screen I saw Lucas Appleton sitting in the exact middle of an otherwise empty row of seats. He was the only one in the room.

"Sit," he told me. No greeting. No handshake. Like Kelly had said, an abrupt man. I took the seat next to him.

"I'm running a real piece of crapola," he said, gesturing toward the screen. "All about these dickhead teenagers trapped in the basement of a collapsed office building after an earthquake. Called *Deadly Earth*. It's deadly, all right."

"Is the picture one of yours?" I asked.

"You gotta be kidding! I make *quality* stuff. You saw *Demons By Darkness*." He snorted. This piece of shit never deserved to get released."

Appleton stripped the cellophane from a long thin cigar and sighed deeply, sticking the cigar in the right corner of his mouth. "Gave up smoking," he said. "I don't light these. Just use 'em as pacifiers."

I didn't say anything to that.

"We're coming to the part of this turkey I wanted you to see. Watch for a kid in the background. Young girl. Her leg is supposed to be caught under a fallen beam . . . Ah, *there* she is — the groaning kid in the ripped blouse." He leaned over an intercom, popped a switch. "Freeze it, Sid."

The projectionist in the booth behind us locked the girl's image in place on the screen.

"What about her?"

"Take a good look. Get her fixed in your head. This was made about three years ago, so she'd be fifteen. She's eighteen by now. Name's Justina Phillips. She's not registered with the Guild or repped by an agent, so maybe this was just a one-shot for her."

I stared at the frozen image of the dark-haired teenager. "So . . . what's this got to do with me?"

Instead of replying, the producer hit the intercom switch again. "Lights, Sid."

I blinked as the overheads went on.

Appleton stood up. "Follow me," he said.

We walked out of the projection room and down another side hall to his office. It was the size of Grand Central Station. But rather starkly furnished. A giant wall poster of *Demons By Darkness* filled most of the wall behind an iceberg-white desk.

He stood by the desk, nodding toward the poster. "So . . . what do you think? I personally designed it myself. Told the artist just what to paint. Classy, eh?"

Under the film's main title, a drooling purple demon with wild red eyes was perched on the stomach of a terrified girl who'd been chained to a table. He had a glittering knife raised, ready to cut her throat. Another demon, also purple, was directly behind her, pulling her head back by the hair to bare the vulnerable white arc of her neck.

Hovering over the scene were the ghostly eyes of Alex DeMarco, his face shining from background darkness.

FIENDS! FREAKS! FLESH EATERS!
APPLETON PRODUCTIONS
PRESENTS
THE SCREEN'S REIGNING
MONARCH OF TERROR . . .
D e M A R C O !
IN A FILM OF
FURY, FEAR, AND FASCINATION

"I thought up all those 'F' words," declared Appleton. "It's called alliteration when you do that."

"Yeah, I know. I do a little writing myself."

"So what you think?"

"Very . . . classy," I said, knowing that was what he wanted to hear.

Appleton settled into a tall scoop-backed cream-colored leather chair behind the desk, shifting the cigar to the left side of his mouth. "So you want to know what *you* have to do with Justina Phillips?"

"Is that her real name?"

"Yes. I checked." He slid open a drawer, reached inside for a manila envelope, and thrust it across the white desk at me.

"It's all there. Everything I could find out about her. Along with an 8×10 glossy I had blown up from the frame. But like I said, she's three years older now."

"So?"

"So she has definite potential. Great eyes, sensuous mouth, a special look. I could build her into a star. But first, of course, I need to find her. That's what I'm hiring you for."

I shook my head. "You've got the wrong boy," I told him. "I'm no detective, I'm an investigator in the field of the paranormal. That's a long way from a private eye. I don't find lost teenagers."

He ignored this. "I had her last known address checked in Santa Monica. She's not there anymore. Called her parents, and they don't know where she is — and don't seem to give a shit. They haven't laid eyes on her since she left home at fifteen right after doing the bit part in *Deadly Earth.*"

"That's pretty young," I said. "To leave home at that age. You'd think her parents would be going nuts with no contact."

"Anyhow . . ." continued Appleton, "we got zip on where Justina is now. Gonna be up to you."

"I told you — I'm not the one for this."

"Even for a five thousand cash retainer? Plus a fat bonus if you find her."

"You've just talked me into it." I grinned. "But why not hire a licensed private detective?"

"I'm a man of instinct," he said, flipping the well-chewed cigar into a snaptop desk tray. "And my instinct tells me you're right for this job." He stood up. "It's as simple as that, Mr. Kincaid." And he walked around the desk to clap me on the shoulder. "Do we understand one another?"

"I think we do," I said.

I left Murdock Studios carrying the manila envelope.

And five thousand dollars of Lucas Appleton's money tucked snugly away in my wallet.

Over lunch in Hollywood at Musso & Frank's (they make great au gratin potatoes), I studied the material inside the envelope. There wasn't much. Clipped to Justina's photo, an actor's pay sheet for *Deadly Earth,* signed by her. A typed transcript of a radio talk show in which she plugged the pic between dog food commercials. And a very brief list of known contacts. These included the director who worked with her on the film, and the studio flack who got her the radio bit spot — plus her parents, Mr. and Mrs. Edwin G. Phillips. They lived in San Diego.

Took me the rest of the afternoon to get down there and find their place — an impressive two-story ranch style home on a quiet cul de sac near Balboa Park.

Mrs. Phillips answered the door.

She was as tall as I am, just under six feet — but she carried her height with poise. Cool gray eyes. Hair as neatly trimmed as the box hedge on her porch. Dressed in a mint green slacks-and-blouse combo you don't get at a Sears sale. A small, perfectly cut diamond mounted in gold at her throat was modestly impressive. Mrs. Phillips personified what Lucas Appleton thought his poster had: class.

She'd been expecting a salesman from some insurance company, and when she found out I wasn't him, it took some fast talk to get me invited inside.

"I *told* those people at the studio I don't have any idea where my daughter is," she said in a voice as cool as her eyes.

We were seated on a large studio couch in the Phillips living room. Late afternoon sun had turned the drapes to gold flame, and a spear of sunlight illumined a large framed photo on the grand piano. Mr. and Mrs. Phillips, posed hand-in-hand.

"I understand that you can't supply information you don't have," I said in my I'm-really-a-nice-fellow voice. "I was hoping you could direct me to someone who might know where she is. Maybe a boyfriend?"

"If Justina has a boyfriend, it's no concern of mine," she said stiffly. "I have no leads for you, Mr. Kincaid, and I regret the inconvenience of your trip."

That would have ended it — but I decided to take a wild shot. "Just when did you and your husband adopt Justina?"

She flushed, stood up, staring at me. "How did you know about that?"

I walked over and picked up the framed photo from the piano, studying it. "This photograph of you and Mr. Phillips — and the one I have of Justina — there's absolutely no family resemblance. Everything's different. Eyes, nose, the shape of the chin — everything."

She crossed to a heavy brass-studded chair and sat down on it, looking pale. "We adopted Justina shortly after her birth at St. Joseph's Hospital. She was . . . born out of wedlock. Her birth parents weren't married."

"Did you tell her she was adopted?'

"Yes, but not until her fifteenth birthday. She was furious with us for what she termed 'withholding the truth.' She packed and left that same day." Mrs. Phillips looked down at her hands; her face was set, unforgiving. "We have not seen her since."

"No contact at all?"

"A letter last Christmas, requesting money. She listed a post office box as an address."

"What did you do about the letter?"

"We destroyed it. My husband and I feel that Justina has acted in a most ungrateful manner. We gave her clothes, a good home, a solid education — and she rejected us."

"Did you give her love?"

Mrs. Phillips looked up at me. Then, slowly: "We tried to. Edwin and I are not emotional people."

A moment of awkward silence. Then: "Do you know the name of her birth mother?"

"On the certificate it was Leona Stoddard. I have no idea if that was her real name. Frankly, I have no interest in the woman."

"What made you adopt Justina?"

"It was Edwin. We were childless — but Edwin wanted to be a father. Heaven knows why, since he never had any time for Justina. Personally, I never wanted a child."

I looked into those cool gray eyes. "I guess that's pretty obvious," I said.

After I left the Phillips house I took a long chance and drove to St. Joseph's Hospital where Justina had been born; it was in the suburb of Chula Vista. I had a strong desire to see if anyone at the place remembered her birth eighteen years ago.

All hospitals look alike, smell alike, sound alike; St. Joseph's was no exception. Only difference: this one was staffed by nuns.

I got lucky. The nun who'd been on floor duty at the time of Justina's birth was still on staff there. Sister Irma.

When we sat down in the patients' reception area, she reminded me of an undersized Santa Claus: just five feet, but fat and jolly, with twinkling eyes. She looked about fifty.

"I've always loved working around babies," she told me, hands tucked primly away inside the wide sleeves of her old-fashioned nun's habit. "If the Good Lord hadn't called me to His service, I would have mothered a large family. But then . . . ." And she twinkled. ". . . *all* the babies I've taken care of through the years are mine. Silly, I suppose, yet I can't help thinking of them that way. But then, aren't we all part of God's greater family?"

"And you *do* remember the Stoddard baby?"

She nodded. "Indeed I do. A lovely little thing — like one of God's angels."

"Do you recall what her mother was like?"

Suddenly the brightness vanished from her face. Her eyes darkened. "Yes . . . I do remember the woman," she said softly. "It's a blessing she never raised that poor child."

"What makes you say that?"

"She had true *evil* in her, Mr. Kincaid," declared Sister Irma. "Her eyes . . . they were . . . quite horrible. There is a perfect word to fit them: demonic."

"And the baby's father?"

"I don't recall his name," she said, "but I know that he drove a cab in the San Diego area. He visited the hospital only once, when I attempted to stir his conscience, asking him why he had not married the mother of his child."

"What did he say?"

"He told me it was none of my business. I got very angry, may the Good Lord forgive me, and followed him out to his cab, shouting at him." She looked as if she were still feeling the guilt of this act eighteen years later. "I watched him drive away and I have always remembered the number of his taxi. It was 636 — a Star Cab vehicle."

She sat stiffly, drained of good humor by the memory.

"Did you personally care for the baby?"

"Oh, yes. I took a special interest in her. Whenever I was on duty I'd see to her first. Never gave me any worry. An absolute angel. After they took her away, I found out she'd been put up for adoption. And that's the last I heard of her." She looked at me in sudden concern. "Is the dear girl all right?"

"I hope so. Her name is Justina Phillips — and I'm trying to locate her for a job." I stood up. "You've been very kind, Sister. I appreciate your talking to me."

"I'm curious, Mr. Kincaid."

"Yes?"

"Why did you come *here*?"

"I wanted to talk to someone who'd actually seen her birth mother. Thought I might find out more about Leona Stoddard. If I could find her, she might lead me to Justina. They *could* be back in touch. That often happens with adopted children."

The nun paled; she lowered her eyes. "If you ever *do* come face to face with that awful woman . . ." Her lower lip quivered. ". . . may God protect you!"

And Sister Irma hastily made the Sign of the Cross.

The Star Cab Company was near the Coast Highway, at the bottom of Grand in downtown San Diego. I'd be getting there after dark.

On the way, I kept thinking of how it must feel to grow up in a loveless environment. Love doesn't always have to come from one's parents; I'd lost both of mine when I was six. They'd died in a desert flash flood near the Hopi Reservation back in Arizona, where they'd worked for the U.S. Bureau of Indian Affairs. The Indians adopted me, and I grew up on the reservation. I never felt unloved. One of the Hopis, an old, half-blind medicine man, became a real father figure to me. Gave me a great amount of affection. And wisdom. Through him, I absorbed the metaphysical Hopi view of life — which headed me into the world of the paranormal.

But, for Justina, once her birth mother abandoned her, she never found love. Mrs. Phillips had made it clear that she lacked any kind of emotional tie to the girl — and her busy husband obviously didn't, either. They didn't give a damn for their daughter. No wonder she took off on her own at fifteen; discovering she was no blood relative to the Phillips freed her to go.

Had she attempted to locate her birth

mother or father?

What kind of emotional state was she in?

Was she, for that matter, still alive?

A Navy town, San Diego was big during the Second World War. As a port city, it got a lot of wear and tear, and the downtown area became seedy and unattractive. Until the City Council voted a major face lift — ugly to beautiful. San Diego's city fathers can be proud of the job they've done with the new downtown area. All big cities should look so good.

I parked the Honda behind Star's red brick office-and-garage, walked in and asked to see the owner.

"Hey, Harl!" yelled a beefy mechanic working on one of the cabs. "Somebody's here to see ya."

Harl waddled out of his glass-walled office, fat as a spider, wearing a greasy pair of white overalls a size too small for him. "I'm Harley Pike. What can I do for you?"

I'd gotten the name of Justina's father from the hospital, so I knew who to ask for. "I'm trying to locate a driver of yours, Al Devits. Worked here in '73."

"That's a long time back," said Pike, scrubbing at his cheek with black-nailed fingers. "I wasn't around in those days. Long time back."

"Can't you check your records?"

"I guess," he said, and sighed. "Come on back to the office and I'll see if I got something on this guy. D–E–V–I–T–S, is it?

"Right." I trailed him to his office at the far end of the garage. It was like Pike — overloaded and greasy.

He blew the dust off a yellowed record book, opened it, thumbing through the entries. "Yeah . . . here he is . . . Albert A. Devits. Drove for us into '75." He looked up at me. "You want his address back then? It's a forwarding — from where he moved from here."

"Sure," I said.

He gave it to me — a small apartment in a pink stucco building behind what used to be the old MGM Studios in Culver City. It was late when I got to the place, and I hoped I wasn't getting anybody out of bed. I wasn't. The guy who answered my ring was Al himself. He was watching the midnight news on TV.

Devits told me he'd been living here since he moved up from San Diego in the fall of '75. He was in his mid-fifties, with a lean, acne-pocked face and sad eyes, like a beagle. He looked worn and defeated. An ashtray overflowing with dead cigarette butts told me he was a chain smoker.

"I don't do no work of any kind these days," he told me in a smoke-fogged voice as we sat facing one another in his small living room. He tapped his right leg. "Fake," he said, smiling. His teeth were tobacco-stained. "Lost the real one in the service. I live on a vet's pension."

"Sorry," I said.

"Don't be. It's no big deal. I live okay." He got out a fresh pack of Camels. "Mind if I smoke?"

"I'd rather you wouldn't."

"Okay." And he put away the cigarettes.

"I came here to ask about your child."

"Got no children." He grunted. "Never married."

"I'm talking about the baby girl Leona Stoddard delivered at St. Joseph's in 1973."

"Oh, *that*," he said. His voice was raspy, like a file on wood. "I try not to do any thinkin' about that."

"You know nothing about what happened to her?"

He shifted, leaning forward to adjust his right leg. "Mister, I never seen that kid but once. For maybe five minutes in the hospital. Don't know nothin' about her. Don't want to. Her mother . . . was bad enough."

"What do you mean?"

"I mean that woman gave me the willies, just bein' around her. Somethin' wrong with her."

"In what way?"

"Dunno exactly. Just . . . that she wasn't *natural*. I got no words for it."

"Did you see her again after the birth of the baby?"

"Hell, no! Never!" Devits shuddered. "I made a mistake mixin' with her in the first place. But she had . . . funny eyes. She could look at you . . . and it was like you were . . ."

"Hypnotized?"

"Yeah, that's it, hypnotized. Eyes like hers — you don't forget."

"Do you have a photo of her?"

He got up, favoring his bad leg, limped to a shelf, removed a shoe box. Opened it and got out a photo.

"That's Leona," he said, handing it to me. "See what I mean?"

Even though it was only a 5×7 snapshot, Leona Stoddard's eyes seemed to burn out of the photo, intense and darkly lustrous. She looked about twenty-five with full, sensual lips and a mass of dark hair framing the pale oval of her face. Striking. And definitely the mother of Justina Phillips. In black ink, on the bottom strip of the photo, she had scrawled, "Yours, Leona."

"I took that picture myself a week after we met. That's the whole time we were together — that week back in '72. Didn't see her again till she got to the hospital. I went over to get me a look at the baby, but I couldn't see anythin' of me in the kid. She had Leona's hair and eyes. I saw her, and then I left. And I haven't seen either of 'em since."

"How did you and Leona first meet?"

"In my cab. She called from the U.S. Grant Hotel in downtown San Diego. I picked her up outside the hotel to take her somewhere . . . The next thing I know — we're in bed together."

"Did she have some kind of job in those days?"

"Not that I knew about. I remember she said she was an actress. In the movies. But I wouldn't know about that. I never go to movies."

"Mind if I keep this photo?"

"You're welcome to it. I don't want to look at that face of hers . . . ever again."

As I was leaving I asked Al Devits one final question: "I can understand your feelings for Leona — but aren't you curious about what happened to your daughter?"

"She don't exist far as I'm concerned," he said. "I don't want nothin' to do with *anythin'* that come out of Leona Stoddard."

The next day I spent some time accessing the files of the Academy of Motion Picture Arts and Sciences in Beverly Hills.

There was no separate listing for "Stoddard, Leona," but in a book of film history I ran across what I was *certain* was a photo of her. The actress was languishing in the arms of Rudolf Valentino in a tent setting for one of his desert love sagas.

Same face. Same dark hair. Same arresting, intense eyes. But the caption named her as "Louise Collins" — and the film was a silent, made back in the 1920s when Valentino was the rage. If Louise Collins and Leona Stoddard *had* been the same woman, she'd have been in her seventies when Al met her.

But the resemblance was incredible.

"Could be Louise Collins was Leona's mother," Kelly said over dinner that night in a booth at Musso's. She was comparing the snapshot of Leona with a Xerox copy of the photo from the Valentino film.

"I checked that angle," I told her. "Louise Collins died in a plane crash in 1930. Never married. No kids."

She handed the photos back to me. "Leona *could* have been illegitimate — same as *her* daughter."

"Maybe." I shook my head. "But anyone would swear they're the same woman. How could she be an identical twin to her mother?"

"Happens all the time. My younger

sister looks almost exactly like Mom did at her age."

"Well, it doesn't matter now. I'm giving up on Leona Stoddard. I need to move in a new direction. Justina's parents are obviously not going to help me find her."

"Then what *are* you going to do?" Kelly asked. She looked terrific. Her hair was combed back in a low ponytail fastened with a black satin bow. She was wearing more makeup than usual — violet eye shadow for one thing — and on her it looked great. Kelly's tight green dress matched her eyes. She looked every bit as good as any of the actresses sitting in the booths around us. I realized that I'd been neglecting her; we hadn't made love in more than a week.

"I'll tell you what I'm going to do. I'm going to drive you home, lock the car, and spend the night in your apartment." I grinned at her. "How does that sound?"

"Like you're horny." And she grinned back at me.

Next morning, I phoned Lucas Appleton at the studio, telling him that so far I'd had no luck in tracing Justina, but I was determined to keep trying. (After all, it was *his* money.)

"You stay right on this, Kincaid," he told me. "I'll be leaving tomorrow for Oregon. Three days. I'll be back by Tuesday."

"Hopefully, by then, I'll have better news for you."

"Contact me Tuesday morning," he said. "It's vital to find this girl."

I put down the phone thoughtfully. What was so "vital" about finding an unknown bit player who may or may not have enough talent to make it in films?

That was when I began to suspect that there was more involved here than screen acting.

But *what*?

I figured it was time to use one of my paranormal contacts. I happen to believe we're all psychic, to an extent, but that some people possess this talent to a much greater degree than others.

I decided to consult a professional.

Naturally, as with any profession, there are phonies. I've encountered (and unmasked) a lot of them in my business. However, Irene Hopwood was genuine. I'd made use of her particular talents in the past, and was convinced she had powers far beyond the ordinary.

She worked out of a lovingly renovated Victorian house in downtown Los Angeles, one of those tall, ornate gingerbread-and-stained-glass jobs that used to crowd the Bunker Hill area before most of them were torn down to make room for big-bucks avant-garde highrises.

Her office was on the lower floor, facing the street.

Irene saw people only by appointment — and I'd made one. For that night, at 10 p.m. (She was never at her best by daylight and claimed that darkness aided her psychic powers.)

"David! How very nice to see you again!" Tasteful jewelry glittered on her fingers and wrist as she extended her hand to me. I pressed it warmly.

"Been a while," I said.

"Please, come in." She led me inside to an old-fashioned parlor. A pot of Earl Grey tea and a plate of big cookies (she knew I loved chocolate chip) were laid out on an antique table.

I made small talk as we sat down. Then, sipping her tea and munching a chocolate chip cookie, I got around to what had brought me there.

"I'm looking for a young woman. Eighteen. Name's Justina Phillips." I opened my leather briefcase, handed over the 8×10 glossy Appleton had given me.

She studied the image. "Arresting eyes," she murmured. "Quite intense." Then she looked up at me. "Do you have an object of hers — a ring, or a bracelet perhaps?"

"No," I said. "I was hoping you could hone in on the name and face and come up with something — maybe get a mental image of her present whereabouts."

She stared at the photo, closed her eyes, softly repeating: "Justina . . . Justina . . . Justina . . ."

I leaned forward. "Anything?"

Slowly, she shook her head. "Nothing. As you know, my own talents work mainly through psychometry. To receive the most accurate vibrations, I need an object owned by the subject, preferably something the subject has worn or otherwise touched a lot. Photos which have been handled by the subject *can* carry vibrational auras, but I'm not receiving any from this one."

"She never touched this," I said.

"Well, then, I'm going to need more. An item of her clothing . . . something *tangible*."

I reached into my briefcase, took out the signed snapshot of Leona Stoddard, gave it to her. "Try this. It's a photo of her mother."

"Yes. I can see that in the eyes . . . so powerfully intense." Irene traced her fingers slowly over the face in the snapshot. Then, as if it were white hot, she pulled back abruptly, allowing the picture to slip to the polished wood floor.

I picked it up. "What's wrong?"

Her breathing was rapid and shallow; she sat rigidly in the chair, hands fisted. "I feel a . . . terrible darkness in this individual . . . a sense of perversion . . . of *foulness*!" She stood up. "I'm blocked. That's all I can give you."

I didn't question her reaction, but it disturbed me.

I returned Leona's snapshot to my briefcase. "I may be back," I said.

At the door, Irene gripped my arm. I could feel the strength of her fingers. "A warning, David. There is . . . a force here . . . powerful and horrific. You're moving toward it — and it can destroy you."

Her words had definitely shaken me.

By the time I was back inside the Honda, fumbling for the ignition key, I found that my hands were moist with cold sweat.

I was tired, very tired, as I reached the end of Las Virgenes Road. I wanted nothing more than a good night's sleep to clear my head, to give my conscious mind a period of quiet restoration.

As I rolled the CRX into the gravel driveway fronting my house I saw something move just at the edge of my vision. Something in the yard, among the trees. A dark mass, shifting ominously.

I stopped, cutting the Honda's engine. Silence. Just the throbbing dirge of crickets. The darkness pressed in thickly around me like a stifling shroud.

Since I live in a remote, semiwilderness area, the intruder could well be a night animal — perhaps a prowling mountain lion. If so, he'd be more afraid of me than I'd be of him. Best to make sure.

As I was reaching for my flashlight in the glove compartment I saw a pair of eyes, red and luminous, glowing from the shadows.

They moved closer.

I clicked on the flash, swinging the arc of light toward the intruder. And gasped. My beam illuminated the stark, oval face of Leona Stoddard, lips pulled back in a snarl, eyes hot and probing. Her hair was tangled and filth-matted.

Horribly, incredibly, only her *face* was human! The lower part of her body, glistening wetly in the powdery beam of light, was that of an enormous insect — and its multiple legs, like those of a giant centipede, began to propel it rapidly toward the car.

Panic and revulsion welled through me. I snap-locked the door, desperately keying the ignition. The engine sputtered and died. I tried again.

Too late. The thing had reached my side of the Honda and now its plated insect legs were scrabbling at the window. Powerfully, they smashed at the glass which gave way in falling shards, exposing me to the bloated horror outside.

"You are *mine!*" hissed the Leona-thing, dipping her head through the shattered window to fasten razor teeth in my right shoulder. I screamed in shock and pain as, sharklike, she ripped away a gouting chunk of my flesh.

I slammed the metal flashlight against her head, but the blows had no effect.

Ripping free of her, blood erupting from my savaged shoulder, I threw myself across the seat to dive out the passenger door.

Landing on my knees in the sharp gravel, I lunged up, began running for the dark bulk of the house.

The Leona-thing scrambled spider-quick over the top of the Honda and launched itself at me. Its loathsome body struck my back, slamming me to the ground. I twisted around, throwing both arms across my face.

Again, the evil hiss of Leona's voice: *"Mine!"*

And her slashing teeth severed my left arm at the elbow; the whole lower portion, hand, wrist, and forearm, gone! As a welter of crimson cloaked my body, I watched, in numb horror, as she devoured my flesh, snapping the bones of my fingers like breadsticks.

She darted toward me once again, and I closed my eyes, my nostrils filled with the sharp, metallic insect odor of the Leona-thing . . .

I sat up, blinking, shaking wildly, saliva running from my open mouth. Sweat, not blood, soaked my face and chest.

Christ, what a nightmare!

I knew I was all right, safe and unharmed, in my own bedroom, with an early pale rose sunrise staining the lower edge of the sky outside the window — but the horrific demon figure of Leona Stoddard had been so vivid and tactile that I found it difficult to believe I was still alive.

And I'd analyzed enough dreams to know that this one was a warning.

A few hours later a telephone call put me back on Justina's trail.

It was Mrs. Phillips, phoning from San Diego to tell me she thought that perhaps Bobbi Graham might be able to help me in my search.

"Who's he?" I asked.

"Graham is female," said Mrs. Phillips, her voice tight and strained. "Justina was . . . involved with her. I was ashamed to tell you."

"Involved? You mean sexually?"

"Oh, no, nothing like that." A hesitation on the line. "It's . . . a drug thing."

"Tell me about it."

"After she dropped out of school, Justina got in with a bad crowd. She became close friends with this Graham girl, and it was Bobbi Graham who introduced her to hard drugs."

"How hard is hard?"

"Cocaine mostly — and some others I don't know about. And she didn't just decide to go off on her own; we *asked* her to leave. Demanded it, really. The psychologists call the process 'Tough Love.' So she went to Los Angeles with the Graham girl. I'm sure they lived there together."

"That would figure, at her age."

"When you asked about Justina . . . well, I just didn't want to get into this drug problem. I trust you'll understand."

"I *do* — and I appreciate your calling me."

"If Justina can get an acting career started for herself, then I don't want to stand in her way," she said firmly. "I may not love her in a conventional sense, Mr. Kincaid, but I do care about her welfare."

"Do you have an address for Bobbi Graham?"

She did.

In Venice.

I drove there.

Venice, today, has the reputation of being a "doper's heaven." You can get anything from rock cocaine to ice — the latest mind-blaster — on the streets of Venice, so from what Mrs. Phillips had told me, I wasn't surprised Bobbi Graham lived here.

Originally, emulating the grand Italian city that had inspired it, Venice had been designed as a graceful community of sparkling canals (with gondolas, yet!), trim green lawns, immaculate streets, and bright-painted pastel houses. That was a long time ago. Now it was worth your life to be caught there on certain streets after dark. The canals were scummed and rancid (you could smell them all the way to Wilshire), filled with rusty water and floating debris best left undescribed.

Bobbi Graham was renting a small, weather-wracked frame house between one of the canals and the ocean, an eyesore among eyesores.

I got out of the Honda and walked across the blistered weed patch that had once been a front yard and knocked on a paint-chipped screen door.

Bobbi was waiting for me, as she'd promised. I heard her voice from inside. "Walk in. The door's open."

I stepped into a cramped, trash-littered living room. Bobbi was slouched in a sagging, near-colorless sofa (it had once been orange), watching television with a sleepy black cat in her lap. The cat regarded me with slitted, smoked-yellow eyes, yawned hugely, then went back to sleep.

Bobbi lifted the animal from her lap and got up to switch off the TV. Aside from assorted trash, the faded sofa, a single wooden kitchen chair, and the TV set were the only items in the room.

"I was watching Geraldo," she said. "Ever watch his show?"

"I was on it once, but no, I can't say that I *watch* it," I said.

Her eyes took on new life. To most people, anybody who's been on television is a celebrity.

"He rounds up some really freaky people. Like, just before you got here, he was interviewing a defrocked priest who owns a string of condom factories in the East. Guy was a real kick."

Bobbi had flopped back on the sofa and I took the chair. She was barefoot, in ragged jeans and a beaded shirt with most of the beads missing. Her face was pinched and narrow-boned, with small bloodshot eyes. She wore no makeup, and her greased, pasty skin was proof that she needed to improve her diet.

"Just who *are* you, anyway?" she asked me.

"I'm an independent investigator."

"You mean, like a cop? If you're a cop, I don't do drugs anymore, so you're wasting your time."

I smiled at that. "I'm no cop. I work in the field of the paranormal."

"Like ghosts and stuff?"

"That's part of it."

"Then why are you nosing around after Justina? She's no ghost."

"I'm glad to hear that."

"Well . . . *why* then?"

"I just need to find her. Personal reasons."

She narrowed her eyes, then smiled. Bobbi had a nice smile; it softened her face, brightened it. "You're kinda cute. How old are you?"

"Thirty-one."

"I'm twenty. Guess that maybe makes you too old for me." She shrugged. "Okay . . . so what do you want to ask me about Justina?"

"Do you know where she is now?"

"Nope. She *was* living here with me, until about three months ago, but we had us a fight, so she split." Bobbi picked up the cat again, began stroking its charcoal back.

"What was the fight about?"

"You *sure* you're not a cop?"

"Swear to God."

"Okay . . . it was about doing drugs. She wanted to quit. Claimed they were bumming her out. Thought maybe she was losing her mind."

"So did she quit?"

"I guess so. She went to this rehab house in Hollywood to get help. That's where she met Lyle."

"Who's Lyle?"

"A guy who worked there. Maybe he still does. Lyle Anmar. She told me they had a thing going for awhile, but I dunno if it lasted. Maybe you should ask Lyle."

I nodded. "Maybe I should. Got an address for the place?"

"It's somewhere on Western, near Hollywood Boulevard. Called 'The New Beginning.' Justina phoned me from there a couple of times."

"I'll find it."

The cat jumped down from her lap and came over to rub against my leg. "He likes me," I said.

"He's just hungry. Thinks you'll feed him. Homer's a real glutton. Eats all the time. I'm gettin' a beer. Want one?"

"No thanks."

She went into a small, grubby kitchen and fetched a Coors, popping the can and returning with it. "Last time Justina called from this place, she wanted me to come over and join some program they have. Get me clean. I told her to screw off. *That'll* be the friggin' day — when I go to some friggin' rehab house!"

"Then you still do drugs?"

"Shit, yes." She shrugged her thin shoulders. "Anyhow, that was the last time I heard from her. I don't know where she is now."

"One more thing," I said.

"What?"

"When she was here with you . . . did she ever talk about her mother? Her *birth* mother?"

"Only that she was pissed at being deserted, being put up for adoption the way she was. She figured her Mom had

to be a primo bitch to do a thing like that."

"She ever show any interest in locating her real mother?"

"Not that I saw. She was too pissed at her."

"What about her life with the Phillips — was she happy when she was with them?"

"For awhile. She had this picture of a birthday party they gave for her down in San Diego at Balboa Park. When she turned ten. They hired a couple of clowns and even rented a kids' merry-go-round. She said that was the happiest day of her life."

"The picture — did she take it with her?"

"No. It's still around here with some of the other stuff she left. Wanta see it?"

"Yeah."

"Okay, if I can find it." She put her can of beer on the floor while she dug into a large cardboard box by the wall near the kitchen, pulling out various papers, shaking her head. Then she tried another box. This time she turned to me in triumph, holding up the photo. "Got it."

It was a color shot the size of a postcard. Young Justina was posed, smiling, between two clowns. She looked pink and healthy. I was about to hand it back when a figure caught my eye. A man. Standing behind them in the far background, staring toward the camera.

Somehow, he looked familiar, but I couldn't place him. The figure was too small and indistinct.

"Can I borrow this?"

"Promise to bring it back?"

"Promise."

As I was leaving, Bobbi stopped me. She looked haunted. "If you find Justina, tell her . . ." She hesitated, tears welling in her eyes. "Tell her I still love her."

"I'll tell her," I said.

In Hollywood I dropped off the picture at Professional Photo Processing, telling them I wanted a blowup . . . and what about enhancing the figure in the background? They said I could pick it up in the morning. To them, it was just another job.

I had no trouble finding the number of the rehab house in the Hollywood phone book. When I got them on the line they told me, yes, Lyle Anmar still worked the night shift there. Starting at eleven. I said I'd drop by before midnight.

The delay gave me time to catch a late dinner at Gorky's. Russian food, like Russian literature, leads to introspection. Alone with my thoughts, I realized that finding Justina Phillips had become a personal quest; I'd developed an emotional interest in the girl, a mix of curiosity and compassion. I found myself hoping she was all right, that the rehab people had provided the help she needed.

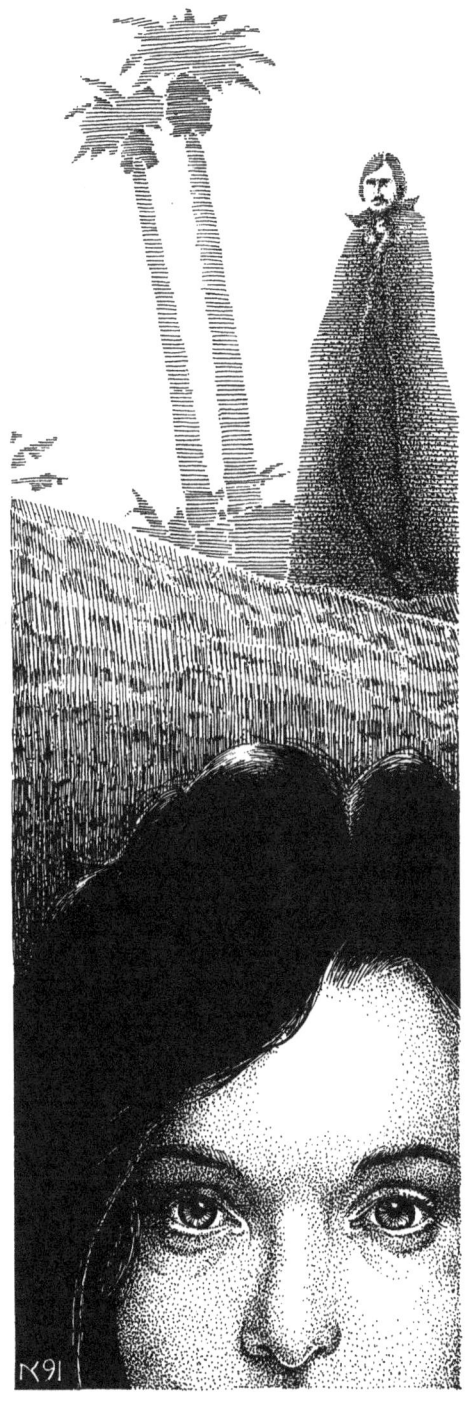

The New Beginning was on Western, just a block down from Hollywood Boulevard. A big rambling converted Spanish-style apartment complex that had been a respectable enough address before this section of town had gone to seed. Now it was smack in the middle of a ghetto area, and its newly-painted turquoise exterior contrasted sharply with the dingy, dirt-encrusted buildings around it on the same block. Scrawled graffiti were everywhere in sweeping, bold patterns — street gangs marking their turf with spray paint the way cats mark their territory with scent.

Like Venice, not a great place to be caught after dark. But Lyle Anmar worked here and we needed to talk.

The door buzzer summoned a bent-backed old man with maybe three strands of hair left on his freckled head. He blinked at me through bottle-thick glasses, running a rusty tongue over cracked lips. "Help ya, mister?"

"I was told that Lyle Anmar works

the night shift. I'm here to see him."

"Then you best talk to Sylva. She's the one in charge. Don't know the young folks by name." He coughed raggedly. "Been a long time since I could remember names." He beckoned to me. "Step inside. I'll go fetch Sylva."

She was in her mid-twenties, dark and pretty. Her eyes were direct but weary; they'd seen a lot. "You the one who called about Lyle?"

I nodded. It was 11:30; I figured he'd be in. He was.

"In the rec room," she said. I followed her down a long, freshly-painted hall. She opened a door and we walked into a wide room crowded with video games, pinball machines, and faded pool tables. Three of the videos were in action. "He's the tall guy," said Sylva, and left me there.

Lyle was at one of the green tables, neatly sinking the eight ball into a corner pocket. He was at least six-three, rangy and raw-boned, with a thin blond beard and long hair tied behind in a ponytail. His opponent was a teenaged girl in ragged slacks and a gray pullover. She looked nervous and strung out.

"Like to talk to you," I said to Anmar. "I'm David Kincaid."

"And I'm busy." He was chalking his cue stick as the girl took her turn. She didn't sink anything. I waited, watching him run the table, socking home the last three balls.

"Want another game?" he asked the girl.

"Not with you," she said. "I never win when I play with you." And she wandered off to one of the pinball machines.

Anmar racked his stick, then swung to face me. He seemed as tall as the Empire State Building, but a lot skinnier. "So what d'ya want to talk about?"

"Justina Phillips," I said.

"Buzz off." He reached for the leather jacket he'd draped over a chair.

"This is important," I said.

"Why should I talk to you?" His mouth was sullen, his eyes a frosted blue.

"If you think I'm a cop, you're wrong," I told him.

"I don't give a flying fuck *who* you are." He started out of the room.

I stopped him at the door. "Talk to me, Lyle. You're the only lead I've got."

"To what?"

"To Justina. I need to find her. There's a chance she could get into films, make some really good money, have a decent life. If you care about her —"

"And what makes you think I do?"

"Bobbi Graham said you and Justina were involved."

"That little twat don't know shit about me." His tone was as cold as his eyes.

"I thought you were here because you wanted to help people," I said, allowing sudden anger to color my voice.

"So?"

"So you may be able to help Justina. If you'll just talk to me about her."

He seemed to relax; his eyes softened. "Okay, mister. It just happens I *do* care about her, even if she doesn't care about me."

"She broke up with you?"

"Sure as hell did. Once she got her head straight she told me we were history."

"Then she's clean?"

"She was — when she left here," he said.

"You ever do drugs with her?"

"Not with her, I didn't. I was clean when I came here. In fact, I helped her get straight."

Two of the video players were looking at us.

"Can we sit down somewhere?" I asked. "There's a lot more I'd like to know."

"Yeah . . . all right. You want some coffee?"

I nodded. "Fine." Actually, I don't drink the stuff, but whatever it took . . .

We sat down over coffee in a deserted kitchen area behind the rec room.

By now, Anmar had opened up; in fact, he seemed anxious to talk about his relationship with Justina. He said she'd come here because of what her dreams had done to her.

"That's how she got into drugs in the first place," Lyle said. "She told me she began using because she thought it might help her escape the nightmares. But it didn't help — just made the dreams worse."

"Did she say what they were about?"

"No. She didn't want to talk about them. But she did say one thing . . ."

"Yeah?"

"Said they were all weird. *Supernatural,* she said."

"You mean — ghosts?"

"Demons," Lyle told me. "Justina said a lot of them were about demons — but she wouldn't go into details. I know they were real bad, though. Scared her a lot." He hesitated. "But there was one thing I could never figure."

"What was that?"

"We have a VCR here — and she was always renting horror videos — all of the Alex DeMarco movies. She'd watch them over and over. I told her they were probably giving her the nightmares, but she said she had to watch them."

"*Had* to?"

"Like she was . . . *compelled* to do it. But she never said why. It was all pretty crazy."

I thought about that. Then I backtracked, asking him how he got hooked on drugs.

"I was riding with the Henchmen when it started," he said.

"The motorcycle gang?"

"Yeah. They're a mean bunch, but for awhile they were like . . . a family to me. But when I found out what they were into, I got out. I knew I had to get my head straight."

"What *are* they into?"

"A lot of stuff — but the worst, for me, was the girl thing. They supply young girls to local pimps. Pick up an out-of-town chick right off the bus, then sweet-talk her into riding with them. Find out she's on the run and can't be traced. Next thing you know, she's history. Gone. Like she never was."

"You know the names of the pimps they supply?"

"No. I was never into that part of it. And, like I say, when I found out what was going down I split."

"Justina ever run with the gang?"

"No. Never. There's no connection."

I made a mental note to have my cop pal, Mike Lucero, check out the Henchmen. Then I asked: "Do you have any idea where Justina might be right now?"

He shook his head. "She could be anywhere. Or nowhere."

"Meaning?"

He looked at me. "How do we know she's still alive?"

"We don't," I said.

The next morning I picked up my enhanced birthday photo of Justina — and recognized the figure in the background of the shot.

Alex DeMarco.

It was just too coincidental — Justina's fascination with his films and then my finding out that DeMarco had been at her tenth birthday party. Maybe he had something to do with what I now thought of as her "disappearance."

But first, before I could talk to him, I had to find his address. They don't list major film stars in the phone book.

I drove over to Murdock Studios, telling the gate guard I had a package to deliver. He waved me inside.

Appleton was still on location in Oregon. His thin-lipped secretary told me she wasn't allowed to give out any personal information on the stars. So I lied. I told her Appleton had *asked* me to see Alex DeMarco as part of the investigation he had hired me to conduct. So, very reluctantly, she gave me DeMarco's address and phone number.

Score one for Kincaid.

I went to a nearby pay phone and punched in the number. Got a servant on the line. Asked to speak to Mr. DeMarco. I told him Lucas Appleton was calling. It worked.

"Hello, Lucas?" The same deep-velvet movie voice.

"This is David Kincaid," I said. "I work for Mr. Appleton. I'd like to see you as soon as it's convenient, Mr. DeMarco."

"What about?"

"A personal matter. Something I'd rather not get into over the phone. But I could drive over this afternoon."

"Uh . . . very well. You have my address?"

"Of course . . . on Glendower Avenue."

"Then I'll expect you at three," he said. "Sharp."

They call DeMarco's place "The House of Horrors," befitting its owner's dark profession, but until I got inside I didn't fully appreciate the name.

Twenty-three hundred Glendower is in the Hollywood Hills, above Griffith Park, and I traveled around a lot of tight, winding curves to reach it. The actor was waiting for me at the gate of his house, holding the leash of a fierce-looking black Doberman who obviously didn't like strangers. The dog was showing me his fangs and growling murderously.

"I have to meet all of my guests personally," said DeMarco. "Otherwise, Bruno considers them intruders. If you were to get inside the gate without me, it's likely he'd tear your throat out."

"I wouldn't like that," I said.

"With Bruno, I don't need a gate-alarm system." And he patted the dog's head. He smiled faintly, then sent Bruno away with a sharp command. We entered the House of Horrors.

It was creepy, to say the least. Floor-to-ceiling oil paintings of Count Dracula, the Wolfman, and Frankenstein. Horror masks pegged to the walls. Rows of signed photos of Boris Karloff, Lon Chaney, Bela Lugosi, Vincent Price, and Barbara Steele. Framed posters celebrating some two dozen fear flicks starring DeMarco.

And a life-sized replica of King Kong's head in the middle of the living room.

The room was dim, with heavy amethyst-colored brocade drapes swagged across the windows.

"I find that sunlight fades the colors," DeMarco said, indicating his paintings and posters. "Please, be seated, Mr. Kincaid. May I offer you something to drink? I often have a brandy in the afternoon."

"Maybe a soft drink," I said. "Anything you've got is fine."

DeMarco snapped his fingers and a tall cadaver of a man instantly appeared at his shoulder. Dressed in black, with a close-shaven head and a blunt, unsmiling face, he seemed to blend in perfectly with the outré surroundings.

"My usual — and a root beer for the gentleman," DeMarco ordered. The skeletal figure nodded tightly, then drifted back into the shadows.

DeMarco was wearing a blood-red silk dressing gown trimmed in black. Matching slippers covered his feet. His face was as relaxed and as friendly as a vulpine face like his can ever get. The eyes were, of course, dark and penetrating.

"Now . . . what brings you to the house of DeMarco?" he asked, settling back into a rich assortment of emerald-and sapphire-colored tasseled-silk pillows.

"Mr. Appleton has hired me to find a young woman named Justina Phillips," I told him. "I thought you might know her."

He smiled. "And what leads you to such a conclusion?"

I reached into my leather briefcase. "This photo." I handed the color blowup to him.

"Ah . . . and is this the young lady?"

"Yes. It was taken in 1983, on her tenth birthday."

He looked at me. "And since I seem to be hovering in the background of the picture, you assume that I know her?"

"*Do* you?"

"Unhappily for your search, the answer is no." He handed the print back to me just as our drinks were wheeled in on a French Baroque tea cart. The genuine item. Definitely not a reproduction. My root beer looked a little silly sitting in its glass of gilded crystal.

"I don't understand," I told him.

"How I could be in the picture?" He inhaled the fragrance of the brandy, turning the antique snifter slowly in his right hand. "The explanation is quite simple, Mr. Kincaid. In 1983 I was in San Diego making a film. On that particular day we were shooting a sequence in Balboa Park. As I recall, it had to do with my roaming through the trees as a werewolf . . . or some such nonsense. Thus, the young lady's birthday had nothing to do with me. I obviously glanced in the direction of the party when the photo was taken. Pure happenstance."

"Then you don't know anything about Justina Phillips?"

"Indeed, I do not." He sampled the brandy.

I took a swig of my root beer.

"Justina is a big fan of yours," I told him. "She's watched videos of your films over and over."

He nodded. "I have many dedicated fans, for which I am most grateful. They allow me to maintain my rather self-indulgent lifestyle."

"I just thought there might be a connection . . ."

DeMarco stood up, putting his brandy glass on the cart. "If you will excuse me, I have some personal matters that need attending." He smiled. "We *have* concluded our little conversation, have we not?"

"Yes . . . we have." I stood to shake his hand. The flesh was cold, almost clammy. "I thank you for your time, Mr. DeMarco."

"Not at all. Edward will see you to the gate."

Now the man in black was at *my* shoulder.

He walked me to the front gate without uttering a word.

Spooky. Definitely spooky.

What Lyle Anmar had said about the cycle gang stuck in my mind: that the Henchmen were into the very sick business of selling underage females. Not that it was any big surprise. Dope and prostitution provide a solid income for many outlaw cycle gangs across the country.

It was time, however, to find out more about the Henchmen, since it was possible they were tied into Justina's disappearance. A long shot, but possible.

So after I left DeMarco's place I drove out to the beach, to the Malibu Sheriff's Station to see my buddy, Mike Lucero.

We go back a ways. When I met him, Mike was a hard-headed cop who possessed an abiding contempt for the paranormal, having termed it (on several occasions) "wacko stuff." When I'd tell him about raising my vibrational energy by using the natural psychic power vortex surrounding Sedona, Arizona — or conducting seminars in Pasadena on out-of-body experiences — he'd shake his head. "Why don't you go find a *real* job? I hate to see a friend of mine involved in all this crap."

Yet we *were* friends, and the world he outwardly scoffed at had formed the basis of our friendship. I'd used my special knowledge to help him on a variety of cases — including referring him to psychics who supplied him with what turned out to be vital information in the solution of several homicides. He still kidded me about my "oddball" life, but these days he had to admit there might be something to it. His mind was opening. Not *much,* admittedly, but Mike's a very stubborn guy.

The truth is, I think he believes a lot more than he's willing to admit about the world of the paranormal. After all, he grew up in one of those superstitious mountain villages in northern New Mexico where they still believe in witches. He told me once that his parents were convinced that if you took a long tail hair from a horse and put it in a pail of water, it would turn into a snake within two weeks. Claimed they'd seen it happen with their own eyes.

Mike's office in the Malibu Station was cluttered and musty. When I walked in he met me at the door with a bear hug. He's an emotional guy, and for people he really cares about he doesn't mind showing open affection. Big and tough and tender, that's Mike.

As usual, he couldn't resist a verbal jab at my profession: "Talked to any little green men from Mars lately?"

"I've told you, there *are* no green men — or women — on the planet Mars."

"Yeah, you did at that." He grinned at me. "How the hell you been, Davey?"

No one else calls me Davey. I hate that name. But I let Mike get away with it. All part of our quirky friendship.

"I'm fine," I told him. "You still having trouble with your prostate?"

"Jeez, I *never* should have told you about that," he groaned.

"If you'd just do what I told you . . ."

"I know, I know. Gobble a handful of fresh pumpkin seeds every day and no more prostate trouble."

"It works," I said. "It really does."

He sat down at his battered oak desk. "How come you're here in the middle of the afternoon? You need some cop help, huh?"

"See," I said brightly, "I told you, you

are psychic!"

He grinned at that. "So what can I do for you, chum?"

"You can give me some info on the Devil's Henchmen."

"They run out of the north Valley . . . Sylmar. Not my beat."

"But you can punch up their stat file. Basic data. That's all I'm asking for."

He did that. The data on the computer screen confirmed what Lyle Anmar told me. They were into a variety of unsavory activities. Several of the gang had prison records connected with drugs, prostitution, armed robbery, and criminal assault. Their current leader was a mean piece of business named Billy "Grinder" Mead. Early twenties, spiked hair, big-boned with muscles to match. He had a long record of his own, but had served only minimal jail time. Obviously, he was a sharp operator.

"Talked to an ex-Henchman," I told Mike. "He said the gang was supplying out-of-town runaways to local pimps."

Mike shrugged. "So what else is new?"

"There's no way of stopping them?"

"Sure there is," he said. "Sometimes a cop gets lucky. Catches 'em with the pimp and the girls as the deal's going down. But that doesn't happen often. And even when it does, sticking a few scumballs in the slammer doesn't put a dent in anything. Life goes right on. Like with the drugs and the robberies. That's what keeps the gang in pocket money. They take the risk because they know the odds are always on their side." He leaned back in his cracked leather chair, sadness clouding his face. "It's a losing battle, but we cops have to keep up the fight. If we didn't, if we weren't around to hassle these creeps, things would be a hell of a lot worse than they already are."

I thanked him for his help with the Henchmen file, and we talked about getting together for dinner at my place, me and Kelly and Mike and his wife,

Carla. A good lady.

"Soon," I promised. "We'll do it soon."

"Okay, Davey, I'm holding you to that. Even Carla can't cook posole the way you can."

He gave me another bear hug and I was out of there.

I decided it was time to pay a personal visit to the Henchmen. Not that I had any solid reason; I was just following a gut hunch that told me this was the thing to do, that the Henchmen were somehow related to my bizarre search for Justina Phillips.

Thanks to Mike Lucero, I was registered as an official Sheriff's Consultant, and Mike had helped me obtain a police permit for the snub-nose Smith & Wesson .38 Special I took along that night. Just in case. I was no gunfighter. Despite a fair amount of practice, I was just barely adequate when it came to hitting the vital areas on a target. I hoped I wouldn't have to shoot anybody.

According to what I'd found out from Lucero, the Henchmen favored a particular Valley hangout — a bar on Sepulveda, near the old San Fernando Mission.

I took the 405 North and parked on the boulevard, directly in front of Bernie's Joint. That was the name of the bar, outlined in a dust-caked scrawl of blinking red neon above the entrance. This was definitely a Triple-B establishment: booze, broads, and bikers. I counted at least a dozen motorcycles, waxed and gleaming, lined up alongside the building, so I figured that most of the Henchmen were inside. This gang was exclusive. Lucero's computer listed only fifteen current members. Nothing like the massive membership of the Hell's Angels.

I tucked the .38 into a clamshell belt holster, buttoned my jacket, and stepped into Bernie's.

The bar was rank with smoke and beer fumes. It wasn't tough spotting the Henchmen. A cluster of them were ranged on tall stools along the bar, each wearing the distinctive club colors — grimy blue-denim sleeveless vests with a horned red skull stitched on the back above the words DEVIL'S HENCHMEN. They were being entertained by several well-endowed gang-mamas wearing Lycra tank leotards with glossy tights. One of the Henchmen, a muscled gorilla with red hair frizzing his bare arms, ambled over to me. "What you want, dude?" He wore a steel bike chain for a belt.

"I want to see Billy Mead."

He lowered his close-shaven bullet head. "The Grinder's occupied."

Mead was sitting at the far end of the bar, a wide-shouldered giant of a man, guzzling beer and playing feelie with a pair of dyed-blonde bimbos.

Ignoring the gorilla, I walked over. "Hi, Billy," I said.

He swung toward me. His face was bloated with drink, and his red-rimmed pig eyes squinted through the smoke haze. His spiked hair was rainbow colored, and a pair of snakes coiled in a purple tattoo on his right hand. "Who the fuck are you, man?"

"I know Lyle Anmar. He used to ride with you."

"That paper-ass!" Mead wiped a white foam of beer from his wide lips. "He ain't worth shit on a short stick."

"Yeah, I know he split with you boys."

"He couldn't cut it," scowled Mead. "No balls. What did that chickenshit tell you about us?"

I slipped past his question. "He had a girl for awhile, *this* girl . . ." I showed him the 8×10 glossy. "Her name's Justina Phillips."

His face paled. Obviously, the name had meaning to him. My hunch was right; there *was* a connection.

"I never seen her. How come you got her picture?"

I didn't answer that one, either. "I

33

thought you might know something about her."

"You better walk out of here right now, dude," Billy told me. "While you still got legs, that is." He drew a heavy-bladed hunting knife from his boot. "Or do you want me to fuckin' cut you in half?"

"Okay, no sweat. I'll leave." I was suddenly scared and nervous. The tension in the room was as thick as the tobacco smoke.

A voice grated behind me: "Let's give him somethin' to remember us by!"

I swung around to face the red-haired gorilla. He had the bike chain in his hand, spinning it like a rodeo roper.

"Back off, Red," I told him, flicking the .38 free of its holster and aiming it at his beer gut. "I came here for information, not trouble. Since you boys can't help me, I'll leave. I don't want a hassle."

Silence. The Henchmen along the bar were all glaring at me. But they didn't move. A .38 is apt to quiet things down a lot.

I left Bernie's Joint as rapidly as possible.

And I didn't start breathing easy again until I was rolling down Sepulveda in the Honda with the wind cool and welcome against my sweating face.

By the following morning I was into some disturbing thoughts. Suppose Justina had been one of the girls "sold" by the Henchmen? They could have seen her with Lyle and taken her after the breakup. Was she back on drugs? On the street? Alive? Dead?

I was dressed and ready to leave the house for another chat with Mike Lucero when the door buzzed.

I opened it. The last person I expected to see was outside my front door, standing there in the sunlight. She said, "Hi. I hear you've been looking for me."

It was Justina.

She was staring at me with those dark, intense eyes. "Aren't you going to say anything?"

"Uh . . . sure, sure. Come on in. I'm just . . . surprised."

"You didn't figure on my coming here, huh?"

"No . . . I didn't. Where did you get my address?"

"From Bobbi. She said you'd been looking for me, and she had one of your cards. So I came on over. Hope you don't mind."

"God, no. I'm just happy to see you're okay."

We sat down in the living room. Both of us a little nervous. I'd spent so much time and emotion trying to locate the girl who sat facing me that the situation seemed more dream than reality.

Justina was wearing a striped black-and-white tank top, red shorts, and high white heels. Her ears sported large red enamel earrings, and there were red plastic bracelets on both wrists. Her oval face was pale. No lipstick. Which made her dark eyes even more striking. "Are you a detective?" she asked me.

"No," I said. "I'm just a hired hand. I was paid to find you."

"By who?"

"Lucas Appleton. He's a movie producer over at Murdock Studios in Burbank."

"What's he want with me?"

"He saw you playing a bit part . . . in that earthquake thing you did."

"So?"

"So he thinks you have 'major potential.' Wants to sign you up for his next film. He says he can build you into a star."

Her face twisted in disdain. "Me? A *star*? That's a load of crap."

"I'm no judge of who looks good in front of a camera," I told her. "But Lucas Appleton knows —"

"Knows what?" she cut in. "Does he know *me*? He just wasted his money sending you after me."

"Then . . . you don't want the chance at a career?"

"Shit, man, I just want to *survive*." She lowered her head in defeat. "I'm so screwed-up that just getting through another day takes everything I've got. I can't hold down any kind of a job right now — let alone trying to be an actress." Her eyes were agonized. "I'm being torn apart inside." She shook her head. "But you don't know what I'm saying. No way you could."

"Are you doing drugs again? Is that it?"

She pushed a strand of dark hair back from her face with a nervous hand. "No, it's not drugs. It's this other thing . . ."

I leaned toward her, meeting her eyes. "Want to talk about it? I'm a good listener."

"Why should I talk to you?"

"Why not? I've invested a lot of time and trouble in trying to find you. Don't you think you could at least tell me *why* you've been running away — and just what you're running from?"

Justina got up, walked to the window, staring out into the morning brightness. Then she wheeled to face me, lips trembling, tears in her eyes. "I don't *know* what I'm running from," she said in a wavering voice. "When the dreams began, I ignored them at first. Then they kept getting worse, turning into nightmares. I used drugs to try and escape them, but that didn't work. So I stopped. With some help. Then I drank for awhile . . . stayed drunk for a week . . . but that didn't help, either. The dreams just keep getting worse. More and more . . . real."

She walked over to my studio couch and sat down limply, biting her lower lip to keep back the tears.

I sat down next to her, taking her hand. She seemed so young and vulnerable, a defeated child lost in the forests of nightmare. "I really want to help," I said.

She nodded. "I believe you, but . . . I don't know why you'd care about what

happens to me."

"Maybe because I don't like to see anyone hurting as badly as you are. In the last few days I've done a lot of thinking about you, Justina. I'm trying to understand you."

"You want to know about the dreams?"

I nodded. "Maybe if you tell me about them, they'll seem less real. I saw Lyle Anmar and he mentioned them. Said they dealt with the supernatural. With demons."

"Just one demon," she said. "It doesn't have a name . . . or if it does, I don't know what it is. This . . . this thing . . . keeps getting stronger. In the early dreams it was in the background — but in each new dream it's getting closer, becoming more real . . . more *horrible*."

"Does it threaten you?"

"Not exactly. It's like . . . it wants to . . . to change me."

"Change you how?"

"I don't know. But it seems to have a *purpose*." She scrubbed at her tear-streaked eyes. "Now, even in the daytime when I'm not dreaming, I can see its face. Grinning at me — as if it knows some special secret."

"This might be an aftereffect of the drugs you took. Sometimes drugs can make dreams seem very real."

She shook her head vigorously. "It was there *before* the drugs. I *told* you . . ."

"You need help," I said. "And I'm not the one who can help you. I know a clinic where you can receive proper treatment."

Justina pulled back from me so abruptly that one of her earrings popped loose, landing on the couch. She ignored it, staring at me with eyes gone suddenly cold. "You don't *really* want to help me," she snapped. "You just want to put me away somewhere like a crazy person. Well, I'm *not* crazy!" She stood up, still glaring at me.

"I never said that. I was only —"

"Go to Hell, Kincaid!"

She ran from the room and was out of the house before I could reach the door to stop her.

Gone.

Back into hiding.

From the demon inside.

Another night. Another victim . . .

The sour taste of vomit was in her throat and her eyes were red and swollen; her naked skin was bleeding from a dozen abrasions. She knew she would die very soon now, her flesh slashed and savaged, her body ripped asunder by daggered teeth.

She was barely sixteen, yet these were the final moments of her life. What a fool she'd been to run away, to leave Ohio, her home, her parents, her younger brother and sister, to come here to California, to run into a death more horrific than she could ever have imagined.

She retched again in dry heaves that tore at her raw throat. Then she sprawled forward, her face against the slimed stones of her cell. Saliva dribbled from her caked, broken lips.

Why me? The question roared in her mind, spinning in endless circles within her brain.

Why me?

Dear God, why me?

Why?

Why?

Lucas Appleton had returned from his location shoot in Oregon when I walked into his office. He smiled at me around one of his unlit cigars. "How are you, David?"

Not that he cared, but I said I was fine.

"The picture's going great," he declared. (That accounted for the smile.) "We're a week ahead of schedule and half a million under budget. Me and the director, we see eye to eye on this baby all down the line. Last director I used was a fag sonuvabitch." He sat down behind his white desk. "Okay — to business. Have you been able to trace the Phillips girl?"

"She traced me," I said, thinking what an offensive toad Appleton really was. The more he shot off his foul mouth, the less I could stomach him. It was good not to be working for him anymore.

He frowned at me. "What do you mean, she traced *you*?"

"Showed up at my house this morning. I told her all about your job offer. She declined."

He leaned forward across the desk. "Where is she now? I *need* to know."

"What difference does it make where she is?" I said. "She doesn't want to make your movies. Period." I put a slip of paper on his desk: my personal check for four grand.

He picked it up, stared at it numbly.

"The other thousand I'm keeping for my time and expenses," I told him.

"I don't care about the damn money!" The producer was red in the face; a muscle jumped along his jawline. "Kincaid, I *demand* that you tell me where the Phillips girl can be found."

I said to him what Justina had said to me before she left; I told him to go to Hell.

And headed for my CRX.

I had dinner again that night with Kelly. She'd just sold a major essay to *Esquire* disputing the *auteur* theory in American cinema and was in a bubbly mood. When I told her about seeing Justina and about my subsequent meeting with Appleton, she seemed as relieved as I was that the job was over. Ultimately, Kelly declared, the girl must deal with whatever personal demons (or demon) pursued her.

I was very quiet throughout our dinner together, feeling guilty about not being able to help Justina. And I couldn't do anything about it now because I didn't know where she'd gone or how to reach her. She'd vanished again, like a puff of smoke, into the immense hive-swarm of Greater Los Angeles.

Also, I knew she didn't *want* my help.

But that didn't change how I felt about her. I couldn't get Justina Phillips out of my mind; her dark eyes continued to haunt me.

I apologized to Kelly for being such a lousy dinner companion and begged off for the rest of the evening, telling her I had to get back on target with my own career. I was going home to prep notes on a seminar I was due to conduct the following month in Palm Springs.

"Would I want to go?"

"Up to you," I said. "Subject is 'The Third Eye: Seeing Beyond the Obvious.' "

"I'll pass. I've already read most of your papers on the Third Eye."

Kelly understood about cutting our date short; she was actually very sweet about it.

I was the moody one.

It was after midnight and a wind from the ocean was rattling the pine trees outside the house. I was working in my den on the seminar, trying to focus on my notes, when a sound from the rear of the house caught my attention.

The wind? I didn't think so. This had been a loud, thumping sound. As if the kitchen door was being forced.

I got up quickly, leaving the den and heading for the kitchen. When I reached it I saw the dim form of a man directly outside the window. He began smashing at the glass with a wooden baseball bat.

I'd left my .38 in the Honda's glove compartment, and it was the only gun I owned, so I reached for a kitchen knife just as the intruder leaped through the shattered window.

He was on top of me before I had a chance to use the knife. We slammed to the floor together in a writhing tangle of arms and legs, the kitchen knife spinning away from me on the polished linoleum.

He was a big guy in a black-knit ski mask, strong as a sumo wrestler. My eyes bugged as he locked a meaty arm around my neck and started squeezing. Red sparks began dancing inside my head and I knew I had to act fast before the killing pressure got to me. I drove my left elbow back into his balls with enough force to elicit a heavy grunt of pain. That broke the chokehold, and I rolled free, managing to scoop up the fallen kitchen knife.

I lunged for him, blade extended, but he smashed my left kneecap with the wooden bat and I dropped the knife again, clutching at my leg. Now he loomed over me, eyes glittering through the holes in the ski mask. "Where is she?"

"Who?" I gasped, holding my knee. "Where's who?"

"The Phillips girl. Lucas said you saw her yesterday. Where *is* she?"

"I don't know," I told him. "You can beat the crap out of me, but it won't change the fact that I don't know where she is."

"We'll see if you're telling the truth," he said, ramming the bat into my stomach. It took me a while to get back enough breath to say, "I don't know. Dammit, man, I *don't know.*"

He swung the heavy bat toward my head. I could see it arcing down at me, could even see the grain of the wood, as if everything moved in slow motion. Then it exploded against my skull and a yellow plume of fire roared across my brain.

I opened my eyes. Mike Lucero was patting my bleeding scalp with a wet bath towel. I was on the studio couch; obviously, he'd carried me there.

"Hi, pal," I said shakily. "What brings you over? It's pretty late for a social call."

"Somebody spotted a guy riding hellbent away from here on a red Harley," Mike told me. "Looked suspicious, so he phoned the Sheriff's Station. Since it was your address, I figured I'd come check on you."

"Glad you did," I said. "But since when are you working nights?"

"Since we got backed up on cases," he said. "I came in tonight to help out."

"So . . . Doctor Lucero, am I still alive?"

"You look like a Mack truck rolled over you," he growled. "I'm calling an ambulance."

"Oh no, you're not." I sat up, holding the towel against my head. "We're going after the bastard that did this."

"You know who he is? You see his face?"

"No, he was wearing a ski mask. But I recognized his voice and I saw the snake tattoo on his right hand. It was Billy Mead."

"The Grinder!" Mike shook his head. "Why would Mead attack you?"

"He wanted to find somebody I've been looking for. A girl. Figured I knew where she was."

"Do you?"

"No, and that's what I told him. But he didn't seem to believe me." I stood up gingerly, testing my left leg. The knee throbbed painfully, but I could walk. I put aside the towel; my head had stopped bleeding. "I'll tell you the full story on the way to get Mead."

"I'd better call for backup."

"No, Mike, it's just you and me on this one. I don't want any cops around when I get my hands on him."

"What about *me*? I'm a cop, for God's sake!"

"You're my friend. There's a difference."

"I'd have to be one crazy son of a bitch to go out against the Henchmen with a smashed-up spook hunter in the middle of the frigging night."

But that's exactly what he did.

We took Mike's police cruiser. Our first stop was Bernie's Joint on Sepulveda. When we walked in, we found several Henchmen at the bar. Mead wasn't among them. The bikers glared at us sullenly, poised for action, until Mike flashed his badge. Then they backed off fast. Cop trouble was the last thing they wanted.

It turned out that the bartender knew Billy's home address and with a little persuasion (Mike threatened to rip off his head), he gave it to us.

We drove over there. To a seedy apartment building just two miles from Bernie's. Mead was on the second floor, number 212, and Mike didn't bother to announce us. He just put his shoulder into that flimsy wooden door and smashed through, gun in hand. I was right behind him with my .38 Special out and ready.

We heard a female shriek from the inner bedroom; a well-rounded blonde in a black net bra and tight red hot pants ran past us into the hall. She took off down the stairs while we headed for the bedroom.

Billy was in there, sitting cross-legged on the mattress, buck naked. He had a sawed-off leveled at us.

"Put down that shotgun," Mike ordered, his .45 aimed at Mead's hairy chest. "I'm with the Sheriff's Department, and you're under arrest."

"For what?" Billy demanded.

Of course he recognized me, and he knew damn well why we were there. But he was a mean piece of goods and his grip on the sawed-off didn't waver.

My throat was dry. If Mead triggered that shotgun we'd be perforated dog meat.

Mike didn't seem shaken by those twin barrels staring at us. His .45 was no match for a sawed-off at this range, but Lucero backs down to nobody.

"I told you," he said coldly, spacing his words: "Put . . . down . . . that . . . weapon!" He let the barrel of the automatic drop an inch. "Or do you want me to blow your balls off?"

"You got nothin' on me," whined Mead. "An' you got no call to come bust-assin' in here with guns. I got my goddamn rights!"

"You gave those up when you came at me tonight with a baseball bat," I said, my .38 pointed at him. I was gripping it so hard my fingers ached.

"How do you know it was me?"

"The tattoo on your right hand," I said.

"I'll tell you just one more time, punk," rasped Mike. "Either you put down that weapon or —"

He didn't get a chance to finish the threat. Billy did a wild roll off the mattress, firing as he hit the floor.

The rolling action threw off his aim and the double shotgun charge took out the top half of the bedroom door, but it didn't touch Mike or me.

Lucero triggered his automatic. Twice. Both rounds socked home in Mead's body. The first skidded across his ribs, but the second got him square in the chest.

He dropped the shotgun, clawing at his bleeding upper body, eyes rolled white with shock.

Mike holstered the .45 and stood over Mead. His voice was level now, the hardness gone. "I'm sorry you made me do that, Billy," he said. "Real sorry."

"That makes . . . two of us," gasped Mead. Blood bubbles were already breaking at his lips; he didn't have long.

"Got a phone here?" Mike asked.

Billy shook his head.

"Stay with him," Mike told me. "I'm going out to the car and call for an ambulance."

I nodded — and Mike quickly exited the bedroom. Billy was trying to tell me something. I knelt down next to him, leaning in close to hear the words.

"It . . . wasn't *me* . . . I was . . . sent."

"Who sent you?"

"Wanted . . . her . . . Justina . . . real bad . . . maybe be . . . one of his girls."

"Are you talking about a pimp?"

A faint shake of his head. "These girls . . . they were . . . *special.*" He coughed raggedly, red froth at his mouth. "Just . . . one a month . . . young, pretty ones . . . he pays high . . ."

"Who? Who's been paying you for these special girls?"

Billy tried to form more words, but couldn't. Blood ran steadily down his chin. He was fading fast. I could hear sirens in the distance as Mike returned to the room.

"He gonna make it?"

In answer, the biker's head fell back. Mead's body twitched once, a spastic death twitch — and then he was gone.

Maybe he'd learned enough this time around so his next life wouldn't be so lousy. I hoped so.

Mike looked at me. His eyes were troubled. We didn't say anything as the sirens got louder.

I decided not to tell Lucero what Billy had said about the "special girls." It was something I wanted to deal with on my own.

Took me a long time that night to get to sleep; I had a lot of anger inside me.

When Lucas Appleton showed up at his studio office at ten-thirty the next morning I was there waiting for him. I'd gotten rid of his thin-lipped secretary a half-hour earlier, telling her that the producer had a head cold and wouldn't be coming in. She was to drive over to his house for some emergency dictation. I didn't want her around when I had my little talk with Appleton.

When he walked in I was sitting in his cream-colored leather desk chair. He looked surprised to see me — as well as annoyed because I was in his chair. I stood up, walking around the desk to face him.

"I'm here because of Billy," I said. My tone was edged.

Appleton lifted an eyebrow. "Billy? I don't know anyone named Billy."

"Not anymore you don't. Billy's dead. And in case you're wondering, he didn't get a thing out of me last night when you sent him to my place."

"Look, Kincaid, I don't know what the hell you're talking about."

"Oh, I think you do," I said, grabbing him by his shirt front and slamming him hard against the office wall. "I think you know *exactly* what I'm talking about, you sick son of a bitch!"

"How dare you manhandle me!" he sputtered.

"You're lucky I'm not taking a baseball bat to your head! That's what your biker boy did to me."

I shoved him backwards onto the couch and he landed with a thump solid enough to dislodge his mirrored shades.

His eyes were wide and frightened; I was getting to him.

"Billy Mead used your name when he broke into my place last night," I told him. "His exact words were: 'Lucas said you saw her yesterday.' Meaning Justina. Obviously, you sent him to beat her address out of me."

"That's insane!"

"There's more. Before he died, Mead told me he's been supplying 'special' girls to someone who's paying a high price for them — and that this buyer wanted Justina Phillips 'real bad,' as he put it." I stood above Appleton, hands fisted. "*You're* the buyer. Everything fits. You never intended to *hire* Justina, you wanted her for the same perverted reason you wanted these other girls."

"Get out of my office!" The producer's face was puffed and livid. "You can't come in here and accuse me of such nonsense! I don't buy women!"

I was about to go for him again when two big security guards, alerted by the racket, grabbed me, painfully twisting my arms behind my back.

"You want this creep arrested, Mr. Appleton?"

"Uh . . . no." Appleton looked badly shaken. "Just . . . have him kept off the lot. He's mentally unbalanced. Now get him out of here."

They did that, fast-walking me to my Honda and making sure I exited Murdock Studios.

I knew why Appleton hadn't pressed charges against me. He was afraid I'd tell the cops what I told him. But I couldn't. Not yet. Because I had no proof that he was the buyer. I was certain in my gut that he was the one, and by facing him at the studio I'd hoped to force an admission out of him. But that hadn't worked.

There was one key question that I kept asking myself, over and over: was Lucas Appleton buying these girls for himself — or for someone else?

I felt I *had* to find Justina — that a demonic force was closing in on her and that I might, somehow, be able to avert its course.

The weather reflected my mood; the day had suddenly darkened. Heavy clouds from the Mexican tropics had rolled in like a host of towering, bloated figures in soot-black clothing. A rainstorm was brewing, unseasonal for August in L.A. Usually we don't get rain in the summer.

When I returned home there was a message from Kelly on my answering machine. She was off to Paris, on assignment for a fashion magazine, and would see me when she got back.

An hour later, under a shrouded sky, I was on the freeway, headed for downtown, carrying in my coat pocket what I hoped would provide a lead to Justina.

I was relieved to find Irene Hopwood at home. When I rang the bell from the porch of her big Victorian house I saw her image rippling through the stained-glass front window as she answered the door. She opened the screen, giving me a warm smile. We exchanged hellos.

"I tried to call you first," I told her, "but you were out. I took a chance anyhow and came on down here."

"I just got home," she said. "Been shopping all afternoon. If you've got feet as wide as mine, finding the right shoes can be a real hassle. Maybe if I were a better psychic I could visualize them and know just where to look."

"May I talk to you?" I asked.

"Of course, David." She gestured me in. "You know you're always welcome. But I'm afraid I didn't buy any of those chocolate chip cookies you like so much."

I grinned. "I'll manage to survive without 'em."

We sat down on two smoked-orange velour chairs in her parlour. The day's gloom was aborted by a pair of tall, heavily-scrolled Victorian bronze lamps. They cast a warm yellow radiance over the room.

"At least I can offer you tea," Irene said.

"No, thanks. I just came to show you this." I took Justina's red earring from my coat pocket. It glittered in the lamplight. "Belongs to the young woman I talked to you about last time. Justina Phillips. She left it at my place."

"Then you *did* find her?"

"No, she came to me. And then promptly disappeared again. I was hoping the earring might help me locate her."

Irene's face was somber. "I'm sorry to hear you're still involved with her. I warned you that by searching for this individual you were moving into a very dangerous area — toward a destructive force of darkness."

"I remember," I said. "And, believe me, I don't discount your warning — but I feel that she *needs* me, that somehow I must reach her before she's destroyed."

"And what if *you're* destroyed with her?"

"That's a chance I'm willing to take. I don't have all the answers, Irene. And I don't *know* what I'll be going up against. But I have to try."

Irene looked at me steadily, concern in her shaded gray eyes. "In her mother's photo, I sensed great evil. Perhaps the two have now united."

"That's possible," I admitted.

"Then you still want me to 'read' the earring?"

"I do. She was wearing it when she came to see me, so it should carry strong vibrations."

I handed the enameled red earring to Irene. She accepted it hesitantly, as if it might burn her flesh. "We're dealing here with demonic powers. Are you *certain* you want me to proceed?"

I nodded. "I'm certain."

She pressed both hands firmly around the object, leaning forward, picking up the earring's vibrations as they began to resonate within her own force field.

She closed her eyes. A ripple of movement shook her body and her breathing deepened. "This person is . . . is . . ."

"Yes? What do you see?"

"Darkness. There is a terrible darkness surrounding her. It's . . . palpable. A *physical* presence. There's a name . . . Sargoth." Abruptly, she opened her eyes. "This is very bad, David. Dangerous. I don't like what I'm getting."

I didn't tell her who Sargoth was; that would have disturbed her even more. "Do you sense danger for Justina?"

"I don't know. The negative vibrations — I can't separate them. The darkness is overwhelming."

"I need to find her as soon as possible," I said. "Try and give me a location."

She pressed the earring to her forehead and closed her eyes again. "A beach. A house . . . facing the ocean. White. The house is painted white."

"But where is it? We've got a helluva long coastline!"

"It's here . . . in this area. Southern California. The Los Angeles area. She . . . she's with a friend. A female."

Maybe Justina was back with Bobbi Graham in Venice. But that building didn't face the ocean — and it wasn't white.

Irene told me she could get no more and seemed anxious to return the earring to me. Like ridding herself of a poisonous snake.

When I left Irene Hopwood I was frightened. I told myself to give it up, to stop searching for Justina, to allow her to work out her own destiny. I knew I was entering an area of serious personal risk, possibly beyond my limits. When you're in a boat and spot a whirlpool churning the water ahead of you, the last thing you do is row toward it. You pull back to keep from being sucked under. That's how I felt — that if I kept up this senseless quest I'd be sucked under, whirled into darkness.

By the time I reached my Honda a hard rain had begun, sizzling on the pavement like grease in a skillet. The sky was ominous and sullen, and the late afternoon sun had retreated behind thickly-massed clouds. It was smart enough to get out of a storm's way.

I wasn't.

Back home I did some basic research in my library. (Of which I am immodestly proud. Over 25,000 well-chosen volumes I began collecting when I was ten, most of them relating to the paranormal and supernatural.) Sargoth was listed in *A History of Demonology* as the progenitor of a ghoulish brood of shape-change demons dating back to Neolithic times. They were said to have a strong taste for human flesh. Such a creature was known as a "broxa."

Could it be possible that Justina's mother was one of these? A lineal descendant of Sargoth, the Father of Demons? Was *she* the demonic presence that haunted Justina's dreams?

"Kincaid," I said aloud, firmly shutting the book, "I think you're round the bend on this one."

It wasn't that I didn't have a healthy respect for the supernatural; I believe that there are many forces in this bizarre, wonderful universe of ours which exist on planes beyond the rational. But I had personally never encountered a demon, anymore than I'd seen a flying saucer. Still . . . I ripped a page from the book, folding it into my pocket.

I decided to quit thinking about broxas and check out my idea that Justina might once again be living with Bobbi Graham. Maybe they'd moved to a new location facing the ocean.

"She'd never move back with me," Bobbi declared when I reached her on the phone. "Our life styles are too spaced out. There's no way we could cut it together anymore."

"Okay," I said. "You've got my home number. Contact me if you hear from her."

With my next call I struck pay dirt. Lyle Anmar knew about a friend of Justina's who had a house right on the beach in Trancas.

"Her name is Linda Galvin," he told me. "She's a commercial artist. Paints stuff for all the major greeting card companies."

"What's she like?"

"Ash blonde. Good looker. In fact, she'd be a real knockout except for the pink scar along the right side of her face. Said she got it when she was a kid — in a car accident."

"Could Justina be living with her?"

"Maybe. They're close pals. But, like I told you, I've been totally out of touch."

I thanked Anmar, telling him that he'd been a big help.

The phone book provided me with Linda Galvin's address.

I drove there.

The darkness was closing in.

As I swung the CRX onto Pacific Coast Highway the storm was in full force. Rain smashed down from a charcoal sky.

Trancas is an upscale beach community a few miles north of Malibu. Several well-known film personalities have homes in the area. Steve McQueen used to live there when he was married to Ali MacGraw. Obviously, Linda Galvin was doing just fine with her art. Losers don't live in Trancas.

Her house was typical. Long, low, rambling — an ultra-modern stone-and-glass job built right on the sand, with a wide porch facing the ocean.

And it was white.

I came in from the beach side. Thunder rumbled overhead like cannon and the sea was in turmoil, sending in its battalions of wind-crested waves like troops charging an enemy shore.

The steps leading up to Galvin's porch were slick with rain and blown sand. I tapped on the sliding glass door and waited, getting out my Sheriff's Consultant ID. Nobody answered. The house was totally dark inside. I tapped again, louder this time. Still no reply.

I leaned close to the cold glass, trying to peer in, but I couldn't make out anything. The interior was as black as the dark side of the moon.

I tried the sliding glass door. It was unlocked. Which bothered me. People in Trancas don't go away leaving their houses open.

Something was wrong inside.

Should I go back to the Honda for my .38? Or should I phone Mike Lucero? But what would I tell him? I wasn't even sure that Justina was living here. That was a guess, based on what Lyle Anmar had told me.

I slid the glass door open. It whispered smoothly back along oiled runners and I stepped inside. Immediately, I recognized a strong, overwhelming odor. Newly-spilled blood. I groped my way to a table lamp and snapped it on.

Blood was everywhere. Spattered on walls, smeared across furniture, streaked along wood flooring. Someone had been butchered in this room like a steer in a slaughterhouse.

Numbly, I snapped on another lamp. This illuminated the killing site — behind a long, sectional sofa. The beige rug was soaked in dark crimson — and *part* of a body was there.

A human arm, ripped violently from the shoulder, was lying near one of the polished oak end tables. The flesh was soft and rounded, and a bracelet still adorned the wrist. The arm of a young female. (*Justina?* Had I arrived too late to save her? Had a monstrous creature from her dreams materialized to destroy her?)

Then I saw that a smeared blood trail led toward the rear of the house. The killer had obviously dragged the body out of the living room and along a short hallway. I followed the gory trail to a closed door at the end of the hall. A bathroom.

Opening that door was one of the most difficult and unnerving acts of my life. It required full willpower to force my hand to turn the knob.

The raw smell of blood and body wastes assaulted my nostrils, overpowering and horrible. I fumbled for the wall switch, activated it. The sudden glare of fluorescent brightness shocked my eyes.

She was in the tub. What was left of her, that is. Much of her body was missing, whole chunks of it, as if a Great White had been at her, slashing and devouring. Gobbets of flesh had plugged the drain and the corpse was literally swimming in blood.

I'd never seen anything like this. I gagged. A sour wave of bile welled up from my stomach, causing me to double over and spew the contents of my last meal over the blood-puddled tile floor.

Most of the head was intact, although it lolled grotesquely sideways, almost bitten through at the neck. Ash blonde hair was clotted with blood and I could clearly see the long pink scar along the right side of the face.

The dead girl was Linda Galvin.

I'd been right about Justina; she *had* been living here in Trancas. I found her clothes in one of the closets, including the striped black-and-white tank top she'd worn at my place.

But where was she now?

Walking back toward the living room, I saw that a message had been scrawled in blood on the wall near the hall doorway. Reading it, I knew suddenly, chillingly, where I'd find Justina.

I had one more thing to do before I left this place of death. I went into the kitchen, opened the fridge, took out a carton of milk. I emptied it into the sink, rinsed it out with cold water, and carried it back into the hall. . . .

I called the Malibu Sheriff's Station from an outside phone, with rain threading the sides of the glass half-booth. I asked for Mike Lucero and they told me to call him at home, that he was back on days.

His wife answered, and I asked Carla to put Mike on the line, telling her that it was urgent.

"What's up, Davey?" His voice was solid and reassuring.

"A young woman named Linda Galvin was butchered tonight at her beach house in Trancas," I told him.

"Jesus! *Butchered?*"

"That's the only word for it."

"Give me the address." I did that, and he said he'd call it into the station.

"I need to ask a favor, Mike. A big one."

"So ask."

"I think I know who killed Linda Galvin," I said. "But I need you with me when I check it out. Just the two of us."

"Again?" He groaned. "Hey, Kincaid, you're not Batman and I'm not Robin the Boy Wonder. If you know where the killer is, then we send in cops to deal with the situation."

"I can't be sure I'm right. It's a wild theory based on a lot of stuff you wouldn't understand. But if I *am* right, then cops with guns won't do any good. It's going to take more than bullets to finish this."

"What the hell are you talking about?"

"If I told you what I'm talking about, you'd refuse to help me. Trust me, Mike. I *need* you with me tonight. I don't want to do this alone."

"Do *what?*"

"You'll find out when I see you. Please. Meet me. I'm asking you as a friend."

Despite his better judgment, Lucero met me exactly one hour later in Griffith Park. The storm was still bad, and rain slashed down like bright swords in front of our headlights.

I waved Mike over. He left his car and climbed into my Honda, shaking rain from his hair and glaring at me as I started the engine. "Where are we going?"

"To the House of Horrors," I said.

I braked the Honda to a quiet stop at twenty-three hundred Glendower, cutting the lights and engine. The sound of drumming rain intensified and the night darkness moved in, thick and menacing, around us.

On the way up the hill I had told Mike what I'd found in Trancas, and why I was convinced that a demon had murdered Linda Galvin.

He stared at me. "Demons don't exist, Davey, and you damn well know it."

"This one does," I said. "Or I should say, *they* do."

"They?"

"There's more than one inside the house. Broxas. Witch-demons. Flesh eaters. Part of a breed dating back to Neolithic times. Very strong — and very dangerous."

I had taken along the page I'd removed from *A History of Demonology*. Now I showed it to Lucero. "This is what we'll be dealing with." The steel engraving portrayed two fanged demons locked in combat.

Mike nodded. "You were right, by God, what you said earlier — that if you'd told me any of this crap over the phone I'd have refused to meet you tonight."

"But it's true, Mike."

"It's bullshit!"

"Come inside with me and I'll *prove* it. They're in the house, Mike, and we have to kill them."

"Oh, yeah?" And he snorted. "And just how do you kill a frigging demon?"

"I know how. But you've got to help me."

"Whose place is this?"

"It belongs to Alex DeMarco."

"The horror actor?"

"He's more than an actor," I said. "And more than human. He's a broxa."

"You're *serious* about all this, aren't you?"

"It's life or death, Mike. Justina Phillips is in there. I've come for her — and I'm going inside with or without you."

He sighed. "Okay, I'll tag along. To make sure you don't get yourself in trouble with DeMarco. Maybe I can explain to him that you're not really a cat burglar, you're just a nut on the supernatural."

"You'll see I'm telling this straight once we're inside," I said, opening the car door.

I got out, carrying the milk carton and a long three-cell metal flashlight.

"What's with the milk?"

"It's not milk, it's blood. And we're going to need it."

"You planning to give DeMarco a transfusion?"

I ignored the wisecrack. "There's a dog named Bruno guarding the place. A black Doberman. I can handle him."

I said this as I was picking the gate lock with a thin sliver of steel, a trick I'm very good at.

"We don't even have a search war-

N91

rant," groaned Lucero. "We're gonna get our ass sued!"

"Stay out here until I take care of the dog," I said. "And keep your gun ready in case you have to shoot him." I stepped through the gate.

"This I gotta see," Mike said.

Right on cue, Bruno came galloping out of the night, black on black, his muscled body shining with rain, teeth bared, snarling savagely.

I devoutly hoped my theory about the creature was right. If it wasn't, Mike would have to put a .45 slug through him to keep him from tearing my throat out. I waited until he was almost on me before I flipped open the carton, whipping it toward him.

A long twine of blood spattered over him and he fell back, howling wildly. Instantly, his body dissolved into the wet night grass.

Mike was bug-eyed. "I don't believe what I just saw," he intoned softly. "That dog . . . he . . . he just *melted*!"

"It wasn't really a dog," I told Mike, holding the gate open for him. I didn't have time to explain that Bruno was a familiar, a creature attendant to a witch-demon, who in this case had assumed the form of a dog. The best way to kill one is with the blood of a broxa victim, and Linda's had done the job neatly. "*Vamanos!* We need to act fast if we're going to surprise DeMarco."

And we moved rapidly toward the house.

We got lucky. One of the lower-story windows was unlatched and we were able to enter the house without setting off any alarms.

I led Mike along a gloomed hallway toward the library. (I'd passed by it the first time I visited DeMarco.) My .38 was still in the Honda; I'd forgotten to put it in my coat. I hoped I wouldn't need it, that if any gunplay was necessary, Mike's .45 would provide us with ample firepower.

The house was cemetery-quiet. The sound of the outside storm was heavily muted, as if God had turned down the volume.

"You sure DeMarco's at home?"

"Bank on it. I know that Justina is here — and where she is, he'll be."

We entered the library. The room was huge, with a deep stone fireplace. I estimated there were at least five thousand volumes packed into the ceiling-to-floor bookcases which lined the room.

"There's a tunnel in here that leads below," I said. "We just have to find it."

"How do you know about a tunnel?"

"There was an article in *Contemporary Architecture* about the guy who built this place," I told him. "It mentioned a tunnel behind one of the bookcases leading down to a wine cellar. I think that's where they are."

I was checking out each bookcase, trying to locate the right one.

"This is Looney Tunes," Mike said. "I feel like a damn fool."

"Got it!" I said in triumph. A large bookcase near the fireplace swung back to reveal the wide mouth of a tunnel, with steps in cut stone leading downward. It smelled damp and fetid. Below us, a faint glow from the cellar tinted the walls.

"Told you they were down there," I whispered.

"There's a light on all right," Mike admitted. "But we don't know *who's* down there."

I put a finger to my lips. "*Real* quiet," I warned as I entered the tunnel. "And be prepared for anything."

Mike followed me down the curved stone stairs with his .45 out, so I knew he was serious.

The tunnel got brighter as we descended. We could hear sounds now — the horrific sounds of teeth on bone, of ripping flesh . . .

I knew what they signified. A blood feast was in progress and the victim was undoubtedly one of the homeless young girls picked up by the Henchmen and sold to Appleton, who passed them on to DeMarco as a sexual diversion. Of course, I was sure Appleton had no idea of their actual disposition — that they were used not for sex, but to slake a demon's monstrous hunger. That was Alex DeMarco's little secret.

The tunnel ended — and we now had a clear view of the feast as we pressed into the deep shadows at the edge of the wine cellar.

My sense of revulsion was blunted somewhat because I had known what to expect, and because I'd already seen what had been done to Linda Galvin — but Mike was visibly shuddering. His face was ashen and his mouth twisted at the horrors confronting us.

Justina *was* with DeMarco, and when I saw her there, I realized that my quest had been without hope, that I could never have saved her.

The transformation had been completed.

She was in a bestial half-crouch, hunched naked over the newly-slain corpse of a young girl. Her body was covered in gore as she gnawed at a detached leg bone, eyes glittering, her hair matted with blood.

She still maintained human form, as did Alex DeMarco, naked beside her, sharing this celebratory meal with his demonic offspring.

The message on the wall in Trancas, scrawled there in her victim's blood, had told me where Justina had gone after slaughtering Linda Galvin:

Tonight I have achieved my destiny.
I know who my real mother is.
I am going to her now.

At last, mother and daughter were united.

Alex DeMarco had been Leona Stoddard . . . just as, in an earlier era, he had been actress Louise Collins. As a shape-change witch-demon, he was able to

transform himself — at will — into a fully-functioning man or woman. As Leona, he had given birth to Justina. But he knew she had to be left alone and allowed to mature gradually. The dreams first, then the reality. DeMarco had kept track of her for awhile (the photo at her tenth birthday party), but had lost contact as she grew older. As she neared her final transformation, he wanted her badly. That's why he had Appleton and the Henchmen looking for her. They didn't know *why* DeMarco wanted her. Since they regularly supplied young women, Justina would be just another of many.

But, at full maturation, she had found her true parent. Blood had called to blood, and she *knew,* instinctively, where to go.

To the house of Alex DeMarco.

I'd been putting all of this together in the back of my mind, but until I found Linda Galvin's half-devoured corpse it didn't lock into place for me.

Tonight, at this moment, it was all too real.

Back at the Trancas house I'd filled the milk carton with the dead girl's blood, dipping the carton into the tub until it was full. My plan was simple: pour a circle of Linda's blood around the demons, then set it afire. A broxa cannot pass through a circle of victim's blood — and broxas *can* be destroyed by fire.

Now I realized that my plan had an inherent problem: how could I immobilize the two demons long enough for me to pour the blood circle? Finding them down here in the wine cellar, however, solved my problem; there was only one exit — through the tunnel. All I had to do was pour a line of blood across the floor in front of the tunnel and put a match to it. The demons would not be able to cross this line, and they'd burn with the house.

I heard a shout from above. I had entirely forgotten about DeMarco's man, Edward. His cry alerted Justina and DeMarco. Like predatory animals, their heads lifted, eyes probing the cellar, picking us out of the darkness.

"Kill the sonuvabitch!" I yelled at Lucero as Edward rounded the tunnel's final curve and came at us with an upraised ax.

Mike didn't hesitate. He fired directly into Edward's face — and the cadaverous creep dropped the ax as Lucero's bullets took his head apart.

At least *he* was no demon.

Justina and DeMarco were watching us calmly, sure of themselves, figuring there was no way we could escape. They were too fast and deadly.

"Bastards!" screamed Lucero, swinging his gun toward them. The roar of the big .45 was deafening in the walled cellar. But, just as I expected, the heavy rounds were totally ineffective; bullets cannot harm a broxa.

He gaped at them, believing, at last, that I was right, that what he now faced was truly demonic.

They were amused. Their gore-smeared lips pulled back in grotesque smiles. I'd never seen smiles like that.

But I still had my plan . . .

I pushed Mike toward the stairs, yelling "Blood! Stay back!" I raised the carton — but I wasn't quick enough. They sprang forward like a pair of jungle cats, knocking the carton from my grasp and pulling us away from the tunnel. Mike tried to fight, viciously clubbing at them with the barrel of his gun, but the blows were useless.

We were thrown heavily to the cellar floor. When Mike lunged upward again, DeMarco delivered a crushing blow which knocked him senseless. He lay face down, unmoving. But Mike wasn't dead; I could see him breathing.

DeMarco finally spoke. "Did you really think you could trap us down here, Mr. Kincaid? That is quite impossible. We are far stronger than you might imagine."

Justina leveled her dark eyes on me. "We could easily smash our way out of this cellar without having to cross your line of blood," she said.

DeMarco moved to the nearest concrete wall, lashing out with his right fist. The wall cracked open, a deep fissure splitting the concrete.

"I'm impressed," I said, fighting to maintain emotional stability. Terror was forming at the edge of my mind. I couldn't give in to it; I *had* to keep my wits clear.

"You should never have followed me," Justina said, her voice cold as the grave. "It will cost you your life."

"It's *your* life you should worry about," I said. A new plan was forming. A desperate one.

Her eyes flashed. "What do you mean?"

"Violent death is part of your heritage," I said. "A parent broxa is driven to devour its young once the offspring has reached maturity. Like the Black Widow spider devours its mate. Why do you think DeMarco wanted so badly to find you? You'll be dead before sunup, torn apart by your own loving parent."

"He lies!" hissed DeMarco. "He's trying to set us against one another so he can escape."

"You're younger and more powerful than he is," I told Justina. "You've just come into your full strength. You can destroy him and avert your fate."

She laughed scornfully. "And why should I believe anything you say of the broxa? You fear us. You know how horrible your death will be at our hands."

"Then consider this," I said, snatching the page with the reproduced steel engraving from the pocket of my coat and tossing it to her. "From *A History of Demonology*. It proves what I've told you."

She stared at the engraved illustration, showing a young broxa being torn apart by its parent demon. The caption verified my words.

DeMarco ripped it from her hand. "Don't listen to him. He seeks to divide us!" He swung his head toward me, eyes blazing. "And shall die for it!"

He pulled me toward him, his mouth wide, head dipping for my throat. His teeth glittered like blood-stained daggers under the cellar lights.

I fought desperately to break free, but his strength was awesome; I was helpless in his grip. The terror in my mind swept in to engulf me. In another second he'd tear my throat out.

Suddenly, DeMarco jerked back, screaming in pain. Attacking behind him, Justina had torn a sizable gobbet of raw flesh from his left shoulder.

He released me, pivoting to clash with his angry offspring. They were snarling at each other, the sounds only half-human.

This was my chance. I closed my fingers around the fallen carton of blood. It was intact; I hadn't had time to open it before it had been knocked to the floor.

I edged around the grappling demons as they writhed in slashing battle. I opened the carton and began pouring the blood circle. Completed, it totally surrounded them, a barrier neither could cross.

I got my arms around Mike's chest and dragged him to the stairs. He was groaning, beginning to come around. I pulled a matchbook from my coat. Fumbled it open. Struck a match. Then I seized the fallen book page that DeMarco had discarded and ignited it, creating a small torch in my hand. I flipped it at the edge of the crimson circle.

Blood from a broxa's victim will burn like jet fuel and the entire area erupted into sudden flame.

Yet DeMarco and Justina paid no heed to the conflagration. Lost in a death struggle, they had now reverted to their loathsome demon forms, scaly and terrible, locked together, tearing savagely at one another with tooth and claw.

Near the tunnel entrance, Mike had regained full consciousness and staggered to his feet, a hand braced against the wall. "What the hell's going on?"

"Up the stairs!" I yelled at him. The fire was spreading rapidly. "Move!"

We plunged back into the tunnel, coughing and choking from the dense smoke, climbing steadily upward as the fire raged below.

By dawn, despite the best efforts of L.A. City firefighters, the House of Horrors was totally destroyed. Only black ash and scorched stone remained.

The storm was over and the sun rose into a cloudless summer sky.

My search for Justina Phillips had ended.   Ω

When you move, beware of the Curse!

Escape the awful emptiness of the Undelivered *Weird Tales*®!
A few weeks before your actual move, as soon as you know your new address, send us your old address (including ZIP code) and your new address (again — please! — with ZIP code).
Many thanks; we can't afford to lose you!

We are at:
Weird Tales®, P.O. Box 13418, Philadelphia PA 19101-3418

ZUKALA'S LOVE SONG

Along the sky my chariot ran,
    And the star-things ran before.
I raced the breeze over star-lit seas
    Till the very wind gave o'er;
But my soul grew lone, and my heart grew sad,
    Sad as the sighing sea,
For there was never a girl or lad
    To laugh in the skies with me.

I hid my wings in a scarlet cloak,
    I lowered my burning eyes,
And I went on foot with a lilting lute,
    A beggar from the skies.
I tuned my lute to a song of love,
    I edged my song with mirth,
And my feet drank deep of the waving grove
    And deep of the dust of earth.

And maidens flung me silver coins,
    And women praised my voice,
And when dawn was past, I found at last
    The rose-white girl of my choice.
She flung me a rose when I sang to her,
    And its roots sank in my breast;
But oh, she flung me a deathly rose
    When she put my love to jest.

I sang her songs like a dew drop's fall
    And songs like a bugle peal;
But her heart was cold, and the world grew old,
    And the heart of me turned to steel.
I rent to shreds my scarlet cloak,
    I raised my terrible eyes,
I spread my wings till they hid the sun,
    And mounted again to the skies.

I left my scarlet cloak to lie
    Like a rift of blood on the sward,
But I did not break the lute I bore,
    For that was the soul of a bard.
Then from the blue empirean deeps
    Where Nothing conquers All,
I raised a hand to the tiny world
    As a giant grasps a ball;

ZUKALA'S LOVE SONG

And I seized the woman that I loved,
    She screamed in my embrace;
And I brought her to me, white and still
    From the fear of that rush through space.
She lay in the hollow of my hand
    And shrieked to hear the truth:
That I who laughed to see her writhe
    Was one with the beggar youth.

Then into the bowl I flung her soul,
    And the stars in glittering dress
Laughed, crowding in with their cosmic sin,
    To jeer at her nakedness;
For the golden plates that hid her breasts
    And the silk that covered her loins
I rent and flung to the trailing mist
    As a drunkard scatters coins.

Blue and dim on the topaz rim
    Where the silence drinks the night,
Forgotten moons like crazy loons
    Hovered into her sight;
And out of the deep where shadows sleep
    That never knew the sun,
Strange eyes aflame, the dark stars came,
    Whispering, one by one.

And with burning eyes that hid her thighs
    As fire-flies cover a tree,
They kissed her face in a hot embrace,
    And she whimpered upon her knee.
Then I swept the band with a jade-nailed hand,
    And the slim of her waist I gripped,
And the stars fell out of her hair like moths
    And through my fingers slipped.

High on a lone sapphirean throne
    I sat me down with a laugh,
And in wild alarm she clung to my arm,
    In fear she clutched at my staff.
A million miles beneath her seat
    Rippled the topaz seas,
And there were stars below her feet
    And moons between her knees.

— **Robert E. Howard**

THE HELL BOOK

by Jason Van Hollander

art by Bob Eggleton

In a scholarly book entitled *The Function of the Nightmare,* there is a whole chapter devoted to the dream drawings of Eli Needleman. These pen and ink creations by my one-time neighbor first appeared in the underground comic books of twenty years ago; they were hellish and revelatory even then. At the time I was a college student — an idler, an ingester of certain consciousness-altering substances. It was during an overlong party in my freshman year, just before sunrise, that I first encountered Eli Needleman's artwork swarming through the pages of *Yellow Dog, Migraine Funnies* and the now infamous "banned" issue of *Zap Comics* Number 666. I couldn't believe my eyes when I saw Eli Needleman's signature at the bottom of the splash panel: these were nationally distributed publications, after all. I thought his signature was a hallucination. I sniffed at the bowl of the pipe I'd been puffing away at for God knew how many hours, then I blamed the Moroccan Trance music blasting from the stereo. Eli Needleman! For years I'd avoided him and his whole crazy family. With alarming clarity I recalled Eli's laughter, a kind of wheezing honk that I found embarrassing.

Dropping the comic books, I staggered to the bathroom of whoever's loft I was at and took a cold shower with my clothes on. This measure (I imagined) would force my drug-induced delirium to recede. But the signature on the title panel didn't go away.

Dripping wet, I tip-toed past drowsing and narcotized bodies. As dawn unshadowed the alleyways of Mole Street, I left the party. In my damp hands I clutched someone's copy of *Squinchy Stories.* On the cover was Eli Needleman's representation of Hell — a Disneyland of flaming torments: beings with briefcases and swishing bifurcate tails; despairing legions of young soldiers about to fling themselves into pits — done in the thick black holding lines familiar to aficionados of comic-book art.

The imagery was topical for the time — anti-this and anti-that, condemnatory. Eli Needleman damned everything in this world to Hell. This particular issue of *Squinchy Stories* I still possess; you can still see the whorls of my college-aged fingerprints (ingrained from that unsobering shower) on the glossy, gaudy, three-color cover. Though twenty-some years have passed, the drawings have lost none of their power.

Over the years I collected much of Eli's available work — minor contributions to *Snarf* and *Umbilicus Review* . . . and the entire four-issue set of *Hell Comic Book*s (which Roche, in the aforementioned *Function of the Nightmare,* details in his chapter on Needleman, "The Dream Bible of Hell"). It is with these *Hell Book*s that I am most intrigued. Here, within these yellowing pages, are to be found caricatures of all of Eli Needleman's family and neighbors. I am represented in one of the earliest panels — as an eight-year old "betrayer," too embarrassed by Eli's mentally-ill mother to remain friends. Indeed, half of the first *Hell Book* charts his mother's descent into madness. We see Eli's mother in the mental institution; her dialogue with her reflection in the "Looking-Glass Canticles" is especially disturbing. My own mother, who visited her, appears as an ineffectual "concerned neighbor" — a *bourgeois* only too eager to get back to her soap operas and shopping. The lascivious activities of Eli's older sister are graphically depicted in the next issue. Her eventual murder by a biker gang is treated in excruciating detail. What is most horrible (in my opinion) is the chronicle of her lingering consciousness as she strangles to death on a wire noose in a shed somewhere in Chester County. Her tunnel-like "Journey of Despair" begins at this point. This is where she encounters the malefic efficiency responsible for the sorrows of the Needleman clan; and the name of this efficiency is given: it names itself.

Eli Needleman.

Horror piles on horror. By the third issue of *Hell Comic Books* we are drawn into the dream world of Eli — an infernal place. "Hell," Eli declares, "is our own self." Rightly, Professor Roche reminds us of the famous Miltonic lament — *Which way I fly is Hell; myself am Hell.* Roche goes on to observe that

in this realm we are privy to the innermost *acharné* visions of Eli Needleman. Gone is any traffic with the outside world — the sanitive and salving world of other people. He allows himself to be subsumed by an aching and ceaseless despair. He is in his own Hell. He enlists demons in a conspiracy *against himself.* Even these degraded creatures are appalled at the depths of his self-treachery. Needleman's capacity for suffering seems boundless. . . .

Professor Roche likens the fourth and last published *Hell Comic Book* to a "poisonous dream" which has

a demoralizing effect on all who dare to read it. Yet it is mesmerizing, a stunning document of a fallen and lost soul. Such a work completely transcends the tawdry genre of the underground comic book, and perhaps that is why this last *Hell Book* remains in print. Herein, Eli Needleman dreams of a Bible of Hell which he illustrates. For ink he uses his own blood. [The comic itself is printed in dark red ink.] Instead of a pen Needleman resorts to his own long, black-lacquered fingernail, sharpened into a nib. In the very heart of Hell he constructs his studio. Demons and damned souls are at his disposal. Every professional consideration is extended to Needleman so that his monstrous task might proceed unhindered. By the emanations of a Hades-red sun, he [the fictional Needleman] limns panel after panel in his customary style . . . a kind of varicose line with meticulous, spidery crosshatching. Throughout, there is an engaging repartee with an ambassador from the court of Hell — a Duke. (A "Somber Eminence" — whom we take to mean Satan — never makes an entrance.) Much time passes, the decades are as hours. When the fictional Needleman thirsts he is given a goblet and a razor. He is bidden to open his own veins so that he might drink. When he hungers he is given a knife and serving tray of wrought iron — for similar purpose. In the end Needleman gnaws at his own flesh. His delight is immediate! He savors the meal as he has savored nothing else in his life. Ultimately, he devours himself. *Yet the work continues.* His own wastes and disgorged parts, animated by worms and worse things, arise so that he can continue the task of illuminating the saga of Hell — a saga that we all know is endless . . . .

The author of *The Function of the Nightmare* makes the paradoxical assertion that the four *Hell Books* are redeemed by their own moral collapse — "because they are a valid document of those antipodal areas of the human experience, they will endure!" Professor Roche goes on to place Needleman in the same "constellation of dark stars as Artaud and Baudelaire and Bosch and Beddoes." The vitiating influence of the "Dream Bible of Hell" on the susceptible is explored at length: a dozen deaths by suicide are attributed to this fourth and final issue. Ample documentation is provided for the specialist. *Hell Comic Book* Number 4, in its thirty-six page entirety, has been reprinted the Asphyx Press several times since its initial publication in 1970, and is available at $2.50 the copy (not including shipping and handling).

——— - ———

Nowhere in the fabled (and oft-re-printed) fourth "Dream Bible" do I appear; only in Issue the First am I to be found — which is out-of-print. I stashed away a few copies of this first issue. In it, I am depicted in unflattering though historically accurate terms. I am depicted as one of the few urchins who bother to show up at a birthday party for Eli; next I am depicted as I wave goodbye after a mere five minutes of listless partying. Seven panels are allotted to this callous tableau. Two entire pages are devoted to the infamous "restaurant episode," where I am portrayed in the act of vomiting on a street corner (the result of an overripe beef-stew). Just as I deposit the half-digested stew into the gutter Eli and his family stroll by. His mad mother has a furlough from the squirrel factory. She is agog at my distress. Gleefully, she approaches my parents and asks in a shrill squeaky voice:

"Who's trying to kill your son?"

Both families are depicted in the heavy cloth garments of an autumn night circa 1959. Details abound. We see rocket-finned cars, penny-loafers, black men with processed hair. We see Mrs. Needleman's decaying teeth. We see plane tickets in the pocket of Eli's father; 1959 was the year he abandoned his family. But it is the image of myself, filtered through Eli Needleman's angst-laden consciousness, that fixes my gaze until my eyeballs congeal.

In truth, who can resist their own image? Seeing myself represented in a gen-yoo-ine *underground comic,* which had a print run of some twenty-five thousand copies (I checked), conferred upon me a meager notoriety, 'way back when I was a freshman. My fellow matriculators presented me with *Hell Books* for Eli, my illustrious and Hell-bound good-buddy, to autograph. It was all very strange, and for a while I enjoyed the attention. But eventually I

realized I was obscured by Needleman's considerable umbra and that I had no public significance beyond my appearance as a cartoon in his first book-length effort. I was merely the shadow's shadow, as it were.

This realization defeated me. No longer was I willing to represent myself as Eli Needleman's neighbor or one-time friend. Years would pass before I resumed acknowledging my connection to the creator of the *Hell Books.*

———— - ————

After graduation — after being away for four years — I returned to my parents' house. I didn't know what to do with myself that particular jobless and moneyless summer, so I read and loafed and sun-bathed. One afternoon I noticed Eli Needleman carrying a shopping bag. Very much aware of his legendary status, I sat up in my chaise longue and wondered how to react. He was bespectacled, tall and gawky. I remember exactly how he was dressed: long-sleeve shirt with every button buttoned, black Sansabelt slacks, black shoes (ideal for immigrant grandfathers). I wore cut-off jeans and nothing else. He noticed me but said nothing. I didn't call out to him. Time had worked its sundering alchemies on us. For a long minute I completely forgot about the hellish comic books he penned. "He looks like a jerk," I remember saying to myself.

But after dinner, as I took the trash out, I saw him again. He was stuffing envelopes into the trash can. Impetuously, I walked over to him. The sun was setting behind me so that my shadow was absurdly elongated and raced ahead of me; and my arms were shadowy claws stretching the length of the driveway, groping towards him. As I approached Eli, he squinted. The surface of his face was brilliant, almost blinding; the glare blighted his features. When I told him how much I admired his *Hell Books*, he produced a honking wheeze and covered his eyes.

"I'm working on a new volume right now," he told me; and there was wariness in his voice.

"Could I take a look?" I asked.

He licked his thin lips, which were chapped. "It's not ready for publication. . . . "

So saying, he dropped another batch of envelopes into the trash. These, I determined, were fan letters (written in care of Asphyx Press). Not a single one was opened.

"You have a lot of admirers," I ventured.

He told me he supposed so. He looked at his wristwatch, made a remark about a deadline. Before he excused himself I asked him about his mother and he bristled ("If you're so concerned about her why don't you ask her yourself?") Vanquished by Eli's pique I returned home, resolving never to approach him again. My parents were in New Brunswick visiting relatives, my college friends dispersed into their various continuums. I remember eating a Swanson's turkey TV dinner. Throughout this bland and lonely meal I smarted from the sting of Eli's remark. Gloom enveloped me. I was the scion of a horribly middle-class family; I was boring. Eli, even with a heritage of madness and scandal, had triumphed! Before I went to bed I re-read my *Hell Books* and then I plunged into a sleep fraught with nightmares.

I dreamt about Eli's mother that night. In the dream she prowled the moonlit driveway. She lifted her thin shift to defecate on the cold cement; finishing, she pulled the garment over her head and bared her emaciated flesh. Unclad, tall and cadaverous, she slunk to our trash cans and to our back door, where she proceeded to rattle and test the back door.

You could hear the doorknob turning;

you could hear the squeak of the unlocked door —

Awakening in a sweat, I sat up and pressed my face to the screen window. The marmoreal figure I sought in the moonlight was not visible. Yet I swore the trash cans rattled.

Raccoons — ?

We lived next to a park. Raccoons and rodents came out at night to nibble the garbage. Occasionally, I'd see them — fat silvery-gray mounds. The mounds would scurry across the driveway. Or they'd scoot into the park, noiseless and swift. In the cool selenial glow none of these creatures could be seen. Yet the subtle clattering continued.

I fretted about the back door. I couldn't remember locking it. It was nearly two in the morning. Sleep would be impossible unless I made sure it was latched. Pulling on my underwear, I went downstairs only to pause in the kitchen. I gaped at the door leading to the basement: *I couldn't rid myself of the notion that someone waited behind it.*

The Needlewoman.

That had been the taunting epithet for Eli's mother. She'd paraded around naked before . . . very occasionally, on mild nights, in the park or driveway. She was too scrawny and too tall to excite erotic reaction. It was always revolting, tragic, a spectacle you'd clamp a pillow over your face to forget. And the prospect of the Needlewoman — this crazy naked woman — capering in my basement was unbearable.

Goosebumps formed on my bare skin, fine hairs on the nape of my neck bristled as I pondered this. Steeling myself, I opened the door and flicked on the basement light. My heart thundered as I ran down the stairs, flailing my arms. Any second I expected to see the Needlewoman brandishing a carving knife. I held my breath and dared to check the back door.

Closed it was, but not locked.

You absent-minded, lame-brained

idiot — !

Hating my forgetfulness, I turned the deadbolt. A metallic twang resulted, an unfamiliar noise, but the door seemed locked. Then I walked upstairs, turning off the light on the way to the kitchen. A dismal thought occurred to me: *What if the Needlewoman managed to get upstairs while I was asleep!* There were dozens of places to hide . . . .

Once and for all I had to put my fears to rest.

I dressed and left the house by the front door. It only took a few minutes to walk around the block: I was determined to see if there was a woman's shift in the driveway. Checking this would constitute a kind of proof. Or I could rattle their back door and see if it was locked!

As I walked in the moonlight these measures began to seem comical to me. My fears seemed ludicrous; I was twenty-one years old, a college graduate — a seasoned survivor of innumerable chemically-induced inward journeys. Well did I know the vagaries of paranoia. In the driveway my feet tangled in a gauzy material. Laughing, I didn't bother to examine it. My rationalization was that it probably fell from a clothesline. Adjacent neighbors left damp wash to dry in the night.

As a lark I decided to peek in the back door of the Needleman residence before returning to my bed. Fan mail sprouted from the trash cans like monstrous blossoms — *I was only here a few hours ago,* I reminded myself. When I peered into the cracked windowpanes of their back door I saw two moon-silvered reflections: my own and that of Eli Needleman, who snuck up behind me.

"Three encounters in one day," he intoned. "I guess you really like my artwork."

Too shaken for speech, I nodded.

"Why do you like my artwork?"

I answered as best I could. He gave me a look lacking all human expression; I assumed he was satisfied I'd spoken the truth. Then he gestured to their weed-clogged back patio. "Mother and I are enjoying the evening," he said mildly, nasally. "Why don't you join us?"

"Are you sure it isn't too late?"

"Are you afraid to be seen with us — ?"

To this baiting challenge I replied: "Absolutely not."

Rusted lawn furniture was grouped in the center of the patio. In a sagging chaise longue reclined Eli Needleman's mother, dressed in an ill-fitting gown of ocean-green. It might have been a prom gown; I thought of Eli's murdered sister. In a shrill musical voice Eli's mother said something to me — a pleasantry, a greeting. It was garbled, whatever she said, because she was chewing and licking her lips. I was too dazed by her deep yellow smile to pay close attention. Each tooth was capped in gold, all glinting in the moonlight as she busily chewed. Next to her was a small barbecue with a suitably infernal glow. On the grill a fondue bubbled away in a copper pan. From time to time, as she spooned away at the hot concoction, she smeared lipstick across her mouth and beyond it somewhat. The red slash divided her face in two; fondue clung to the gold teeth. "Mother can't sleep so I'm keeping her company," Eli explained, offering me a chair.

"I guess you sleep during the day."

"I dream but I don't sleep." He sat down next to me. "It's very restful out here," he said, shifting topics. "I really like the park, the animal noises, the crickets. Everything is so *interesting.*"

Fidgeting, I agreed the park was interesting.

"I'd go in there at night," he continued, "but I'm afraid the Park Guards wouldn't understand. They'd arrest me. I'm widely regarded as a 'subversive influence.' Think of the headlines:

Communist-Hippie Underground Cartoonist Caught Ritually Molesting Chipmunks in Park after Midnight."

I laughed or pretended to laugh — I can't remember which. The expression on Eli's face, I noticed, hadn't changed.

Eli's mother broke in: "My son is a very famous artist. Ask him to show you his room!"

This I did. Complying, Eli ushered me through the back door and into the unlighted basement. Damp it was; the floor was gritty. A pervasive smell of kerosene and rot and charcoal bothered me. On the second floor I saw a wedding portrait of his parents — a monochrome brown photograph so gaudily tinted with Marshall Oil Paints that they looked like Polynesian clowns in formal attire. The television set had been left on; it was set at no particular channel. "Do you remember the last time you were here?" Eli Needleman asked me.

He meant the birthday party. "Well," I finally replied, "I guess I haven't been here for about twelve or thirteen years."

"Time is very strange . . . . "

On the way upstairs I surveyed the ancient living room. All the rest of the furniture was slightly boxy, constructed of glass, chrome, formica'd wood. It occurred to me these were display fixtures: before his desertion Eli's father had been a buyer for a department store. Reaching the third floor I shook off a clogging sense of *déjà-vu*. All the houses on our block had been built from the same plans, after all. Eli's room was in the same relative position as my own; indeed, this house was a distorted, shabby mirror-image of my home.

My discomfort grew. Being in the Needlemans' house after all these years unlocked decayed memories; and it occurred to me that this place was the bad place of my nightmares. Nausea evoked this place; childhood illnesses evoked this place; a bout with blood-poisoning and the resultant delirium took me here. Those silent straining messages which finally caused me to cry at my grandmother's funeral, evoked this place. Tripping on psychedelic drugs evoked this place; convulsing on opium evoked this place.

Drug-filtered reality was less warped than this place.

Next to the bathroom was his sister's bedroom. The door to this room was covered with gaudy Op-Art wallpaper. Nails were driven through the molding. To enter you'd need a crowbar. I was invited into the adjacent room — Eli's studio, which was my room in the unaltered continuum of my parent's house. Candy-bar wrappers littered his floor. Two display sconces flickered red bulbs of low wattage: the real illumination came from a buzzing Tensor lamp, which rested on a drawing table of wrought iron. Very odd, very old, this table. A ceiling the color of old cheddar screamed for paint; but most alarming was the wall-sized mural, a cartoon-panelled monstrosity. The window overlooking the park formed but one of its many "modules," and through this I could see Mrs. Needleman gobbling the dregs of fondue. All the other modules were Eli's artwork: Van Gogh crucified on an easel; halo'd rats in a paradisiacal sewer; a kilted skeleton piping lung bagpipes; B-52s with fœtus-bombs, fecal dirigibles, swastika poker decks. Crematoria fancies; gangrenous japes. Sections of the mural were devoted to the imagery of Hell. The largest panel showed Eli working on an oversized black book while flames flickered in the background; demons were looking over his shoulder.

"Would you like to see the real *Hell Book*?" asked Eli Needleman all at once.

"The real one — ?"

"Not the published versions. This is the real thing. I've been working on it . . . for years. Would you like to see it?"

Appalled, appreciative, I nodded my assent. What is the appeal of evil? At the time I thought evil was only a mental sensation, a color. It didn't occur to me, then, as I waited for Eli to get the book, that the fascination with evil was a response to a subtle summons. What is the call of evil? And what is its name?

Eli spoke and I heard my name. On the drawing table of wrought-iron he lowered the book — reverently, it seemed to me. "There are no chairs," Eli apologized. "I work standing up." Before touching the book I glanced out the window. The trees rustled like titan wraiths. The weed-grown back yard looked restful. There was the Needlewoman, in the gown of her dead daughter. Breezes rippled the sea-green dress.

"No chairs," I repeated, dully.

Averred Eli Needleman: "After father died we had to economize."

"You know, it was so strange . . . seeing myself in the first *Hell Book*."

"This *Hell Book* is a lot stranger."

So saying, he slid the book towards me, positioning it under my fingers. The book was covered in a thick black hide. It was twice the size of a photo-album. I turned the pages — a kind of vellum, thinking how expensive each sheet seemed.

" . . . the finest materials," he crooned. "It's my life's work, it's what I'm about." On my neck I felt his odorless breath . . . "It's what I am," he whispered.

The artwork was familiar yet unfamiliar — a subtle variation of his technique. The line work was lustrous black lacquer . . . "Beautiful work," I murmured.

"Yes, yes." He stepped away but I barely noticed. I was entranced by the panels, the artwork, the depth and clarity of Eli's obsession. I began in the middle of the book. A story began to unfold — a sequence of images: Eli as a child. Eli begging his father for a walk in the park. Father and son putting on their coats. It is late autumn. The year is 1959.

"Go on, go on."

Obedient, I turned the page and saw more drawings: Eli and his father leaving through the back door; father and son in the driveway and into the yard and into the park. Father and son speaking about the park and how interesting it is at night. A Park Guard on horseback passing by; father and son hide concealing themselves behind a tree, an ancient elm that I'm able to recognize —

The topographic details were so perfect. "Eli, I'm really impressed," I heard myself say.

"Go on."

On the next page the colors changed: now all the cartoons were rendered in blood red and I became unaware that I was reading and everything flowed in my mind, image after image: Eli and his father standing on precipitous hill above a creek. The child bending over to pick up a fist-sized rock; the child striking the father on back of the head. The father tumbling into the creek. Still clutching the rock, Eli jumps in. The water is bitter cold. Again and again the child smites the father's skull with the rock. Somehow, the ten-year-old boy drags the soggy body into a culvert and stuffs it into a pipe. The end of the pipe is sealed with rocks and gravel. And all the while demonic creatures cheer Eli on. He is one of their own. A celebratory dance transpires —

Slamming the book closed I continued to see terrible images from the *Hell Book*. I shut my eyes tightly to blot out the scarlet visions *yet they continued!* A threshold had been crossed: I'd lowered myself into the Pit and was trapped forever . . . .

"What's the matter?" Needleman suddenly asked.

Daring to open my eyes I saw the book, the *Bible of Hell,* closed on the table before me. I excused myself. As I fumbled out the room I swore Eli smiled. I don't remember leaving the house but I found myself in the driveway, running to my back door. Madly, it was wide open so I wouldn't venture inside. My next clear recollection was boarding a bus for New Brunswick that same night. I couldn't endure the prospect of being alone in my parents' house. And this was at a time when thousands of soldiers my own age were killing and perishing in a jungle war.

————— · —————

At a comic-book convention not long ago I heard Professor Emmanuel Roche speak at a symposium. On his topic he was eloquent, if misinformed. When the panel discussion was over I approached Roche; he was studying a bus schedule. I introduced myself and revealed my connection to the creator of *Hell Comics*.

"Have you seen Needleman recently?" he asked.

"Not since I graduated from college — and that was twenty years ago."

"I've never met him myself," the professor admitted. "What is Eli Needleman like?"

For years I'd wrestled with this very question. "He's very demonic," I said after a long and reflective pause.

Professor Roche laughed. "Surely you know the difference between satirizing evil and celebrating it."

"If you're cooking a kettle of soup and you jump into the kettle, you become part of the soup . . . . "

"Eli Needleman is a moralist and a visionary."

I didn't press the point. Nor did I regale the professor with my theories about obsessive, repetitive activities and their link to the occult. Professor Roche was an old man, after all. Silent, I recalled that night years before when I waited for Eli to show me his *Bible of Hell*, the real one that will take him forever to complete. And I remembered how agreeable evil's invitation seemed at the time.

What is the call of evil? And what is its name?

Eli spoke and I heard my name. And I responded, fascinated. Ω

! B O O K S ! from WEIRD TALES® LIBRARY

Darrell Schweitzer's epic fantasy, *The White Isle*:
Science Fiction Review wrote: ". . . this story is exceptional . . . memorable for its structure, striking scenes and powerful emotional forces." *Aboriginal Science Fiction* wrote: ". . . a lovely, horrific tale that is worth your while to seek out." With full-color dustjacket and b&w interior drawings by **Stephen Fabian**. $18.95.

Robert Weinberg's occult adventure novel, *The Devil's Auction*:
Joe R. Lansdale wrote: "A rootin-tootin, booger of a book with just about every kind of pulp cliché turned inside out and made fresh as a spring daisy . . ." With full-color dustjacket and b&w interior drawings by **Stephen Fabian.**$18.95.

Keith Roberts's classic of modern fantasy, *Anita*:
The amusing, sometimes terrifying adventures of a teenaged English girl interested in all the normal things — boys, sex, seeing the wide world, boys, new clothes . . . and witchcraft. With a new introduction by the author and a story not in the fabulously rare first edition. By the author of *Pavane, Kiteworld* and others. With full-color dustjacket and b&w interior drawings by **Stephen Fabian**. $20.25.

Send check or money order to Weird Tales®, P.O. Box 13418, Philadelphia PA 19101-3418. In Pennsylvania, add 6% sales tax. To charge Visa or MasterCharge, include your account number, expiration date, and signature. Always include complete address and Zip or Postal code.

THE HORROR WRITER

Shadow shapes,
swimming in fogged darkness,
razored teeth,
   slicing deep, releasing
   crimson heart tides.

Prowling beasts,
beneath a scything moon,
wild of eye,
   lust-hungry for the kill.

Demonic fiends,
claw-fingered, eager
to rend flesh,
   in blood-gored midnight feasts.
   Specter spirits,
summoned from gloomed grave, risen
from dank coffined earth
   to fetid life.

Witch, devil, ghoul,
the tall walking dead,
night companions all,
who join me at the keys,
   Welcome!

Welcome to my world!

—William F. Nolan
art by William F. Nolan

We also publish *Weird Tales®* in hard covers!

Issues 290 through 296: trade edition $20 each (four or more, $12 each).

Issues 291–296: limited to 100 copies, signed by the featured author and artist and the editors: $50 each(four or more, $40 each). (Issue 290 is now sold out in this limited edition)

Issues 297 onwards: limited to 200 copies, signed by featured author, artist, and editors, $30 each (four or more, including prepaid subscriptions for forthcoming issues, $25 each).

We take MasterCard and Visa: we need your card number, expiration date, and your signature on your order. We also accept money orders and checks.

Order from us at Terminus Publishing Co., Inc., P.O. Box 13418,
Philadelphia PA 19101-3418.

Weirdisms

The Witches' Sabbat!
Twice a year, on the
ancient pagan feasts of
Beltane and *Samhain*...

...witches and warlocks
fly through the night sky
to cavort with their
master - *Satan!*

© 1991 Jason Van Hollander

63

THE VISIONS

by William F. Nolan

It's been happening over the past two months. And it happened again today. I saw another one.

I know this isn't a mental problem. I'm not a nut case. In fact, I'm a very ordinary fellow. Work as a road salesman for American Detergent Corporation. Forty-one. Good health. No wife or kids to tie me down so I have no problem traveling for the company the way I do. (I was married once, to a woman named Clara, but let's not go into that. It's a closed door in my life and I don't want to open it again.)

I drum up wholesale orders for ADC. It's a good product, with a proven national rep, so I don't have to high pressure anybody. An easy sell. I started out in this game selling second-rate vacuum cleaners that broke down about a month after people bought them. Resulted in a lot of pissed-off housewives. That was back in my house-to-house period when I'd peddle anything that didn't bite back. And I mean that literally. I once tried to sell white mice as pets for the kids, but they bit the hell out of me (the mice, not the kids) and I had to dump them. Cute little things, but those teeth . . .

I'm getting way off-track here. My purpose is to tell you about what I've been seeing off and on for the past two months.

It started the day I drove into Detroit. Terrible road conditions. Had an appointment with a wholesaler downtown and got there in the middle of a blizzard. Snow coming down thick enough to slice. And with a cutting wind blowing it into my face. I'd had trouble parking, and had to walk more than three blocks in the storm.

I was miserable. Hate cold weather, snow, and ice. Okay for kids, lousy for adults. By the time I'd covered two blocks my hands were frozen (I'd left my gloves in the car). I'd stopped to set down my sample case and blow on my fingers, to try and warm them a little, when I saw the first one.

Chuck Almont.

He was about fifty feet ahead of me, walking toward the corner, bareheaded (Chuck always hated wearing hats) with a white scarf around his neck and his coat collar turned up.

Instinctively, I yelled at him: "Hey! Hey, Chuck!"

But the wind was too strong. Blew away my words before they reached him.

Smiling idiotically, I began to run, trying to catch up, but by the time I'd reached the corner he was gone. Probably into one of the office buildings along the block.

I stood there on the snow-covered sidewalk, shaking all over. Not because of the cold. Because of Chuck. Because I'd been *convinced* it had been him.

And because I knew he was dead.

We all have friends who die on us. Of cancer. Or heart trouble. Or strokes. (One girl I knew got what she figured was a head cold, took some aspirin for it, and was dead within a week. Maybe the same kind of flu that killed the famous puppet guy, Jim Henson.)

Naturally, I told myself that the man on the street wasn't Chuck. Just somebody who looked like him from the back, and walked the way he used to walk with

Copyright © 1991 by William F. Nolan

his head down and his shoulders thrust forward. Couldn't have been Chuck Almont.

Chuck had died three years ago during triple-bypass surgery. His veins had collapsed during the operation. (He'd been a heavy smoker and junk food freak all his life — and he drank so much his liver would have killed him if his heart hadn't.)

Still, trying to sleep that night, I kept opening my eyes in the dark motel room, with the vision of the walking man on the street flashing through my head.

A week later, in Chicago, I saw my second one. A woman. She was just stepping onto an escalator in this busy shopping mall, and I got a clear look at her profile.

Helen Bond.

I pushed my way through the crowd and made the escalator just as Helen stepped off the top. When I reached the upper level I saw her going into a shoe store three shops down. I ran to the shop, hesitating at the doorway, my heart thudding, dry-mouthed with fright.

Helen had died of breast cancer in St. Louis last summer. I'd visited her at the hospital three days before the end. She'd lost her hair (chemotherapy) and looked tired and wasted, with haunted eyes and the cancer etched into the sudden deep lines of her face. Helen knew she was dying and gripped my hand hard as we said our goodbyes.

And here she was, these long months later, alive and walking into a Chicago shoe store.

I stepped into the shop, my eyes raking the customers. There were six women in the place — but none of them was Helen. She'd vanished!

Then I realized that a side door on the right, in the children's shoe section, led to another part of the mall. She'd entered, taken a glance around, then gone out the side exit.

That was the logical explanation.

But it didn't explain how Helen Bond could still be alive the year after her burial. Had to be a mistake on my part. *Had to be.*

The third one was a boy I'd known from my high school in San Diego, California. In my chemistry class. Frankie "Fritz" McKnight. He'd been hit by a bus a week before our senior prom. The front wheel of the bus had crushed his chest, and he was dead by the time the ambulance arrived.

Yet in Hays, Kansas, just two weeks after I'd seen Helen Bond, I saw Fritz step out of a movie theater (one of those multiplex places where you can see six or eight films in the same building).

This time I was real close to him and I knew the vision was real, that this *was* Fritz. Eighteen, tall and gawky, with freckles across his nose. I walked up behind him, touching his shoulder.

"Fritz," I said, my voice strained and uncertain.

"Yeah?" He turned to squint at me, nearsighted, the way he always did. "Who are you?"

"I'm . . . Paul," I said, staring at him.

"I don't know any Paul."

"Puck. That was my nickname in school. Puck Wilson. From Grant High. We were in chemistry together."

Fritz chuckled. "Yeah . . . I remember you." His squint deepened. "But you're a *lot* older."

"That's because . . . I'm . . . an adult now." I was groping for the right words. "When we . . . when you knew me . . . that was a long time ago."

"Yeah, I guess." And he shrugged. "Well, I gotta go. Maybe I'll see ya again. Bye, Puck."

And he walked away, crossed the street, and was lost in the crowd.

I just stood there, rooted to the spot, my breathing rapid, heart going like mad, sweat on my upper lip. I wanted to call out, run after him, ask him how he could still be . . . alive.

But I didn't. I just walked slowly back to my car, climbed in, and drove, in a kind of dream daze, back to my motel.

In the room I sat on the bed, rubbing my head, eyes closed, trying to make some kind of rational sense out of what I'd seen. If Fritz were real (and he *was*) then I'd actually seen Chuck Almont and Helen Bond.

They were *all* real.

The next morning I went to a clinic in Kansas City for testing. I was sure I had a brain tumor and that it had been producing these visions, making them happen.

I paid a thousand dollars for what they call a magnetic brain scan. (Even though I was insured by American, I paid out of my own funds. I didn't want the company to know anything about this.)

They had me stretch out flat on my back, arms tight to my sides, on this kind of a wide metal tube bed on tracks; then they slid me into the heart of the big scan machine — like a fun ride at Disneyland without the fun.

For a full hour I was in there, inside that big magnetic machine, flat on my back, while they scanned and photographed every inch of my skull, top, sides, and bottom. Loud *beep-beep-beep* sounds would engulf me at two-minute intervals, and I was told not to move my head or swallow while the sounds hammered at me. Between sounds I could swallow and move a little — although the space was very confining. Worse than being trapped in an elevator.

When it was over they asked me to come back the following morning and a doctor would tell me what the machine had revealed.

The next day I got the news: no tumor. My brain was A-okay.

I walked out of the clinic utterly depressed. Guess that sounds weird, eh? I *should* have been delighted to find that

I didn't have a brain tumor. But not so. Since I *didn't* have a tumor, that left me with only one other possible verdict: the visions had to be a product of a mental aberration.

I was going insane.

I saw the latest one tonight.

Couldn't work after that visit to the clinic. I phoned my boss at the company and told him I was taking sick leave.

"For how long?" he wanted to know.

"There's . . . no way to tell," I said.

"What the hell's wrong, Paul? You've never been sick before, not once. What is it?"

"Don't know exactly," I told him. "I'm . . . just sick. Can't work." My tone was low, numbed.

"Well, all right then. You've got a month of sick leave coming. But if you're not over whatever's wrong in a month we'll have to replace you. We've got a business to run. Got to keep the product moving."

"I understand."

And the call ended.

That was just over ten days ago.

What did I do after that call? Got on the westbound highway and drove. Going nowhere. No destination. Kept on driving, day and night. Didn't get much sleep. Didn't eat much.

I drove until I hit the Pacific shore. Southern California. San Diego. I hadn't really meant to end up here.

When I visited the site of my old high school (to try and make a connection with the past) all I found was a vacant lot. They'd torn down the school. There was a big metal sign up that said:

COMING SOON!
THE MIRACLE MALL!
OVER FIFTY ULTRA-MODERN
STORES TO SERVE YOU!

But let me get to tonight.

I drove over the long bridge from San

Diego to Coronado. Stopped at the big white wooden Victorian hotel at the far end of the island. Took a room there. Walked down to get some dinner at the hotel restaurant. Moving mechanically. Like a robot. I was in a kind of trance — able to function, dress myself, drive a car — but my mind was in a numbed-out state. I kept repeating, over and over, under my breath: "You're *not* insane . . . you're *not* insane . . . you're *not* insane . . ."

In the hotel dining room: another vision.

Ken Moss was seated three tables over, facing me, his head down, eating.

I didn't question his identity. It was Ken all right. At least, *to my mind,* it was.

Ken Moss had been a test driver for GM, a friend of my father's, who had spun out of control into the guardrail on turn nine at the end of the long straight at Riverside Raceway five years ago. The car, a factory prototype, had been totally demolished. Among other things, Ken's neck and back were broken. He never regained consciousness after the crash.

But he was here tonight, eating dinner on Coronado Island.

I walked over to him.

"Ken," I said softly.

He raised his head, smiling up at me. "Yes."

"You're dead," I said in a flat, emotionless tone. A statement, not a question.

"That's right." He nodded, patting his lips with a white linen napkin.

"You were killed at Riverside."

"Right again," he said. The smile never wavered.

"Then how can you be *here*?" I asked.

"I just *am,*" Moss declared. "I don't have an explanation. It's just a fact. You're here . . . and I'm here."

I turned away and walked rapidly through the lobby, out the wide brass entrance/exit doors, toward my parked car.

I intended to drive off a cliff into the ocean.

No more visions.

I couldn't stand to see another. Life was no longer bearable.

I was unlocking the door of my car when a bald little man in heavy glasses approached me, eyes wide, his mouth open.

"Paul," he gasped. "Paul Wilson!"

I nodded. "I'm Wilson."

And then I recognized him — an executive I'd made a large sale to in Des Moines early last year. With some name like Hastings . . . or Harley . . . I couldn't recall exactly.

"No . . . no . . . you can't be Wilson," he was saying. "I made a mistake. I'm sorry." He began to turn away.

My tone was harsh; I didn't have time for nonsense. "I *said* I was Wilson. Now, what do you want?"

He stared at me. "But . . . that road thing two months ago near Detroit . . . in the blizzard I read about in the papers. I even saw the photo they took."

"What photo?"

"Never mind," said the agitated little man. "I was mistaken. You . . . you're obviously not . . ." And he walked away nervously, quickly.

I stood there, my hand on the car door.

The visions. *All in the past two months.*

They *were* real. The people I'd seen. Real in the sense that I was one of them.

The bald man — *Harris* was his name. Harris was also one, but he didn't know it yet.

I began to laugh. It was really damn funny. A howl. I didn't have to try and kill myself by driving my car off a cliff.

I was already dead.

Ω

THE LUSTSTONE
by Brian Lumley
art by Bob Eggleton

One:

The ice was only a memory now, a racial memory whose legends had come down the years, whose evidence was graven in the land in hollow glacial tracts. Of the latter: time would weather the valley eventually, soften its contours however slowly. But the memories would stay, and each winter the snows would replenish them.

That was why the men of the tribes would paint themselves yellow in imitation of the sun-god, and stretch themselves in a line across the land east to west and facing north, and beat back the snow and ice with their clubs. And *frighten* it back with their screams and their leapings. With their magic they defeated winter and conjured spring, summer, and autumn, and thus were the seasons perpetuated.

The tribes, too, were perpetuated; each spring the tribal wizards — the witch-doctors — would perform those fertility rites deemed necessary to life, by means of which the grass was made to grow, the beasts to mate, and Man the weapon-maker to increase and prosper upon the face of the earth. It was the time of the sabretooth and the mammoth, and it was the springtime of Man, the thinking animal whose destiny is the stars. And even in those far dim primal times there were visionaries.

Chylos of the mighty Southern Tribe was one such: Chylos the Chief, the great wizard and seer whose word was law in the mid-South. And in that spring some ten thousand years ago, Chylos lay on his bed in the grandest cave of all the caves of the Southern Tribe, and dreamed his dream.

He dreamed of invaders!

Of men not greatly unlike the men of the tribes, but fiercer far and with huge appetites for ale, war, and women. Aye, and there were gross-bearded ones, too, whose dragon-prowed ships were as snakes of the sea, whose horned helmets and savage cries gave them the appearance of demons! But Chylos knew that he dreamed only of the far future and so was not made greatly fearful.

And he dreamed that in that distant future there were others who came from the east with fire and thunder, and in his dreams Chylos heard the agonized screams of the descendants of his tribe, men, women, and children; and saw visions of black war, red rape, and rivers of crimson blood. A complex dream it was, and alien these invaders: with long knives and axes which were not of stone, and again wearing horned helmets upon their heads to make them more fearsome yet. From the sea they came, building mounds and forts where they garrisoned their soldiers behind great earthworks.

And some of them carried strange banners covered with unknown runes and wore kilts of leather and rode in horse-drawn chairs with flashing spokes in their wheels; and their armies were disciplined thousands, moving and fighting with one mind. . . .

Such were Chylos's dreams, which brought him starting awake; and so often had he dreamed them that he knew they must be more than mere nightmares. Until one morning, rising from his bed of hides, he saw that it was spring again and knew what must be done. Such visions as he had dreamed must come to pass, he felt it in his old bones, but not for many years. Not for years beyond his numbering. Very well: the gods themselves had sent Chylos their warning, and now he must act. For he was old and the earth would claim him long before the first invaders came, and so he must unite the tribes now and bring them together. And they must grow strong and their men become great warriors.

And there must be that which would remain long after Chylos himself was gone: a reminder, a monument, a *Power* to fuel the loins of the men and make the tribes strong. A driving force to make his people lusty, to ensure their survival. There must be children — many children! And their children in their turn must number thousands, and theirs must number . . . such a number as Chylos could not envisage. Then when the invaders came the tribes would be ready, unconquerable, indestructible.

So Chylos took up his staff and went out into the central plain of the valley, where he found a great stone worn round by the coming and going of the ice; a stone half as tall again as a man above the earth, and as much or more of its mass still buried in the ground. And upon this mighty stone he carved his runes of fertility, powerful symbols that spelled L U S T. And he carved designs which were the parts of men and women: the rampant pods and rods of seed, and the ripe breasts and bellies of dawning life. There was nothing of love in what he drew, only of lust and the need to procreate; for man was much more the animal in those dim forgotten days and love as such one of his weaknesses. But when Chylos's work was done, still he saw that it was not enough.

For what was the stone but a stone? Only a stone carved with cryptic runes and symbols of sexuality, and nothing more. It had no power. Who would remember it in a hundred seasons, let alone years? Who would know what it meant?

He called all the leaders of the tribes together, and because there was a recent peace in the land they came. And Chylos spoke to those headmen and wizards, telling them of his dreams and visions, which were seen as great omens. Together the leaders of the tribes decided what must be done; twenty days later they sent all of their young men and women to Chylos the Seer, and their own wizards went with them.

Meanwhile a pit had been dug away from the foot of the great stone, and wedged timbers held back that boulder

from tumbling into the pit. And of all the young men and women of the tribes, Chylos and the Elders chose the lustiest lad and a broad-hipped lass with the breasts of a goddess; and they were proud to be chosen, though for what they knew not.

But when they saw each other, these two, they drew back snarling; for their markings were those of tribes previously opposed in war! And such had been their enmity that even now when all the people were joined, still they kept themselves apart each tribe from the other. Now that the pair had been chosen to be together — and because of their markings, origins, and tribal taboos, the greatest of which forbade intercourse between them — they spoke thus:

"What is the meaning of this?" cried the young man, his voice harsh, affronted. "Why am I put with this woman? She is not of my tribe. She is of a tribe whose very name offends me! I am not at war with her, but neither may I know her."

And she said: "Do my own Elders make mock of me? Why am I insulted so? What have I done to deserve this? Take this thing which calls itself a man away from me!"

But Chylos and the Elders held up their hands, saying: "Be at peace, be at ease with one another. All will be made plain in due time. We bestow upon you a great honour. Do not dishonour your tribes." And the chosen ones were subdued, however grudgingly.

And the Elders whispered among each other and said: "We chose them and the gods were our witnesses and unopposed. They are more than fit for the task. Joining them like this may also more nearly fuse their tribes, and bring about a lasting peace. It must be right." And they were all agreed.

Then came the feasting, of meats dipped in certain spices and herbs known only to the wizards and flavoured with the crushed horn of mammoth; and the drinking of potent ales, all liberally sprinkled with the potions of the wizards. And when the celebrant horde was feasted and properly drunk, then came the oiled and perfumed and grotesquely-clad dancers, whose dance was the slow-twining dance of the grossly endowed gods of fertility. And as the dance progressed so drummers took up the beat, until the pulses of the milling thousands pounded and their bodies jerked with the jerking of the male and female dancers.

Finally the dance ended, but still the drummers kept to their madly throbbing beat; while in the crowd lesser dances had commenced, not so practiced but no less intense and even more lusty. And as the celebrants paired off and fell upon each other, thick pelts were tossed into the pit where the great stone balanced, and petals of spring flowers gathered with the dew upon them, making a bower in the shadow of the boulder; and this was where the chosen couple were made to lie down, while all about the young people of the tribes spent themselves in the ritual spring orgy.

But the pair in the pit — though they had been stripped naked, and while they were drunk as the rest — nevertheless held back and drew apart, and scowled at each other through slitted eyes. Chylos stood at the rim and screamed at them: "Make love! Let the earth soak up your juices!" He prodded the young man with a spear and commanded him: "Take her! The gods demand it! What? And would you have the trees die, and all the animals, and the ice come down again to destroy us all? *Do you defy the gods?*"

At that the young man would obey, for he feared the gods, but she would not have him. "Let him in!" Chylos screamed at her. "Would you be barren and have your breasts wither, and grow old before your time?" And so she wrapped her legs about the young man.

But he was uncertain, and she had not accepted him; still, it seemed to Chylos that they were joined. And as the orgy climbed to its climax he cried out his triumph and signalled to a pair of well-muscled youths where they stood back behind the boulder. And coming forward they took up hammers and with mighty blows knocked away the chocks holding back the great stone from the pit.

The boulder tilted — three hundred tons of rock keeling over — and in the same moment Chylos clutched his heart, cried out and stumbled forward, and toppled into the pit! — and the rune-inscribed boulder with all its designs and great weight slammed down into the hole with a shock that shook the earth. But such was the power of the orgy that held them all in sway, that only those who coupled in the immediate vicinity of the stone knew that it had moved at all!

Now, with the drumming at a standstill, the couples parted, fell back, lay mainly exhausted. A vast field, as of battle, with steam rising as a morning mist. And the two whose task it had been to topple the boulder going amongst them, seeking still-willing, however aching flesh in which to relieve their own pent passions.

Thus was the deed done, the rite performed, the magic worked, the lust-stone come into being. Or thus it was intended. And old Chylos never knowing that, alas, his work was for nothing, for his propitiates had failed to couple . . .

Three winters after that the snows were heavy, meat was scarce, and the tribes warred. Then for a decade the gods and their seasonal rites were put aside, following which that great ritual orgy soon became a legend and eventually a myth. Fifty years later the lust-stone and its carvings were moss-covered, forgotten; another fifty saw the stone a shrine. One hundred more years passed and the domed, mossy top of the boulder was hidden in a grove of oaks: a place of the gods, taboo.

The plain grew to a forest, and the stone was buried beneath a growing mound of fertile soil; the trees were felled to build mammoth-pens, and the grass grew deep, thick, and luxurious. More years saw the trees grow up again into a mighty oak forest; and these were the years of the hunter, the declining years of the mammoth. Now the people were farmers, of a sort, who protected limited crops and beasts against Nature's perils. There were years of the long-toothed cats and years of the wolf. And now and then there were wars between the tribes.

And time was the moon that waxed and waned, and the hills growing old and rounded, and forests spanning the entire land; and the tribes flourished and fought and did little else under the green canopy of these mighty forests. . . .

Through all of this the stone slept, buried shallow in the earth, keeping its secret; but lovers in the forest knew where to lie when the moon was up. And men robbed by the years or by their own excesses could find a wonder there, when forgotten strength returned, however fleetingly, to fill them once more with fire.

As for old Chylos's dream: it came to pass, but his remedy was worthless. Buried beneath the sod for three thousand years the luststone lay, and felt the tramping feet of the nomad-warrior Celts on the march. Five thousand more years saw the Romans come to Britain, then the Anglo-Saxons, the Vikings, and still the luststone lay there.

There were greater wars than ever Chylos had dreamed, more of rape and murder than he ever could have imagined. War in the sea, on the land and in the air.

And at last there was peace again, of a sort. And finally —

Finally . . .

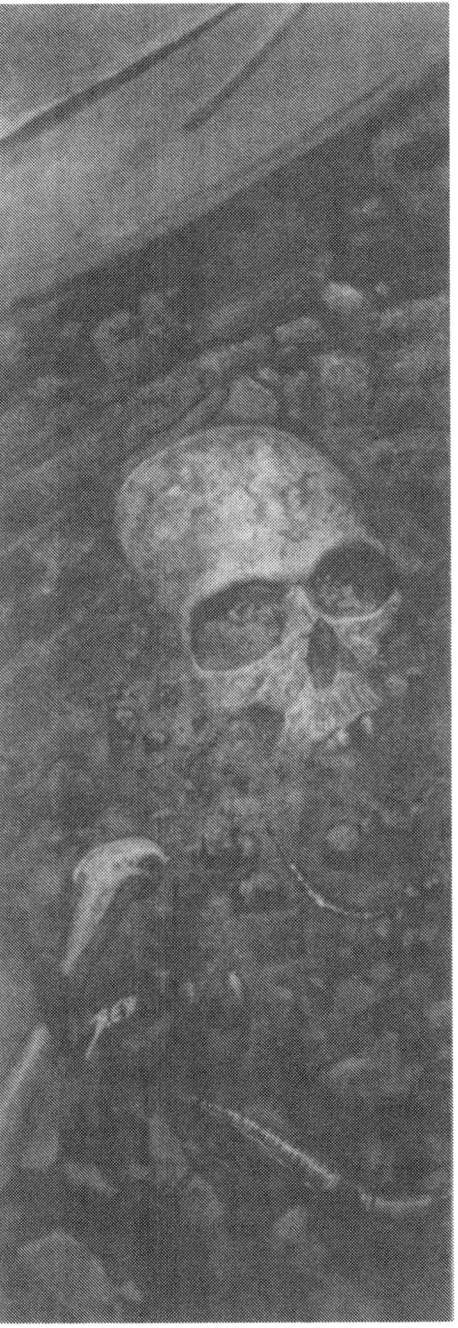

Two:

Gary Clemens was a human calculator at a betting shop in North London; he could figure the numbers, combinations and value of a winning ticket to within a doesn't matter a damn faster than the girls could feed the figures into their machines. All the punters knew him; generally they'd accept without qualms his arbitration on vastly complicated accumulators and the like. With these sort of qualifications Garry could hold down a job any place they played the horses — which was handy because he liked to move around a lot and betting on the races was his hobby. One of his hobbies, anyway.

Another was rape.

Every time Garry took a heavy loss, then he raped. That way (according to his figuring) he won every time. If he couldn't take it out on the horse that let him down, then he'd take it out on some girl instead. But he'd suffered a spate of losses recently, and that had led to some trouble. He hated those nights when he'd go back to his flat and lie down on his bed and have nothing good to think about for that day. Only bad things, like the two hundred he'd lost on that nag that should have come in at fifteen to one, or the filly that got pipped at the post and cost him a cool grand. Which was why he'd finally figured out a way to ease his pain.

Starting now he'd take a girl for every day of the week, and that way when he took a loss — no matter which day it fell on — he'd always have something good to think about that night when he went to bed. If it was a Wednesday, why, he'd simply think about the Wednesday girl, et cetera . . .

But he'd gone through a bad patch and so the rapes had had to come thick and fast, one and sometimes two a week. His Monday girl was a redhead he'd gagged and tied to a tree in the centre of a copse in a built-up area. He'd spent a lot of time with her, smoked cigarettes in between and talked dirty and nasty to her, raped her three times. Differently each time. Tuesday was a sixteen-year-old kid down at the bottom of the railway embankment. No gag or rope or anything; she'd been so shit-scared that after he was through she didn't even start yelling for an hour. Wednesday (Garry's favourite) it had been a heavily pregnant colored woman he'd dragged into a burned-out shop right in town! He'd made that one do everything. In the papers the next day he'd read how she lost her baby. But that hadn't bothered him too much.

Thursday had been when it started to get sticky. Garry had dragged this hooker into a street of derelict houses but hadn't even got started when along came this copper! He'd put his knife in the tart's throat — so that she wouldn't yell — and then got to Hell out of there. And he'd reckoned himself lucky to get clean away. But on the other hand, it meant he had to go out the next night, too. He didn't like the tension to build up too much.

But Friday had been a near-disaster, too. There was a house-party not far from where he lived, and Garry had been invited. He'd declined, but he was there anyway — in the garden of the house opposite, whose people weren't at home. And when this really stacked piece had left the party on her own about midnight, Garry had jumped her. But just when he'd knocked her cold and was getting her out of her clothes, then the owners of the house turned up and saw him in the garden. He'd had to cut and run like the wind then, and even now it made his guts churn when he thought about it.

So he'd kept it quiet for a couple of weeks before starting again, and then he'd finally found his Thursday girl. A really shy thing getting off a late-night tube, who he'd carried into a parking lot and had for a couple of hours straight.

And she hadn't said a word, just panted a lot and been sick. It turned out she was dumb — and Garry chuckled when he read that. No wonder she'd been so quiet. Maybe he should look for a blind one next time . . .

A week later, Friday, he'd gone out again, but it was a failure; he couldn't find anyone. And so the very next night he'd taken his Saturday girl — a middle-aged baglady! So what the Hell! — a rape is a rape is a rape, right? He gave her a bottle of some good stuff first, which put her away nicely, then gave her a Hell of a lot of bad stuff in as many ways as he knew how. She probably didn't even feel it, wouldn't even remember it, so afterwards he'd banged her face on the pavement a couple of times so that when she woke up at least she'd know *something* had happened! Except she hadn't woken up. Well, at least that way she wouldn't be talking about it. And by now he knew they'd have his semen type on record, and that they'd also have *him* if he just once slipped up. But he didn't intend to.

Sunday's girl was a lady taxi driver with a figure that was a real stopper! Garry hired her to take him out of town, directed her to a big house in the country and stopped her at the bottom of the drive. Then he hit her on the head, ripped her radio out, drove into a wood and had her in the back of the cab. He'd really made a meal of it, especially after she woke up; but as he was finishing she got a bit too active and raked his face — which was something he didn't much like. He had a nice face, Garry, and was very fond of it. So almost before he'd known that he was doing it, he'd gutted the whore!

But the next day in the papers the police were talking about skin under her fingernails, and now he knew they had his blood-group but definitely, too. *And* his face was marked; not badly, but enough. So it had been time to take a holiday.

Luckily he'd just had a big win on the gee-gees; he phoned the bookie's and said he wasn't up to it — couldn't see the numbers too clearly — he was taking time off. With an eye-patch and a bandage to cover the damage, he'd headed west and finally holed up in Chichester.

But all of that had been twelve days ago, and he was fine now, and he still had to find his girl-Friday. And today *was* Friday, so . . . Garry reckoned he'd rested up long enough.

This morning he'd read about a Friday night dance at a place called Athelsford, a hick village just a bus-ride away. Well, and he had nothing against country bumpkins, did he? So Athelsford it would have to be . . .

It was the middle of the long hot summer of '76. The weather forecasters were all agreed for once that this one would drag on and on, and reserves of water all over the country were already beginning to suffer. This was that summer when there would be shock reports of the Thames flowing backwards, when rainmakers would be called in from the USA to dance and caper, and when a certain Government Ministry would beg householders to put bricks in their WC cisterns and thus consume less of precious water.

The southern beaches were choked morning to night with kids on their school holidays, sun-blackened treasure hunters with knotted hankies on their heads and metal detectors in their hands, and frustrated fishermen with their crates of beer, boxes of sandwiches, and plastic bags of smelly bait. The pubs were filled all through opening hours with customers trying to drown their thirsts or themselves, and the resorts had never had it so good. The nights were balmy for lovers from Land's End to John o' Groats, and nowhere balmier than in the country lanes of the Southern Counties.

Athelsford Estate in Hampshire, one

of the few suburban housing projects of the Sixties to realize a measure of success (in that its houses were good, its people relatively happy, and — after the last bulldozer had clanked away — its countryside comparatively unspoiled) suffered or enjoyed the heatwave no more or less than anywhere else. It was just another small centre of life and twentieth-century civilization, and apart from the fact that Athelsford was "rather select" there was little as yet to distinguish it from a hundred other estates and small villages in the country triangle of Salisbury, Reading, and Brighton.

Tonight being Friday night, there was to be dancing at The Barn. As its name implied, the place had been a half-brick, half-timber barn; but the Athelsfordians being an enterprising lot, three of their more affluent members had bought the great vault of a place, done it up with internal balconies, tables, and chairs, built a modest car park to one side — an extension of the village pub's car park — and now it was a dance hall, occasionally used for weddings and other private functions. On Wednesday nights the younger folk had it for their disco-theques, (mainly teenage affairs, in return for which they kept it in good repair) but on Friday nights The Barn became the focal point of the entire estate. The Barn and The Old Stage.

The Old Stage was the village pub, its sign a coach with rearing horses confronted by a highwayman in tricorn hat. Joe McGovern, a widower, owned and ran the pub, and many of his customers jokingly associated him with the highwayman on his sign. But while Joe was and always would be a canny Scot, he was also a fair man and down to earth. So were his prices. Ten years ago when the estate was new, the steady custom of the people had saved The Old Stage and kept it a free house. Now Joe's trade was flourishing, and he had plenty to be thankful for.

So, too, Joe's somewhat surly son Gavin. Things to be thankful for, and others he could well do without. Gavin was, for example, extremely thankful for The Barn, whose bar he ran on Wednesday and Friday nights, using stock from The Old Stage. The profits very nicely supplemented the wage he earned as a county council labourer working on the new road. The wage he *had* earned, anyway, before he'd quit. That had only been this morning but already he sort of missed the work, and he was sure he was going to miss the money. But . . . oh, he'd find other work. There was always work for good strong hands. He had that to be thankful for, too: his health and strength.

But he was *not* thankful for his kid sister, Eileen: her "scrapes and narrow escapes" (as he saw her small handful of as yet entirely innocent friendships with the local lads), and her natural, almost astonishing beauty, which drew them like butterflies to bright flowers. It was that, in large part, which made him surly; for he knew that in fact she wasn't just a "kid" sister any more, and that sooner or later she . . .

Oh, Gavin loved his sister, all right — indeed he had transferred to her all of his affection and protection when their mother died three years ago — but having lost his mother he wasn't going to lose Eileen, too, not if he could help it.

Gavin was twenty-two, Eileen seventeen. He was over six feet tall, narrow-hipped, wide in the shoulders: a tapering wedge of muscle with a bullet-head to top it off. Most of the village lads looked at Eileen, then looked at Gavin, and didn't look at Eileen again. But those of them who looked at her twice reckoned she was worth it.

She was blonde as her brother was dark, as sweet and slim as he was huge and surly; five-seven, with long shapely legs and a waist like a wisp, and blue eyes with lights in them that danced when she smiled; the very image of her mother. And that was Gavin's problem — for he'd loved his mother a great deal, too.

It was 5:30 P.M. and brother and sister were busy in workclothes, loading stock from the back door of The Old Stage onto a trolley and carting it across the parking lot to The Barn. Joe McGovern ticked off the items on a stock list as they worked. But when Gavin and Eileen were alone in The Barn, stacking the last of the bottles onto the shelves behind the bar, suddenly he said to her: "Will you be here tonight?"

She looked at her brother. There was nothing surly about Gavin now. There never was when he spoke to her; indeed his voice held a note of concern, of agitation, of some inner struggle which he himself couldn't quite put his finger on. And she knew what he was thinking and that it would be the same tonight as always. Someone would dance with her, and then dance with her again — and then no more. Because Gavin would have had "a quiet word with him."

"Of course I'll be here, Gavin," she sighed. "You know I will. I wouldn't miss it. I love to dance and chat with the girls — and with the boys — when I get the chance! Why does it bother you so?"

"I've told you often enough why it bothers me," he answered gruffly, breathing heavily through his nose. "It's all those blokes. They've only one thing on their minds. They're the same with all the girls. But you're not just any girl — you're my sister!"

"Yes," she answered, a trifle bitterly, "and don't they just know it! You're always there, in the background, watching, somehow threatening. It's like having two fathers — only one of them's a tyrant! Do you know, I can't remember the last time a boy wanted to walk me home?"

"But . . . you are home!" he answered, not wanting to fight, wishing now that he'd kept his peace. If only she was capable of understanding the ways of the world. "You live right next door."

"Then simply walk me!" she blurted it out. "Oh, anywhere! Gavin, can't you understand? It's nice to be courted, to have someone who wants to hold your hand!"

"That's how it starts," he grunted, turning away. "They want to hold your hand. But who's to say how it finishes, eh?"

"Well not much fear of that!" she sighed again. "Not that I'm that sort of girl anyway," and she looked at him archly. "But even if I was, with you around — straining at the leash like . . . like a great hulking watchdog — nothing's very much likely to even get started, now is it?" And before he could answer, but less harshly now: "Now come on," she said, "tell me what's brought all this on? You've been really nice to me this last couple of weeks. The hot weather may have soured some people but you've been really sweet — like a Big Brother should be — until out of the blue, this. I really don't understand what gets into you, Gavin."

It was his turn to sigh. "Aren't you forgetting something?" he said. "The assault — probably with sexual motivation — just last week, Saturday night, in Lovers' Lane?"

Perhaps Eileen really ought not to pooh-pooh that, but she believed she understood it well enough. "An assault," she said. "Motive: 'probably' sexual — the most excitement Athelsford has known in . . . oh, as long as I can remember! And the 'victim': Linda Anstey. Oh, my, what a surprise! Hah! Why, Linda's always been that way! Every kid in the school had fooled around with her at one time or another. From playing kids' games to . . . well, everything. It's the way she is and everyone knows it. All right, perhaps I'm being unfair to her: she might have asked for trouble and she might not, but it seems hardly surprising to me that if it was going to happen to someone, Linda would be the one!"

"But it *did* happen," Gavin insisted. "That kind of bloke does exist — plenty of them." He stacked the last half-dozen cans and made for the exit; and changing the subject (as he was wont to do when an argument was going badly for him, or when he believed he'd proved his point sufficiently) said: "Me, I'm for a pint before I get myself ready for tonight. Fancy an iced lemonade, kid?" He paused, turned back towards her, and grinned, but she suspected it was forced. If only she could gauge what went on in his mind.

But: "Oh, all right!" she finally matched his grin, "if you're buying." She caught up with him and grabbed him, standing on tip-toe to give him a kiss. "But Gavin — promise me that from now on you won't worry about me so much, OK?"

He hugged her briefly, and reluctantly submitted: "Yeah, all right."

But as she led the way out of The Barn and across the car park, with the hot afternoon sun shining in her hair and her sweet, innocent body moving like that inside her coveralls, he looked after her and worried all the harder; worried the way an older brother *should* worry, he thought, and yet somehow far more intensely. And the worst of it was that he *knew* he was being unreasonable and obsessive! But, (and Gavin at once felt his heart hardening), . . . oh, he recognized well enough the way the village Jack-the-Lads looked at Eileen, and knew how much they'd like to get their itchy little paws on her — the grubby-minded, horny . . .

. . .But there Gavin's ireful thoughts abruptly evaporated, the scowl left his face, and he frowned as a vivid picture suddenly flashed onto the screen of his mind. It was something he'd seen just this morning, across the fields where they were laying the new road; something quite obscene which hadn't made much of an impression on him at the time, but which now . . . and astonished, he paused again. For he couldn't for the life of him see how he'd connected up a thing like that with Eileen! And it just as suddenly dawned on him that the reason he knew how the boys felt about his sister was because he sometimes felt that way too. Oh, not about *her* — no, of course not — but about . . . a boulder? Well, certainly it had been a boulder that did it to him this morning, anyway.

And: *Gavin, son,* he told himself, *sometimes I think you're maybe just a tiny wee bit sick!* And then he laughed, if only to himself.

But somehow the pictures in his mind just wouldn't go away, and as he went to his upstairs room in The Old Stage and slowly changed into his evening gear, so he allowed himself to go over again the peculiar occurrences of the morning . . .

Three:

That Friday morning, yes, and it had been hot as a furnace. And every member of the road gang without exception looking forward to the coming weekend, to cool beers in cool houses with all the windows thrown open; so that as the heat-shimmering day had drawn towards noon they'd wearied of the job and put a lot less muscle into it.

Also, and to make things worse, this afternoon they'd be a man short; for this was Gavin McGovern's last morning and he hadn't been replaced yet. And even when he was . . . well, it would take a long time to find someone else who could throw a bulldozer around like he could. The thing was like a toy in his hands. But . . . seeing as how he lived in Athelsford and had always considered himself something of a traitor anyway, working on the link road, he'd finally decided to seek employment elsewhere.

Foreman John Sykes wasn't an Athelsfordian, but he made it his business to know something about the people working under him — especially if they were local to the land where he was driving his road. He'd got to know Big Gavin pretty well, he reckoned, and in a way envied him. He certainly wouldn't mind it if *his* Old Man owned a country pub! But on the other hand he could sympathize with McGovern, too. He knew how torn he must feel.

This was the one part of his job that Sykes hated: when the people up top said the road goes here, and the people down here said oh no it doesn't, not in *our* back garden! Puffed up, awkward, defiant, little bastards! But at the same time Sykes could sympathize with them also, even though they were making his job as unpleasant as they possibly could. And that was yet another reason why the work hadn't gone too well this morning.

Today it had been a sit-in, when a good dozen of the locals had appeared from the woods at the end of Lovers' Lane, bringing lightweight fold-down garden chairs with them to erect across the road. And there they'd sat with their placards and sandwiches on the new stretch of tarmac, heckling the road gang as they toiled and sweated into their dark-stained vests and tried to build a bloody road which wasn't wanted. And which didn't seem to want to be built! They'd stayed from maybe quarter-past nine to a minute short of eleven, then got up and like a gaggle of lemmings waddled back to the village again. Their "good deed" for the day — *Goddam!*

Christ, what a day! For right after that . . . *big* trouble, mechanical trouble! Or rather an obstruction which had caused mechanical trouble. Not the more or less passive, placard-waving obstruction of people — which was bad enough — but a rather more physical, much more tangible obstruction. Namely, a bloody great boulder!

The first they'd known of it was when the bulldozer hit it while lifting turf and

muck in a wide swath two feet deep. Until then there had been only the usual stony debris — small, rounded pebbles and the occasional blunt slab of scarred rock, nothing out of the ordinary for these parts — and Sykes hadn't been expecting anything quite this big. The surveyors had been across here, hammering in their long iron spikes and testing the ground, but they'd somehow missed this thing. Black granite by its looks, it had stopped the dozer dead in its tracks and given Gavin McGovern a fair old shaking! But at least the blade had cleared the sod and clay off the top of the thing. Like the dome of a veined, bald, old head it had looked, sticking up there in the middle of the projected strip.

"See if you can dig the blade under it," Sykes had bawled up at Gavin through clouds of blue exhaust fumes and the clatter of the engine. "Try to lever the bastard up, or split it. We have to get down a good forty or fifty inches just here."

Taking it personally — and with something less than an hour to go, eager to get finished now — Gavin had dragged his sleeve across his brown, perspiration-shiny brow and grimaced. Then, tilting his helmet back on his head, he'd slammed the blade of his machine deep into the earth half a dozen times until he could feel it biting against the unseen curve of the boulder. Then he'd gunned the motor, let out the clutch, shoved, and lifted all in one fluid movement. Or at least in a movement that should have been fluid. For instead of finding purchase the blade had ridden up, splitting turf and topsoil as it slid over the fairly smooth surface of the stone; the dozer had lurched forward, slewing round when the blade finally snagged on a rougher part of the surface; the offside caterpillar had parted in a shriek of hot, tortured metal.

Then Gavin had shut her off, jumped down, and stared disbelievingly at his grazed and bleeding left forearm where it had scraped across the iron frame of the cab. "Damn — *damn!*" he'd shouted then, hurling his safety helmet at the freshly turned earth and kicking the dozer's broken track.

"Easy, Gavin," Sykes had gone up to him. "It's not your fault, and it's not the machine's. It's mine, if anybody's. I had no idea there was anything this big here. And by the look of it this is only the tip of the iceberg."

But Gavin wasn't listening; he'd gone down on one knee and was examining part of the boulder's surface where the blade had done a job of clearing if off. He was frowning, peering hard, breaking away small scabs of loose dirt and tracing lines or grooves with his strong, blunt fingers. The runic symbols were faint but the carved picture was more clearly visible. There were other pictures, too, with only their edges showing as yet, mainly hidden under the curve of the boulder. The ganger got down beside Gavin and assisted him, and slowly the carvings took on clearer definition.

Sykes was frowning, too, now. What the Hell? A floral design of some sort? Very old, no doubt about it. Archaic? Prehistoric?

Unable as yet to make anything decisive of the pictures on the stone, they cleared away more dirt. But then Sykes stared harder, slowly shook his head, and began to grin. The grin spread until it almost split his face ear to ear. Perhaps not prehistoric after all. More like the work of some dirty-minded local kid. And not a bad artist, at that!

The lines of the main picture were primitive but clinically correct, however exaggerated. And its subject was completely unmistakable. Gavin McGovern continued to stare at it, and his bottom jaw had fallen open. Finally, glancing at Sykes out of the corner of his eye, he grunted: "Old, do you think?"

Sykes started to answer, then shut his mouth and stood up. He thought fast,

scuffed some of the dirt back with his booted foot, bent to lean a large, flat flake of stone against the picture, mainly covering it from view. Sweat trickled down his back and made it itch under his wringing shirt. Made it itch like the devil, and the rest of his body with it. The boulder seemed hot as Hell, reflecting the blazing midday sunlight.

And: "Old?" the ganger finally answered. "You mean, like ancient? Naw, I shouldn't think so . . . Hey, and Gavin, son — if I were you, I wouldn't go mentioning this to anyone. You know what I mean?"

Gavin looked up, still frowning. "No," he shook his head, "what do you mean?"

"What?" said Sykes. "You mean to say you can't see it? Why, only let this get out and there'll be people coming from all over the place to see it! Another bloody Stonehenge, it'll be! And what price your Athelsford then, eh? Flooded, the place would be, with all sorts of human debris come to see the famous dirty caveman pictures! You want that, do you?"

No, that was the last thing Gavin wanted. "I see what you mean," he said, slowly. "Also, it would slow you down, right? They'd stop you running your road through here."

"That, too, possibly," Sykes answered. "For a time, anyway. But just think about it. What would you rather have: a new road pure and simple — or a thousand yobs a day tramping through Athelsford and up Lovers' Lane to ogle this little lot, eh?"

That was something Gavin didn't have to think about for very long. It would do business at The Old Stage a power of good, true, but then there was Eileen. Pretty soon they'd be coming to ogle her, too. "So what's next?" he said.

"You leave that to me," Sykes told him. "And just take my word for it that this time tomorrow this little beauty will be so much rubble, OK?"

Gavin nodded; he knew that the

ganger was hot stuff with a drill and a couple of pounds of explosive. "If you say so," he spat into the dust and dirt. "Anyway, I don't much care for the looks of the damned thing!" He scratched furiously at his forearm where his graze was already starting to scab over. "It's not right, this dirty old thing. Sort of makes me hot and . . . itchy!"

"Itchy, yeah," Sykes agreed. And he wondered what sort of mood his wife, Jennie, would be in tonight. If this hot summer sun had worked on her the way it was beginning to work on him, well tonight could get to be pretty interesting. Which would make a welcome change!

Deep, dark, and much disturbed now, old Chylos had felt unaccustomed tremors vibrating through his fossilized bones. The stamping of a thousand warriors on the march, roaring their songs of red death? Aye, perhaps. And:

"*Invaders!*" Chylos breathed the word, without speaking, and indeed without breathing.

"*No,*" Hengit of the Far Forest tribe contradicted him. "*The mammoths are stampeding, the earth is sinking, trees are being felled. Any of these things, but no invaders. Is that all you dream about, old man? Why can't you simply lie still and sleep like the dead thing you are?*"

"*And even if there were invaders,*" the revenant of a female voice now joined in, Alaze of the Shrub Hill folk, "*would you really expect a man of the Far Forest tribe to come to arms? They are notorious cowards! Better you call on me, Chylos, a woman to rise up against these invaders — if there really were invaders, which there are not.*"

Chylos listened hard — to the earth, the sky, the distant sea — but no longer heard the thundering of booted feet, nor warcries going up into the air, nor ships with muffled oars creeping and creaking in the mist. And so he sighed and said: "*Perhaps you are right — but neverthe-*

less, we should be ready! I, at least, am ready!"

And: "*Old fool!*" Hengit whispered of Chylos into the dirt and the dark.

And: "*Coward!*" Alaze was scathing of Hengit where all three lay broken, under the luststone . . .

7:15 P.M.
The road gang had knocked off more than two hours ago and the light was only just beginning to fade a little. An hour and a half to go yet to the summer's balmy darkness, when the young people would wander hand in hand, and occasionally pause mouth to mouth, in Lovers' Lane. Or perhaps not until later, for tonight there was to be dancing at The Barn. And for now . . . all should be peace and quiet out here in the fields, where the luststone raised its veined dome of a head through the broken soil. All *should* be quiet — but was not.

"Levver!" shouted King above the roar of the bikes, his voice full of scorn. "What a bleedin' player you turned out to be! What the 'ell do yer call this, then?"

"The end o' the bleedin' road," one of the other bikers shouted. "That's where!"

"Is it ever!" cried someone else.

Leather grinned sheepishly and pushed his Nazi-style crash-helmet to the back of his head. "So I come the wrong way, di'n I? 'Ell's teef, the sign said bleedin' Affelsford, dinnit?"

"Yers," King shouted. "Also NO ENTRY an' WORKS IN PRO-bleedin'-GRESS! 'Ere, switch off, you lot. I can't 'ear meself fink!"

As the engines of the six machines clattered to a halt, King got off his bike and stretched, stamping his feet. His real name was Kevin; but as leader of a chapter of Hell's Angels, who needed a name like that? A crude crown was traced in lead studs on the back of his leather jacket and a golden sovereign glittered where it dangled from his left earlobe. No more than twenty-five or -six years of age, King kept his head clean-shaven under a silver helmet painted with black eye-sockets and fretted nostrils to resemble a skull. He was hard as they come, was King, and the rest of them knew it.

"That's the place I cased over there," said Leather, pointing. He had jumped up onto the dome of a huge boulder, the luststone, to spy out the land. "See the steeple there? That's Affelsford — and Comrades, does it have *some* crumpet!"

"Well, jolly dee!" said King. "Wot we supposed to do, then? Ride across the bleedin' fields? Come on, Levver my son — you was the one rode out here and onced it over. 'Ow do we bleedin' *get* there?" The rest of the Angels sniggered.

Leather grinned. "We goes up the motorway a few 'undred yards an' spins off at the next turnin', that's all. I jus' made a simple mistake, di'n I."

"Yers," said King, relieving himself loudly against the luststone. "Well, let's not make no more, eh? I gets choked off pissin' about an' wastin' valuable time."

By now the others had dismounted and stood ringed around the dome of the boulder. They stretched their legs and lit "funny" cigarettes. "That's right," said King, "light up. Let's have a break before we go in."

"Best not leave it too late," said Leather. "Once the mood is on me I likes to get it off . . ."

"One copper, you said," King reminded him, drawing deeply on a poorly constructed smoke. "Only one bluebottle in the whole place?"

"S'right," said Leather. "An' 'e's at the other end of town. We can wreck the place, 'ave our fun wiv the girlies, be out again before 'e knows we was ever in!"

" 'Ere," said one of the others. "These birds is the real fing, eh, Levver?"

Leather grinned crookedly and nodded. "Built for it," he answered. "Gawd, it's ripe, is Affelsford!"

The gang guffawed, then quietened as a dumpy figure approached from the construction shack. It was one of Sykes's men, doing night-watchman to bolster his wages. "What's all this?" he grunted, coming up to them.

"Unmarried muvvers' convention," said King. "Wot's it look like?" The others laughed, willing to make a joke of it and let it be; but Leather jumped down from the boulder and stepped forward. He was eager to get things started, tingling — even itchy — with his need for violence.

"Wot's it ter you, baldy?" he snarled, pushing the little man in the chest and sending him staggering.

Baldy Dawson was one of Sykes's drivers and didn't have a lot of muscle. He did have common sense, however, and could see that things might easily get out of hand. "Before you start any rough stuff," he answered, backing away, "I better tell you I took your bike numbers and phoned 'em through to the office in Portsmouth." He had done no such thing, but it was a good bluff. "Any trouble — my boss'll know who did it."

Leather grabbed him by the front of his sweat-damp shirt. "You little —"

"Let it be," said King. " 'E's only doin' 'is job. Besides, 'e 'as an 'ead jus' like mine!" He laughed.

"Wot?" Leather was astonished.

"Why spoil fings?" King took the other's arm. "Now listen, Levver me lad — all you've done so far is bog everyfing up, right? So let's bugger off into bleedin' Affelsford an' 'ave ourselves some fun! You want to see some blood — OK, me too — but for Chrissakes, let's get somefing for our money, right?"

They got back on their bikes and roared off, leaving Baldy Dawson in a slowly settling cloud of dust and exhaust fumes. "Young bastards!" He scratched his naked dome. "Trouble for someone before the night's out, I'll wager."

Then, crisis averted, he returned to

the shack and his well-thumbed copy of *Playboy.* . . .

Four:

"*This time,*" said Chylos, with some urgency, "*I cannot be mistaken.*"

The two buried with him groaned — but before they could comment:

"*Are you deaf, blind — have you no feelings?*" he scorned. "*No, it's simply that you do not have my magic!*"

"*It's your 'magic' that put us here!*" finally Hengit answered his charges. "*Chylos, we don't need your magic!*"

"*But the tribes do,*" said Chylos. "*Now more than ever!*"

"*Tribes?*" this time it was Alaze who spoke. "*The tribes were scattered, gone, blown to the four winds many lifetimes agone. What tribes do you speak of, old man?*"

"*The children of the tribes, then!*" he blustered. "*Their children's children! What does it matter? They are the same people! They are of our blood! And I have dreamed a dream . . .*'

"*That again?*" said Hengit. "*That dream of yours, all these thousands of years old?*"

"*Not the old dream,*" Chylos denied, "*but a new one! Just now, lying here, I dreamed it! Oh, it was not unlike the old one, but it was vivid, fresh, new! And I cannot be mistaken.*"

And now the two lying there with him were silent, for they too had felt, sensed, something. And finally: "*What did you see . . . in this dream?*" Alaze was at least curious.

"*I saw them as before,*" said Chylos, "*with flashing spokes in the wheels of their battle-chairs; except the wheels were not set side by side but fore and aft! And helmets upon their heads, some with horns! They wore shirts of leather picked out in fearsome designs, monstrous runes; sharp knives in their belts, aye, and flails — and blood in their eyes!*

Invaders — I cannot be mistaken!"

And Hengit and Alaze shuddered a little in their stony bones, for Chylos had inspired them with the truth of his vision and chilled them with the knowledge of his prophecy finally come true. But . . . what could they do about it, lying here in the cold earth? It was as if the old wizard read their minds.

"*You are not bound to lie here,*" he told them. "*What are you now but will? And my will remains strong! So let's be up and about our work. I, Chylos, have willed it — so let it be!*"

"*Our work? What work?*" the two cried together. "*We cannot fight!*"

"*You could if you willed it,*" said Chylos, "*and if you have not forgotten how. But I didn't mention fighting. No, we must warn them. The children of the children of the tribes. Warn them, inspire them, cause them to lust after the blood of these invaders!*" And before they could question him further:

"*Up, up, we've work to do!*" Chylos cried. "*Up with you and out into the night, to seek them out. The children of the children of the tribes . . . !*"

From the look of things, it was all set to be a full house at The Barn. Athelsfordians in their Friday-night best were gravitating first to The Old Stage for a warm-up drink or two, then crossing the parking lot to The Barn to secure good tables up on the balconies or around the dance floor. Another hour or two and the place would be in full swing. Normally Gavin McGovern would be pleased with the way things were shaping up, for what with tips and all it would mean a big bonus for him. And his father at the pub wouldn't complain, for what was lost on the swings would be regained on the roundabouts. And yet . . .

There seemed a funny mood on the people tonight, a sort of scratchiness about them, an abrasiveness quite out of keeping. When the disco numbers were playing the girls danced with a sexual aggressiveness Gavin hadn't noticed before, and the men of the village seemed almost to be eyeing each other up like tomcats spoiling for a fight. Pulling pints for all he was worth, Gavin hadn't so far had much of a chance to examine or analyse the thing; it was just that in the back of his mind some small dark niggling voice seemed to be urgently whispering: *Look out! Be on your guard! Tonight's the night! And when it happens you won't believe it!* But . . . it could simply be his imagination, of course.

Or (and Gavin growled his frustration and self-annoyance as he felt that old obsession rising up again) it could simply be that Eileen had found herself a new dancing partner, and that since the newcomer had walked into the place they'd scarcely been off the floor. A fact which in itself was enough to set him imagining all sorts of things, and uppermost the sensuality of women and sexual competitiveness, readiness, and willingness of young men. And where Gavin's sister was concerned, much too willing!

But Eileen had seen Gavin watching her, and as the dance tune ended she came over to the bar with her young man in tow. This was a ploy she'd used before: a direct attack is often the best form of defence. Gavin remembered his promise, however, and in fact the man she was with seemed a very decent sort at first glance: clean and bright, smartly dressed, seriously intentioned. Now Gavin would see if his patter matched up to his looks.

"Gavin," said Eileen, smiling warningly, "I'd like you to meet Gordon Cleary — Gordon's a surveyor from Portsmouth."

"How do you do, Gordon," Gavin dried his hands, reached across the bar to shake with the other, discovered the handshake firm, dry, and no-nonsense. But before they could strike up any sort of conversation the dance floor had emptied and the bar began to crowd up.

"I'm sorry," Gavin shrugged ruefully. "Business. But at least you were here first and I can get you your drinks." He looked at his sister.

"Mine's easy," she said, smiling. "A lemonade, please." And Gavin was pleased to note that Cleary made no objection, didn't try to force strong drink on her.

"Oh, a shandy for me," he said, "and go light on the beer, please, Gavin, for I'll be driving later. And one for yourself, if you're ready."

The drinks were served and Gavin turned to the next party of customers in line at the bar. There were four of them: Tod Baxter and Angela Meers, village sweethearts, and Allan Harper and his wife, Val. Harper was a PTI at the local school; he ordered a confusing mixture of drinks, no two alike; Gavin, caught on the hop, had a little trouble with his mental arithmetic. "Er, that's two pounds — er —" He frowned in concentration.

"Three pounds and forty-seven pence, on the button!" said Gordon Cleary from the side. Gavin looked at him and saw his eyes flickering over the price list pinned up behind the bar.

"Pretty fast!" he commented, and carried on serving. But to himself he said: *except I hope it's only with numbers . . .*

Gavin wasn't on his own behind the bar; at the other end, working just as hard, Bill Salmons popped corks and pulled furious pints. Salmons was ex-Army, a parachutist who'd bust himself up jumping. You wouldn't know it, though, for he was strong as a horse. As the disc jockey got his strobes going again and the music started up, and as the couples gradually gravitated back towards the dance floor, Gavin crossed quickly to Salmons and said: "I'm going to get some of this sweat off. Two minutes."

Salmons nodded, said: "Hell of a night, isn't it? Too damned *hot!*"

Gavin reached under the bar for a clean towel and headed for the gents' toilet. Out of the corner of his eye he saw that Eileen and Gordon Cleary were back on the floor again. Well, if all the bloke wanted was to dance . . . that was okay.

In the washroom Gavin took off his shirt, splashed himself with cold water, and towelled it off, dressed himself again. A pointless exercise: he was just as hot and damp as before! As he finished off Allan Harper came in, also complaining of the heat.

They passed a few words; Harper was straightening his tie in a mirror when there came the sound of shattering glass from the dance hall, causing Gavin to start. "What — ?" he said.

"Just some clown dropped his drink, I expect," said Harper. "Or fainted for lack of air! It's about time we got some decent air-conditioning in this —"

And he paused as there sounded a second crash — which this time was loud enough to suggest a table going over. The music stopped abruptly and some girl gave a high-pitched shriek.

We warned you! said several dark little voices in the back of Gavin's mind. "What the Hell — ?" he started down the corridor from the toilets with Harper hot on his heels.

Entering the hall proper the two skidded to a halt. On the other side of the room a village youth lay sprawled among the debris of a wrecked table, blood spurting from his nose. Over him stood a Hell's Angel, swinging a bike chain threateningly. In the background a young girl sobbed, backing away, her dress torn down the front. Gavin would have started forward but Harper caught his arm. "Look!" he said.

At a second glance the place seemed to be crawling with Angels. There was one at the entrance, blocking access; two more were on the floor, dragging Angela Meers and Tod Baxter apart. They had yanked the straps of Angela's dress down, exposing her breasts. A fifth Angel had clambered into the disco control box, was flinging records all over the place as he sought his favourites. And the sixth was at the bar.

Now it was Gavin's turn to gasp, "Look!"

The one at the bar, King, had trapped Val Harper on her bar stool. He had his arms round her, his hands gripping the bar top. He rubbed himself grindingly against her with lewdly suggestive sensuality.

For a moment longer the two men stood frozen on the perimeter of this scene, nailed down by a numbness which, as it passed, brought rage in its wake. The Angel with the chain, Leather, had come across the floor and swaggered by them into the corridor, urinating in a semicircle as he went, saying: "Evenin' gents. This the bog, then?"

What the Hell's happening? thought Harper, lunging towards the bar. There must be something wrong with the strobe lights: they blinded him as he ran, flashing rainbow colours in a mad kaleidoscope that flooded the entire room. The Angel at the bar was trying to get his hand down the front of Val's dress, his rutting movements exaggerated by the crazy strobes. Struggling desperately, Val screamed.

Somewhere at the back of his shocked mind, Harper noted that the Angels still wore their helmets. He also noted, in the flutter of the crazy strobes, that the helmets seemed to have grown horns! *Jesus, it's like a bloody Viking invasion!* he thought, going to Val's rescue. . . .

It had looked like a piece of cake to King and his Angels. A gift. The kid selling tickets hadn't even challenged them. Too busy wetting his pants, King supposed. And from what he had seen of The Barn's clientele: pushovers! As soon as he'd spotted Val Harper at the bar, he'd known what he wanted. A toffynosed bird like her in a crummy place like this? She could only be here for one thing. And not a man in the place to deny him whatever he wanted to do or take.

Which is why it came as a total surprise to King when Alan Harper spun him around and butted him square in the face. Blood flew as the astonished Angel slammed back against the bar; his spine cracked against the bar's rim, knocking all the wind out of him; in another moment Bill Salmon's arm went round his neck in a strangle-hold. This was no time for chivalry: Harper the PTI finished it with a left to King's middle and a right to his already bloody face. The final blow landed on King's chin, knocking him cold. As Bill Salmons released him he flopped forward, his death's-head helmet flying free as he landed face-down on the floor.

Gavin McGovern had meanwhile reached into the disc-jockey's booth, grabbed his victim by the scruff of the neck, and hurled him out of the booth and across the dance floor. Couples hastily got out of the way as the Angel slid on his back across the polished floor. Skidding to a halt, he brought out a straight-edged razor in a silvery flash of steel. Gavin was on him in a moment; he lashed out with a foot that caught the Angel in the throat, knocking him flat on his back again. The razor spun harmlessly away across the floor as its owner writhed and clawed at his throat.

Seeing their Angel at Arms on the floor like that, the pair who tormented Angela Meers now turned their attention to Gavin McGovern. They had already knocked Tad Baxter down, kicking him where he huddled. But they hadn't got in a good shot and as Gavin loomed large so Tod got to his feet behind them. Also, Allan Harper was dodging his way through the now strangely silent crowd where he came from the bar.

The Angel at the door, having seen something of the melee and wanting to get his share while there was still some going, also came lunging in through the wild strobe patterns. But this one reckoned without the now fully roused passions of the young warriors of the Athelsford tribe. Three of the estate's larger youths jumped him, and he went down under a hail of blows. And by then Allan Harper, Gavin McGovern, and Tod Baxter had fallen on the other two. For long moments there were only the crazily flashing strobes, the dull thudding of fists into flesh, and a series of fading grunts and groans.

Five Angels were down; and the sixth, coming out of the toilets, saw only a sea of angered faces all turned in his direction. Faces hard and full of fury — *and* bloodied, crumpled shapes here and there, cluttering the dance floor. Pale now and disbelieving, Leather ran towards the exit, found himself surrounded in a moment. And now in the absolute silence there was bloodlust written on those faces that ringed him in.

They rolled over him like a wave, and his Nazi helmet flew off and skidded to a rocking halt . . . at the feet of Police Constable Charlie Bennet, Athelsford's custodian of the law, where he stood framed in the door of the tiny foyer.

Then the normal lights came up and someone cut the strobes, and as the weirdly breathless place slowly came back to life, so PC Bennet was able to take charge. And for the moment no one, not even Gavin, noticed that Eileen McGovern and her new friend were nowhere to be seen. . . .

Five:

Chylos was jubilant. *"It's done!"* he cried in his grave. *"The invaders defeated, beaten back!"*

And: *"You were right, old man,"* finally Hengit grudgingly answered.

"There were invaders, and our warnings and urgings came just in time. But this tribe of yours — pah! Like flowers, they were, weak and waiting to be crushed — until we inspired them."

And now Chylos was angry indeed. *"You two!"* he snapped like a bowstring. *"If you had heeded me at the rites, these many generations flown, then were there no requirement for our efforts this night! But . . . perhaps I may still undo your mischief, even now, and finally rest easy."*

"That can't be, old man, and you know it," this time Alaze spoke up. *"Would that we could put right that of which you accuse us; for if our blood still runs in these tribes, then it were only right and proper. But we cannot put it right. No, not even with all your magic. For what are we now but worm-fretted bones and dust? There's no magic can give us back our flesh. . . ."*

"There is," Chylos chuckled then. *"Oh, there is! The magic of this stone. No, not your flesh but your will. No, not your limbs but your lust. Neither your youth nor your beauty nor even your hot blood, but your spirit! Which is all you will need to do what must be done. For if the tribes may not be imbrued with your seed, strengthened by your blood — then it must be with your spirit. I may not do it for I was old even in those days, but it is still possible for you. If I will it — and if you will it.*

"Now listen, and I shall tell you what must be done. . . ."

Eileen McGovern and "Gordon Cleary" stood outside The Barn in the deepening dusk and watched the Black Maria come and take away the battered Angels. As the police van made off down the estate's main street Eileen leaned towards the entrance to the disco, but her companion seemed concerned for her and caught her arm. "Better let it cool down in there," he said. "There's bound to be a lot of hot blood still on the boil."

"Maybe you're right," Eileen looked up at him. "Certainly you were right to bundle us out of there when it started! So what do you suggest? We could go and cool off in The Old Stage. My father owns it."

He shrugged, smiled, seemed suddenly shy, a little awkward. "I'd rather hoped we could walk together," he said. "The heat of the day is off now — it's cool enough out here. Also, I'll have to be going in an hour or so. I'd hoped to be able to, well, talk to you in private. Pubs and dance halls are fine for meeting people, but they're dreadfully noisy places, too."

It was her turn to shrug. It would be worth it if only to defy Gavin. And afterwards she'd make him see how there was no harm in her friendships. "All right," she said, taking Cleary's arm. "Where shall we walk?"

He looked at her and sighed his defeat. "Eileen, I don't know this place at all. I wouldn't know one street or lane from the next. So I suppose I'm at your mercy!"

"Well," she laughed, "I do know a pretty private place." And she led him away from The Barn and into an avenue of trees. "It's not far away, and it's *the* most private place of all." She smiled as once more she glanced up at him in the flooding moonlight. "That's why it's called Lovers' Lane. . . ."

Half an hour later in The Barn, it finally dawned on Gavin McGovern that his sister was absent. He'd last seen her with that Gordon Cleary bloke. And what had Cleary said: something about having to drive later? Maybe he'd taken Eileen with him. They must have left during the ruckus with the Angels. Well, at least Gavin could be thankful for that!

But at eleven o'clock when The Barn closed and he had the job of checking and then shifting the stock, still she wasn't back. Or if she was she'd gone straight home to The Old Stage and so to bed. Just before twelve midnight Gavin was finished with his work. He gratefully put out the lights and locked up The Barn, then crossed to The Old Stage where his father was still checking the night's take and balancing the stock ledger.

First things first, Gavin quietly climbed the stairs and peeped into Eileen's room; the bed was still made up, undisturbed from this morning; she wasn't back. Feeling his heart speeding up a little, Gavin went back downstairs and reported her absence to his father.

Burly Joe McGovern seemed scarcely concerned. "What?" he said, squinting up from his books. "Eileen? Out with a young man? For a drive? So what's your concern? Come on now, Gavin! I mean, she's hardly a child!"

Gavin clenched his jaws stubbornly as his father returned to his work, went through into the large private kitchen and dining room and flopped into a chair. Very well, then he would wait up for her himself. And if he heard that bloke's car bringing her back home, well he'd have a few words to say to him, too.

It was a quarter after twelve when Gavin settled himself down to wait upon Eileen's return; but his day had been long and hard, and something in the hot summer air had sapped his usually abundant energy. The evening's excitement, maybe. By the time his father went up to bed Gavin was fast asleep and locked in troubled dreams. . . .

Quite some time earlier:
. . . In the warm summer nights, Lovers' Lane wasn't meant for fast-walking. It was only a mile and a half long, but almost three-quarters of an hour had gone by since Eileen and her new young man had left The Barn and started along its winding ways. Lovers' Lane: no, it wasn't the sort of walk you took at the trot. It was a holding-hands, swinging-arms-together, soft-talking walk; a kissing walk, in those places where the hedges were silvered by moonlight and lips softened by it. And it seemed strange to Eileen that her escort hadn't tried to kiss her, not once along the way. . . .

But he had been full of talk: not about himself but mainly the night — how much he loved the darkness, its soft velvet, which he claimed he could feel against his skin, the *aliveness* of night — and about the moon: the secrets it knew but couldn't tell. Not terribly scary stuff but . . . strange stuff. Maybe too strange. And so, whenever she had the chance, Eileen had tried to change the subject, to talk about herself. But oddly, he hadn't seemed especially interested in her.

"Oh, there'll be plenty of time to talk about personalities later," he'd told her, and she'd noticed how his voice was no longer soft but . . . somehow coarse? And she'd shivered and thought: *time later? Well of course there will be . . . won't there?*

And suddenly she'd been aware of the empty fields and copses opening on all sides, time fleeting by, the fact that she was out here, in Lovers' Lane, with . . . a total stranger? What was this urgency in him, she wondered? She could feel it now in the way his hand held hers almost in a vise, the coarse, jerky tension of his breathing, the way his eyes scanned the moonlit darkness ahead and to left and right, looking for . . . what?

"Well," she finally said, trying to lighten her tone as much as she possibly could, digging her heels in a little and drawing him to a halt, "that's it — all of it — Lovers' Lane. From here on it goes nowhere, just open fields all the way to where they're digging the new road. And anyway it's time we were getting back. You said you only had an hour."

He held her hand more tightly yet, and his eyes were silver in the night. He took something out of his pocket and she heard a click, and the something gleamed a little in his dark hand. "Ah, but that was then and this is now," Garry Clemens told her, and she snatched her breath and her mouth fell open as she saw his awful smile. And then, while her mouth was still open, suddenly he *did* kiss her — and it was a brutal kiss and very terrible. And now Eileen knew.

As if reading her mind, he throatily said: "But if you're good and do *exactly* as you're told — then you'll live through it." And as she filled her lungs to scream, he quickly lifted his knife to her throat, and in his now choking voice whispered, "But if you're *not* good then I'll hurt you very, very much and you won't live through it. And one way or the other it will make no difference: I shall have you anyway, for you're my girl-Friday!"

"Gordon, I —" she finally breathed, her eyes wide in the dark, heart hammering, breasts rising and falling unevenly beneath her thin summer dress. And trying again: "Tell me this is just some sort of game, that you're only trying to frighten me and don't mean any . . . of . . . it." But she knew only too well that he did.

Her voice had been gradually rising, growing shrill, so that now he warningly hissed: "Be *quiet!*" And he backed her up to a stile in the fence, pressing with his knife until she was aware of it delving the soft skin of her throat. Then, very casually, he cut her thin summer dress down the front to her waist and flicked back the two halves with the point of his knife. Her free hand fluttered like a trapped bird, to match the palpitations of her heart, but she didn't dare do anything with it. And holding that sharp blade to her left breast, he said:

"Now we're going across this stile and behind the hedge, and then I'll tell you all you're to do and how best to please me. And that's important, for if you *don't* please me — well, then it will be good night Eileen, Eileen!"

"Oh, God! *Oh, God!*" she whispered, as he forced her over the fence and behind the tall hedge. And:

"Here!" he said. "Here!"

And from the darkness just to one side of him, another voice, not Eileen's, answered, *"Yes, here! Here!"* But it was *such* a voice . . .

"What . . . ?" Garry Clemens gulped, his hot blood suddenly ice. "Who . . .?" He released Eileen's hand and whirled, scything with his knife — scything nothing! — only the dark, which now seemed to close in on him. But:

"Here," said that husky, hungry, lusting voice again, and now Clemens saw that indeed there was a figure in the dark. A naked female figure, voluptuous and inviting. And, *"Here!"* she murmured yet again, her voice a promise of pleasures undreamed, drawing him down with her to the soft grass.

Out of the corner of his eye, dimly in his confused mind, the rapist saw a figure — fleeting, tripping, and staggering upright, fleeing — which he knew was Eileen McGovern where she fled wildly across the field. But he let her go. For he'd found a new and more wonderful, more exciting girl-Friday now. "Who . . . who *are* you?" he husked as he tore at his clothes — astonished that she tore at them, too.

And: *"Alaze,"* she told him, simply. *"Alaze. . . ."*

Eileen — running, crashing through a low thicket, flying under the moon — wanted to scream but had no wind for it. And in the end was too frightened to scream anyway. For she knew that someone ran with her, alongside her; a lithe, naked someone, who for the moment held off from whatever was his purpose.

But for how long?

The rattle of a crate deposited on the doorstep of The Old Stage woke Gavin McGovern up from unremembered dreams, but dreams which nevertheless left him red-eyed and rumbling inside like a volcano. Angry dreams! He woke to a new day, and in a way to a new world. He went to the door and it was dawn; the sun was balanced on the eastern horizon, reaching for the sky; Dave Gorman, the local milkman, was delivering.

"Wait," Gavin told him, and ran upstairs. A moment later and he was down again. "Eileen's not back," he said. "She was at the dance last night, went off with some bloke, an outsider. He hasn't brought her back. Tell them."

Gorman looked at him, almost said: *tell who?* But not quite. He knew who to tell. The Athelsford tribe.

Gavin spied the postman, George Lee, coming along the road on his early morning rounds. He gave him the same message: his sister, Eileen, a girl of the tribe, had been abducted. She was out there somewhere now, stolen away, perhaps hurt. And by the time Gavin had thrown water in his face and roused his father, the message was already being spread abroad. People were coming out of their doors, moving into the countryside around, starting to search. The tribe looked after its own. . . .

And beneath the luststone:

Alaze was back, but Hengit had not returned. It was past dawn and Chylos could feel the sun warming their mighty headstone, and he wondered what had passed in the night: was his work now done and could he rest?

"How went it?" the old wizard inquired immediately, as Alaze settled back into her bones.

"It went . . . well. To a point," she eventually answered.

"A point? What point?" He was alarmed. *"What went wrong? Did you not follow my instructions?"*

"Yes," she sighed, *"but —"*

"But?" And now it was Chylos's turn to sigh. *"Out with it."*

"I found one who was lusty. Indeed he was with a maid, which but for my intervention he would take against her will! Ah, but when he saw me he lusted after her no longer! And I heeded your instructions and put on my previous female form for him. According to those same instructions, I would teach him the true passions and furies and ecstasies of the flesh; so that afterwards and when he was with women of the tribe, he would be untiring, a satyr, and they would always bring forth from his potent seed. But because I was their inspiration, my spirit would be in all of them! This was why I put on flesh; and it was a great magic, a gigantic effort of will. Except . . . it had been a long, long time, Chylos. And in the heat of the moment I relaxed my will; no, he relaxed it for me, such was his passion. And . . . he saw me as I was, as I am. . . ."

"Ah!" said Chylos, understanding what she told him. *"And afterwards? Did you not try again? Were there no others?"*

"There might *have been others, aye — but as I journeyed out from this stone, the greater the distance the less obedient my will. Until I could no longer call flesh unto myself. And now, weary, I am returned."*

Chylos sagged down into the alveolate, crumbling relics of himself. *"Then Hengit is my last hope,"* he said.

At which moment Hengit returned — but hangdog, as Chylos at once observed. And: *"Tell me the worst,"* the old man groaned.

But Hengit was unrepentant. *"I did as you instructed,"* he commenced his story, *"went forth, found a woman, put on flesh. And she was of the tribe, I'm sure. Alas, she was a child in the ways of men, a virgin, an innocent. You had said: let her be lusty, willing — but she was not. Indeed, she was afraid."*

Chylos could scarce believe it. *"But — were there no others?"*

"Possibly," Hengit answered. *"But this was a girl of the tribe, lost and afraid and*

vulnerable. I stood close by and watched over her, until the dawn. . . ."

"Then that is the very end of it," Chylos sighed, beaten at last. And his words were truer than even he might suspect.

But still, for the moment, the luststone exerted its immemorial influence. . . .

Of all the people of Athelsford who were out searching in the fields and woods that morning, it was Gavin Mc-Govern who found the rapist Clemens huddled beneath the hedgerow. He heard his sobbing, climbed the stile, and found him there. And in the long grass close by, he also found his knife still damp with dew. And looking at Clemens, the way he was, Gavin fully believed that he had lost Eileen forever.

He cried hot, unashamed tears then, looked up at the blue skies she would never see again, and blamed himself. *My fault — my fault! If I'd not been the way I was, she wouldn't have needed to defy me!*

But then he looked again at Clemens, and his surging blood surged more yet. And as Clemens had lusted after Eileen, so now Gavin lusted after him — after his life!

He dragged him out from hiding, bunched his white hair in a hamlike hand, and stretched his neck taut across his knee. Then — three things, occurring almost simultaneously.

One: a terrific explosion from across the fields, where John Sykes had kept his word and reduced the luststone to so much rubble. Two: the bloodlust went out of Gavin like a light switched off, so that he gasped, released his victim, and thrust him away. And three, he heard the voice of his father, echoing from the near-distance and carrying far and wide in the brightening air:

"Gavin, we've found her! She's unharmed! She's all right!"

PC Bennet, coming across the field, his uniformed legs damp from the dewy grass, saw the knife in Gavin's hand and said, "I'll take that, son." And having taken it he also went to take charge of the gibbering, worthless, soul-shrivelled maniac thing that was Garry Clemens.

And so in a way old Chylos was right, for in the end nothing had come of all his works. But in several other ways he was quite wrong. . . .   Ω

SUBSCRIBE TO *WEIRD TALES*®!

In the United States: Six issues, $24. Twelve issues, $46.
In Canada & Mexico: Six issues, $30. Twelve issues, $58.
In all other countries: Six issues, $33. Twelve issues, $64.
Published every three months.

Send check or money order to *Weird Tales*®, P.O. Box 13418, Philadelphia PA 19101-3418. We accept checks on U.S. banks and on Canadian banks in U.S. dollars. We accept checks on United Kingdom banks in pounds at £1 = $2. To charge your Visa or MasterCharge account, let us know your card number, the expiration date, the amount in U.S. dollars, and include your signature. In every case, include your full address and Zip or Postal code.
Our address:
Weird Tales®, P.O. Box 13418, Philadelphia PA 19101-3418
Many thanks!

TO BE A HERO

It always happens to ordinary guys like me
With maybe a secret sorrow
A missing father, a crippled arm
A fragile mother to support
A need for the services of a hero

And of course there is a woman I worship
Passionate and beautiful with wild wild hair
Who does not care about me at all.
Whether she would make me happy
Seems to be parenthetical.

So he comes out of nowhere, tall and dark
A fugitive from his own sad perilous past
He has been a gangster maybe or a jewel thief
Or a spy. He chooses me as a friend
Because I have all the innocence he has ever lost.

He is silent, handsome, he dresses in black
At first sight she falls hard in love with him
And he soft and wary and careful with her.
It is of course necessary that I should be blond
With blue eyes and a boyish grin.

When we fight over her he takes my blows
And won't hurt me even though I know
At least once he has killed a man.
Sooner or later he finds out about my father
Or I lose the farm or my mother dies
And I end up crying on his shoulder.

Or maybe he helps me save the home place
Or maybe I do it myself. I am after all
White hat to his black. He casts a long shadow,
By his side I catch the sun. Just knowing him
Has made me worthy to be a hero.

When his past tracks him down, when he goes away again
And we all know he can never come back,
Because he has made a man of me
He can hand the girl to me on a platter
But what does it matter. I don't want her anymore.
It's him I love.

— Nancy Springer
Copyright © 1991 by Nancy Springer

WEIRD TALES TALKS
WITH WILLIAM F. NOLAN

by Darrell Schweitzer

Weird Tales: You mentioned in the introduction to one of your books that the essential characteristic for a writer of horror fiction is a love of the genre. So, how did your particular love affair with the field begin?

Nolan: Part of that is already answered in "Dark Bedfellows," the memoir I've written for you, how I fell in love with horror fiction by discovering Boris Karloff's *Tales of Terror* when I was a boy in Kansas City. But, before that, it was motion pictures. It was *Dracula* and *Frankenstein* in the early '30s. Those pictures had a tremendous effect on me as a child. The raising of the monster into the lightning in *Frankenstein* is imprinted in my brain, as is Harker's welcome to Dracula's castle and the whole effect and the mood of that sequence. I realized that horror was something I really related to emotionally. I would have to say that motion pictures started it all.

WT: When you became a professional, you gravitated toward screenwriting very quickly. So the fascination with film must have stayed with you all along.

Nolan: Absolutely! When the MGM lion roared I used to sit in the Isis Theater in Kansas City and watch those early pictures thinking that someday my name would be up there on that screen. The first time I sat in the Cinerama dome in Hollywood and watched *Logan's Run* and the MGM lion roared and I saw "based on a novel by" — and suddenly my name was there in giant letters — that was a great moment. I've loved films all my life. I still see two a week even now. Films are part of my life's blood. We live in a visual world, and as I wrote *Logan* I was envisioning it as a film. I write with an imaginary screen running inside my head, and each scene I write is a scene in my film with me playing all the parts, the director, the production designer, the actors, and so on.

WT: Your prose style is very spare. Is this intentional?

Nolan: I never tell more than I need to in a story. I never over-describe anything. In the novella "Broxa" in this issue, I give minimum description to each scene, so that the reader is told just what he or she has to know, and then the imagination takes over from there. I always leave room for the reader's imagination in my writing.

I literally do not understand the kind of British writer who opens the door to an apartment and spends the next five pages describing what's in the room, or writers who take half a chapter to get their character across a kitchen in a breakfast scene. I'm in and out of the kitchen and down the road and into the next county by the time they're reaching the marmalade. I can't write in that manner. I pare my work down to the essentials. I keep revising it until every word has a weight of its own. I try for very spare, economical images. The idea is to let the reader's mind create the rest of the image, so the reader thinks he or she is seeing more than I've actually written.

WT: What you're describing is the

effect of film on prose. Compare this to a writer prior to the film era, say, Arthur Machen, who was gorgeous but very, very leisurely. He could take up half the story for the prologue.

Nolan: I think that in terms of Machen and Charles Dickens and Algernon Blackwood and other early writers, or even Lovecraft to some extent, they were fine for their period. Readers were ready to accept that leisurely pace. When I wrote my first private-eye novel I had my detective moving through Los Angeles like a whirlwind, killing any number of enemies with his smoking .45 and having a great time doing it.

WT: Your new novella, "Broxa" has a considerable mixture of detective and supernatural elements. What do you see as the affinity between these two forms?

Nolan: I'm a great cross-genre mixer. When I wrote the two novels about my Mars-based private eye, Sam Space, I cross-mixed genres — obviously science fiction and the hardboiled detective story. I love to take a form and put a new face on it to make it fresh. In "Broxa," I took the detective form and mixed it with the supernatural genre. I was able to do a semi-hardboiled detective approach within a demonic setting. It's a cross-mix, and I think it's fresher and allows the reader to find new trails to explore, new areas that he or she wouldn't expect to find in this kind of a story. Just about the time the reader thinks he's got one of my stories figured out, I always like to throw a twist into it, to knock him off his pins, as it were.

WT: I suppose the affinities are that the detective story is full of dark images and menace, only in the usual detective story it turns out to be a natural menace. So the affinity has been there from the start. Hence all the psychic detective stories.

Nolan: That's true — but I think I've taken a new route with this novella. I've never read anything quite like it. I tried deliberately to freshen the whole genre

of the private eye and the cliché of the missing-daughter case. The most overworked story in private-eye fiction is when the detective is hired to find a missing daughter. So I used that situation and turned it around. There are things in this novella that I'm sure no reader is going to guess. My wife said to me when I was writing my second private detective novel set in Los Angeles — *The White Cad Crossup* — "You're two-thirds of the way through the book, so who's the killer?" And I said, "I don't know yet." She was shocked. "How can you write two-thirds of a novel and not know who the killer is?" For me, it works. I get right down to the last chapter or so, and then I look at all the different characters and I pick out the one the reader would least expect to be the killer. Then I tailor earlier portions of the novel to fit. It works.

WT: I take it then that you're one of those writers who sits down and gets going, rather than outlining.

Nolan: It depends on the project. I outlined "Broxa" on about twenty-five file cards. What I often do is set up a basic plot skeleton. Then I flesh it out with the writing. I don't want a long, detailed outline, because that spoils the fun for me. I want to discover what is going on, along with the reader. Part of the fun is discovering what my characters are going to do next, letting them take me places that I didn't know they were going to take me. You decide to kill off a character, then you fall in love with the character, and end up letting him live. Vice-versa, you think you're going to like a character, you don't like the character, so you kill him off. There's a god-like feeling to writing. You *are* God. You can create life or destroy it on the page. It's a tremendous feeling of emotional power.

WT: I think the secret, particularly in horror fiction, is to engage the emotions. A horror story that can't do that is nothing. So, how do *you* do that?

Nolan: The first thing the writer has to do with any story is create real people. If you can draw your reader into the story by the reader's believing in your characters, if you can touch psychic nerves with people, touch fundamental truths with characterization, then you can do anything you want with those characters. The reader will go with you.

My first job as a writer, whether I'm doing short stories, novels, or scripts, is to find a way to create believable characters. If I can't do that, the reader's not going to care what happens in my story.

I had one letter just last week, in which someone said they'd read one of my short stories in which I used five very short vignettes, and this reader asked "How do you create such empathy so quickly for your characters?" Well, it's shorthand writing again. You have to make every word count. If you can create empathy in a paragraph rather than a chapter, then do it that way. Some writers require an immense amount of space in order to achieve in-depth characterization, but I do it very quickly. I sketch it in like a watercolorist. I suppose it's my art background. You know, I'm an ex-artist, and I think in visual brushstrokes. That's one way to put it: my style is a series of quick brushstrokes that build the picture stroke by stroke.

WT: Were you a professional artist *before* you became a writer?

Nolan: Well, my first real piece of creative work involved both art *and* writing — for my high school newspaper. Called "Freshman Frankie," it was a comic strip that ran for twelve issues, and it dealt with this little fellow who wanted to be tall, and when he got to be tall nobody really loved him, so he went back to being small again. In other words, *Be yourself. Don't try to be something you're not.* That was the message.

It won first prize in a citywide high school contest back in Kansas City. This encouraged me to go on to the Kansas City Art Institute, where I studied art

for two years. I became an artist for Hallmark Cards for a summer, designing and writing greeting cards. Then when I came out to San Diego in the late '40s, I set up my own art studio in Balboa Park. I painted outdoor murals and did commissioned artwork for various people. So I thought that was what I was going to be, a commercial artist. However, writing was the thing that I always enjoyed doing the most, but it was always in the background. Then in 1952 I realized that it was the *art* that should be in the background. So I reversed the entire course of my life. That's the day I admitted to myself that I really wanted to write for a living, not draw. My drawing now is purely on a hobby level. The writing is the career.

WT: Did you start sending stories out at that point?

Nolan: Yes, the first story I sent out was in 1952. I have a very unusual sales record with regard to my fiction. I've written a hundred and fifteen short stories and I've sold a hundred and fifteen short stories! I've met people who have drawers full of rejected stories, but this kind of thing never happened to me. Sometimes an editor will say, "I know you don't have time to write a new story right now, so just give me one of your trunk stories, something you haven't been able to sell," and I say "I don't have anything," and I mean it. I've written nine novels and I've sold nine novels. I don't understand how people can write ten, twelve, fifteen novels, and still have the guts to keep going when they haven't been able to sell them. It would have destroyed me. I haven't had that problem. I've sold ninety-nine percent of everything I've written in my life, fiction or non-fiction.

WT: You got into screenwriting relatively early, and so when you wrote *Logan's Run* you already had much more polish and discipline than the usual first novelist does. You already knew how to write by then.

Nolan: Oh, sure. I learned by writing fiction first. I wrote in school notebooks from the age of ten. I wrote stories about cowboys and daring air aces and G-men. When I was ten and eleven I would fill notebooks with these lurid stories. They're dreadful things. I go back and read them and they show no jot of talent. But I just kept at it, learning more each year. . . . I made my first sale when I was twenty-five and I had been writing fifteen years — all through high school and into college. But during this time I never sent out anything. When I felt that I was ready to send things out, then I began to sell immediately.

WT: Beyond horror and science fiction, you've written in several other fields, right?

Nolan: Right. Most people don't realize that I've written eight auto-racing books, and over a hundred and fifty auto-racing articles. I've written in the show business field — biographies of John Huston the film director and Steve McQueen the actor. I've written westerns. I've written in the field of aviation, and of course I've done a lot of mystery writing, hardboiled detective, crime-suspense work, a biography of Dashiell Hammett, essays on Raymond Chandler and so forth. The answer is to do a lot of writing before you start sending out material, so you know you've polished your craft.

WT: At the same time, isn't there also a temptation to use this as an excuse for never sending *anything* out? Surely you've known writers like that, whose work is good, but they don't believe it and you have to pry it out of them.

Nolan: That's certainly true of a lot of people. They simply won't work to get the material out. You've got to polish it. I start out with a Flair pen on paper at a coffee-shop counter late at night. I do all my first drafts that way. I'm talking about novels, biographies, scripts, stories, whatever it is. I do them all with a Flair pen on a pad, handwritten. That forms one draft. Then I correct that handwritten draft, and I do another draft on the typewriter. I correct the typewritten draft, going over it very carefully, making yet another draft. I give it to my wife who has a word-processor. I then correct her draft from the word-processor, make a lot of changes, and then put it through the word-processor once again. That's the draft that goes out to market. I don't see any other way to do it.

You've got to maintain a quality level. The writer I want to beat is William F. Nolan. I'm not too worried about Stephen King and Peter Straub and all these people. I'm worried about William F. Nolan. I've got to keep doing better than this guy, or else I'm not going to make it. I challenge myself each time out. Have I done this before? Is this fresh? Can I better the effect of this scene? Can I write a deeper character? Can I write a more shocking bit of dialogue here?

You've got to keep stretching yourself. The little voice inside you has to say, "You know you can do better. Now sit down there and *do* better." I know a fellow who has been writing for fifteen years, and he's done two short stories and part of a novel. That's it, and yet he calls himself a writer. But he isn't. He won't work hard enough. He just won't send out the material.

WT: I was thinking of someone on the order of Emily Dickinson. She never did send most of her material out, and it was all published posthumously. I suppose this can still happen, and sometimes dilettantes write interesting work. So you have to strike a balance between being over-confident and not confident enough. Perhaps a writer needs a genuinely effective way of evaluating his own work. How do you tell when your work is genuinely good? How do you know it's not just ego?

Nolan: Let's talk about ego for a moment. Ego is absolutely the central foundation, the pillar that every writer has to have in his house. He's got to have that pillar of ego. He's got to believe he's good. He's got to believe that other people want to read what he has to say. It takes a lot of nerve to sit down and write something and expect that millions of people will want to read it or want to see it on the screen. You've got to believe in yourself. You have to believe that you have a vision, a fresh story to tell and a fresh way to tell it.

Ego is absolutely central to the continuance of a professional career. I have ego. I believe in myself. If I didn't, I don't think I could turn the work out.

In terms of how I judge it, I put on my editor's coat. I have a coat, the writer's coat, that I take off, and then I put on my editor's coat, and then I look at the story as if I'd never written it at all, as if someone else had sent it to me.

I've edited twenty-three anthologies and was managing editor of *Gamma* magazine in the '60s, and I've been contributing editor and West Coast editor to half a dozen other magazines.

As an editor, I look at this William F. Nolan story and say, "This guy is weak here. He's getting away with sloppy characterization there. He should tighten this sentence. Where's his motivation here?" I am able to be objective about my own work. A lot of writers aren't able to do that. When I put the editor's coat on, I catch a lot of things that the writer thought he could get away with.

WT: What was the story behind the magazine *Gamma*? This was an extremely interesting periodical which had only five issues, seemingly published with great stealth.

Nolan: *Gamma* was a West Coast magazine created by Charles E. Fritch, who was to become a long-time editor of *Mike Shayne's Mystery Magazine* in later years. At the time he had never edited anything. This was in 1963. He got together with another writer named Jack Matcha, and myself, and the three of us launched *Gamma*. We put out five issues over a two-and-a-half-year period. It was supposed to be a quarterly. But we couldn't get the right distributor. Half the time the magazine never reached the newsstands of the country. These terrible distribution problems finally killed the magazine. But we had a tremendous group of writers: Fritz Leiber and Charles Beaumont and Ray Bradbury and all kinds of top people writing for it. The five issues that *do* exist are all of very high quality. I remember we had Shakespeare on one cover and William Faulkner on another. These are not names you usually find in such magazines.

WT: It was as if you were doing again what *The Magazine of Fantasy and Science Fiction* did in 1949, which was produce a science-fiction and fantasy publication which was more literate than anything else on the market, and something you didn't have to make any excuses for.

Nolan: You're on the mark! We used *The Magazine of Fantasy and Science Fiction* as our model. I read the first four or five years of that magazine cover-to-cover. It was like a bible to me. Our publication was a kind of West Coast version.

WT: How much of an influence was Ray Bradbury on your work? Did he ever coach you in the art of writing? One gets this impression from some of his introductions to your work.

Nolan: Well, Ray was a great influence on me, as he has been on many people. Of course I was influenced by a large number of writers, as most of us are. When you ask a writer the question, "Who influenced you?" he'll go down the list. I could do the same thing. I collect over a hundred authors in my own personal library. Bradbury definitely impacted my life at an early age. The first Bradbury story I read was "The Jar" in *Weird Tales*, and I thought that it was an extraordinary piece of work. I said, "Who is this man?" I began to read anything that had his name on it.

When I came out to California in 1950 and met Ray, he had just published *The Martian Chronicles*. I met him in July of 1950 and *The Martian Chronicles* had come out in May. He was just beginning his career, as it were.

But already I had read *Dark Carnival*, and many of his short stories in the pulps, and I told him I wanted to be a professional writer.

He said, "Well, look, when you have a story that you think is good enough, really good enough for a professional magazine to print, you send me that story and I'll give you a detailed critique." Well, it was three years later, when he went to Ireland, that I sent him "The Joy of Living" in an early draft.

He wrote back, "This is a fine story. Don't worry about being a writer. You're already a writer. You've gone through the early stages. You've learned dialogue. You've learned description. But what you haven't learned to do is end your story properly. You have the character doing X, Y, and Z, when he should be doing A, B, and C." He showed me, in a letter from Ireland, exactly how to end this story. And I took his letter and rewrote the ending; and the story became my first professional sale. It was printed in *If, Worlds of Science Fiction,* in 1954.

So Ray has had a great influence in my life. We've had many a long midnight conversation tossing ideas back and forth with Charles Beaumont and with Richard Matheson and with other mutual friends down the years. We formed a sort of West Coast writers' group that has included, from time to time, Ray Russell, Chad Oliver from Texas when he was getting his degree at UCLA, George Clayton Johnson, Ray, myself, Matheson, and Beaumont. We would all meet and stay up into the dawn talking stories, shouting and yelling out our

ideas. I got a tremendous amount of help and moral support from those sessions. I look back on them with great fondness.

WT: For all horror seems to have been your first love, your first sale was science fiction. So what brought you to write SF at that time, as opposed to the *Weird Tales* kind of story?

Nolan: There really was no market for it until Stephen King came along. He really created the modern market for horror. But horror, at the time I was writing in the '50s, didn't have the market that science fiction had, and a professional writer has to go with his market. You have to make a living at it. So I wrote a lot of science fiction, including *Logan's Run* and the Sam Space books, in that period. Now I am writing virtually no science fiction. I am doing almost entirely horror work, which is a return to my first love. I'm back home again now, and I'm going to stay there.

WT: Granting the fact that you *like* writing horror, what would you do if you found editors doing what they did to Frank Herbert late in life, that is demanding the same and more of the same, over and over?

Nolan: I've never had any problems in that regard. I've had fifty-one books published now, and I have several more in the works. Each is different. I don't repeat myself. John Steinbeck taught me that you can do all sorts of books and still maintain the same quality level, without having to repeat the same book over and over. I couldn't write a series of horror novels and nothing else. I will continue to write horror, but I will always write other types of material along with it. I'll always extend my roots out into other genres, because it's just natural for me. Otherwise I'd bore myself and I think I'd bore the reader.

I've written well over a thousand pieces of material, something like seven or eight hundred articles and the fifty books and forty television and film scripts, plus all the short stories. I've spread it out over many genres, but that's what keeps me fresh. That's what keeps the challenge alive in me, when I can switch genres, when I can get excited about a brand new thing.

WT: Would you describe some of the things you're working on now?

Nolan: Let's start with David Kincaid, the protagonist of the novella "Broxa" in this issue of *Weird Tales®*. I'm going to write a series of novels about him and his involvement in various paranormal and supernatural adventures. I've edited the new 1991 anthology celebrating Bradbury's fiftieth year, *The Bradbury Chronicles*. I've finished a professional booklet called *Blood Sky,* with eleven pages of my artwork in it. I have my first horror novel, *Helltracks,* out from Avon, and they are following this up with a collection of my best shock-terror stories, *Nightshapes.* I'm always doing new short stories. I'm due out in about twenty anthologies. I'll have my own horror comic book this year, *William F. Nolan's Beyond Midnight,* and of course I'll continue to work in television, on Movies of the Week. Then there's verse, magazine articles, and checklists. Also, Dell is publishing my *Logan Trilogy* — all three Logan novels — in a new trade paperback in their "Classic Science Fiction" series. I write every day. I write Christmas. I write New Year's. I write Halloween. The key to being a professional and the key to making a success out of this business is to write all the time. I expect to go on doing it for at least another twenty years. Then I just might start to slow down!

WT: Thank you, William F. Nolan.

Ω

THE SHAPE OF THRILLS TO COME!

In *Weird Tales®* 303, our featured author is Thomas Ligotti, with additional stories by Keith Taylor and William Wu.

The next issue, *Weird Tales®* 304, will be a John Brunner issue, with his "Concerning the Forthcoming Inexpensive Paperback Translation of the Necronomicon of Abdul Alhazred". The issue will also have stories by Ramsey Campbell and Tanith Lee.

Next comes *Weird Tales®* 305,
with F. Paul Wilson as the featured author.

Appearing soon: stories by S.P. Somtow, Steve Rasnic Tem, and Darrell Schweitzer, along with more poetry by Robert E. Howard and Ray Bradbury.

THE CREATIVE URGE

by Robert Bloch

art by Bob Eggleton

The typing started.

"What are we doing here?" she murmured.

"Shouldn't we have thought about that before?" he asked.

"When do you mean?"

"Like back on page twenty-seven."

"You must be kidding! We had other things to do there," she said.

"Look, we don't have to do anything we don't want to."

"Oh really? We've no say-so in the matter!"

"One of *those*." He sighed. "Then you believe there's some kind of Author writing this whole thing?"

She nodded. "Of course. Somebody had to create us, didn't He?"

"How do you know it's a *He*? Or even a *She*, for that matter? If there is such a thing as an Author, what makes you so certain we're created in the same image?"

"Because the Author understands us. He knows our thoughts, our feelings —"

"But they're *our* thoughts, *our* feelings. And if the Author does write about us, that doesn't mean He or She *cares* what happens. Or even knows what's *going* to happen."

She frowned. "You're saying there's no plot, He just makes it up as He goes along?"

"Why not? When you come right down to it, what are we? Just a combination of keyboard letters imprinted on paper."

"But there's a pattern to what we do! And if there's a pattern, there must be a purpose behind it."

"Not necessarily. For all we know, we're merely the result of random selection, individual alphabet-groupings which have no reason for being except the whim of the Author."

"Whim?" Her frown deepened. "What about moral responsibility for our welfare?"

"His responsibility ends with the act of creation."

"It's destruction I'm afraid of."

His eyes narrowed. "Then watch what you're saying. Remember, Authors are jealous, suspicious, insecure. They need constant encouragement from editors, flattering blurbs and reviews, praise from readers."

"*They?*" Her voice faltered. "You actually believe there can be more than one?"

"Thousands of them, each with a devoted following." He spoke slowly. "But of course belief in an Author, even worship, doesn't prove anything. For all we know, maybe there is no Author at all. Typed or computerized, we're still just the products of a mechanical process, and perhaps it's the machine itself that created us."

"Someone must operate the machine."

"Suppose it operates automatically?"

"Then where does the power come from?"

"Electrical energy." He shrugged. "Does it matter?"

"It does to me." She hesitated. "And there *is* an Author. I know, because I've heard Him."

"Heard?"

"I'm sure of it. Sometimes when I'm lying here on the page, waiting for what's going to happen next, I become aware of a voice that seems to come from

high above, past the light. I don't understand the message but I'm positive I've
heard it speak my name. I get a feeling
the Author might be talking to Himself,
debating what's right for me to do."

"Why should He be concerned about
you? What's right for Him is all that
counts."

"I'm talking about Good and Evil."

"And in capital letters, too!" He
chuckled derisively. "Don't you understand? The only thing the Author cares
about is what makes the story work.
Work for *Him,* not His characters.
Which means we can be rewarded without reason, punished without reason —
at least no reason we might comprehend. Because there is no such thing as
Good, no such thing as *Evil.*"

"I can't go along with that. The
Author is Good!"

"How do you know? Just because you
think you heard a voice speaking your
name?"

"I *did* hear Him."

"But you've never seen Him."

"Nobody has. He lives on another
plane, and we poor two-dimensional
beings can't hope to —"

He scowled. "Why did you stop?"

"I don't know. I get a feeling that the
Author doesn't want us to talk about
such things."

"You mean, wondering if He's Good or
Evil?" He shook his head. "If the Author
is Good then He'd have no reason to hide
Himself from us. But if He were Evil —"

She glanced up. "Now *you* stopped in
the middle of a sentence."

"Not of my own accord. Maybe He
thought there was too much dialogue."
He lowered his voice to a whisper. "No,
you're right. He doesn't want us to talk
about Him."

"Then let's stop." She forced a smile.
"What use is there in arguing about
whether the Author is Good or Evil?"

He shrugged. "None. Even if you're
right, we'd still have to see Him in order
to know."

"But we *can't* see Him."

"There you go with that old two-dimensional theory again! Everybody accepts it without question, so nobody tries to get around it. I have a feeling that if we really wanted to, perhaps we *could* see the Author. We know He's up there, and you believe you've even heard His voice. I say that if we have the courage to lift our eyes from the page, perhaps we could find His face. If there is an Author."

"I say there is, and He is Good."

"Then let's find out once and for all. No more taking things on faith. We'll see for ourselves. Look up, if you dare."

She blinked. "The light is so bright. Like staring into the sun —"

"Look past it. Above, into the distance." He was staring upwards too.

"See! There *is* something. Way, way beyond."

"Clouds?"

"Not clouds. Hands. Hands with curling fingers. Moving up and down, up and down. And above them, even higher — a face. Hard to make it out, but there's something familiar —"

"Yes, I see it too." She nodded, then gasped. "Now I recognize Him! He's —"

Just in time.

Just in time the typing stopped. The pages, shredded into a thousand pieces, were crumpled into a globular mass and tossed away.

Then, seating himself once again, the Devil began to create yet another world.

Ω

BACK ISSUES OF *WEIRD TALES*® AVAILABLE:

Issue 290: featuring Gene Wolfe & George Barr, plus Ramsey Campbell, F. Paul Wilson, T.E.D. Klein, & Tanith Lee.

Issue 291: featuring Tanith Lee & Stephen Fabian, plus Morgan Llywelyn, Nancy Springer, Brian Lumley, & Harry Turtledove.

Issue 292: Keith Taylor & Carl Lundgren, plus Tad Williams, & Alan Rodgers.

Issue 293: Avram Davidson & Hank Jankus, plus Robert Sheckley, Keith Roberts, Carl Jacobi, & Ian Watson.

Issue 294: Karl Edward Wagner & J.K. Potter, plus Jonathan Carroll, Brian Lumley, & Nina K. Hoffman.

Issue 295: Brian Lumley & Vincent Di Fate, plus Phyllis Ann Karr, Darrell Schweitzer, Robert Sheckley, & Keith Taylor.

Issue 296: David J. Schow & Janet Aulisio, plus Tad Williams, Harry Turtledove, & Michael Rutherford.

Issue 297: featuring Nancy Springer & Frank Kelly Freas, along with John Brunner, Susan Shwartz, & Thomas Ligotti.

Issue 298: featuring Chet Williamson, with a variety of artists, plus stories by Ian Watson, R. Bretnor, Fred Chappell, & Darrell Schweitzer.

Issue 299: Jonathan Carroll & Thomas Kidd, with William F. Nolan, Ian Watson, R. Garcia y Robertson, & Nina Kiriki Hoffman.

Issue 300: Robert Bloch & Gahan Wilson, plus more by Henry Kuttner, Ray Bradbury, Lawrence Watt-Evans, & Michael Rutherford.

Issue 301: Ramsey Campbell & Bob Walters, as well as Stephen King, Robert Bloch, Darrell Schweitzer, & Keith Taylor.

The first seven issues, $4 each; the rest, $5 each; all twelve, $42.

Order from: *Weird Tales*®, P.O. Box 13418, Philadelphia PA 19101-3418 with check or money order. To use MasterCharge or Visa, send us your card number, its expiration date, your signature, and your name and complete address.

THE MAGICIAN

by Ronald Anthony Cross
art by Stephen Fabian

Part One: The Party

It was at a party that Tusci first met Fermo, the one whom he would always think of as *the* magician, for they had parties even here, wherever "here" was.

"What do you call it, here?" Tusci had asked Natania, Mistress of the Aerie (which consisted of a castle floating on a cloud).

"I don't call it anything, my little ferret," Natania had answered, smiling, always smiling her "I-know-a-secret" smile.

Tusci, who had been chased out of his own world and exiled here to live in a city of castles floating among the clouds, which no one had bothered to name, had achieved the exalted position of lowest lackey of the Aerie. He sometimes even took orders from Snide, Natania's apprentice and chief lackey.

"Is your name really Snide?" he had asked the gaunt bald man with the constant sneer and the dark piercing eyes.

"As long as the Mistress chooses to call me so, then so shall it be," he had answered.

Tusci's main job had been the coveted position of trainer of Natania's giant spiders, which as far as he could tell, were as easy to train as any spiders he had encountered elsewhere.

"Oh, well," Natania had answered. "They're very young, they'll grow older and wiser, as will we all."

When he had tried to explain to her that he had not the faintest idea how to train spiders, she had told him it was simple: you used telepathy. Then, when he had argued that he did not know

anything about telepathy, she had laughed aloud and clapped her hands together.

"There you have it," she said. "It's all so simple even you should be able to understand — right, Snide?" Snide snickered and nodded. "You must teach yourself telepathy and stop blaming the spiders, it's all your fault they can't understand."

She turned to leave, but suddenly turned back again as though struck by a new thought. "Oh, by the way, just in case it isn't obvious to you" (Snide snickered again), "let me point out that these are a variety of spider which grow to be quite large. They will grow very fast until they are as big as their mother was." (Their mother had been the size of a small barn.) "And they are hunting spiders. If you do not learn telepathy fast enough, they will surely kill and eat someone. Since you are their trainer, and also since you are the lowest in rank among my servants here — in fact, so low that you have not yet even begun the mastery of telepathy —" (yet another snicker from Snide) "who do you think that someone is most likely to be?"

Tusci had blurted out, "I am the greatest swordsman who has ever walked the world. Any world."

But Natania and Snide merely looked into each other's eyes and shook their heads conspiratorially.

"Come with me," she said, and led him outside onto one of the castle's spiraling balconies which laced around and around the tall slender spire jutting up out of the white, fluffy, phony-looking cloud.

"Look out there," she said.

As if in a dream, Tusci saw a clear blue sky with white fluffy clouds floating in it as far as the eye could see. Most of the clouds had slender elegant castles jutting up out of them.

"It is only *will* that accomplishes this. Look down."

He looked down, and down, shivered. He could just barely make out the sprawl of land down below, so distant he might have been on the moon.

"You surely wouldn't want me to have to train my own spiders. I have enough to do. Besides, look at it this way. You were the greatest swordsman who walked the earth; now you've been promoted to the lowest of my servants." She smiled sweetly. *She really is beautiful,* Tusci thought.

"Thank you," she said, and went back inside, leaving Tusci to return to his spiders. All week long he had been approaching them with bowls full of ground meat (he dared not imagine what kind of meat), and the only result he had gotten from the loathsome creatures was that when he cried "Come," they would come. If you could call slithering, scurrying, scampering, and jumping and snapping at you "coming." And, of course, only when he had the bowl of meat in his hand. Bowl of meat meant "come." No bowl of meat, no come. Period. All this time he should have been using telepathy, great! He should have known that. Divined it from the stars, perhaps. Oh, there were stars here, all right.

So, living among the clouds in a castle, as a servant (the lowest of the servants — an apprentice servant?) to Natania of the Shining Hands, a spider trainer whose ultimatum was "Train successfully or be eaten," he was astounded to hear that such mundane things as parties existed in the life of his mistress.

But yes, in a mood as effervescent as fine sparkling wine, she described the whole lavish affair to be, embellishing her descriptive prose with exquisite sweeping hand gestures.

The group of four who had modestly given themselves the title "Masters of the West" were to attend, each of course accompanied by his or her favorite servants. The other eight were to stay home and concentrate, sort of make sure the world didn't fall apart. *Babysit?* Tusci thought.

"Yes, stay home and mind the baby," Natania said, "good way to put it. Us being the creators and everything else being our baby."

"Who are the four?" And why four?" Tusci asked.

"Why four? Twelve is too many for us in our rather undeveloped states of consciousness. So we are broken up into three groups of four, who, if necessity arises, work together. Each group has its own concerns and obligations, with which I won't bore you.

"As to our group — first and foremost, of course, is me." She smiled so brightly it made Tusci wince.

"Natania, She of the Shining Hands, Mistress of Water, she whom everybody wants, but nobody ever gets, my poor little Tusci." And with a genuinely sad expression she reached out and touched him with her finger on his nose.

"I don't want you," Tusci blurted out, but he felt hot, and confused, dizzy almost. Her touch was . . . magic?

"Then, Fermo the Magician, Master of the Black Cloud. The Dominator.

"Then, Tremmello the Ear, he who hears all, knows all, and tells all, etc.

"Last and least, Chima, she whom everybody gets but nobody wants. No, I'm not being fair. It's just that she's such a whore. Earth Mistress, sex magic, and all that.

"And . . ." (accompanied by huge expansive sweep of hands and arms) ". . . all of their lowly servants and helpers."

Like me, thought Tusci.

"I will not serve drinks," he said through gritted teeth.

"Of course not, my ferret. I've just been teasing you. You're not really a servant — well, not a common servant, anyway. You're the trainer of my pets, my adventurer, and upon special occasions, such as this one, you are automatically elevated to the position of my personal bodyguard.

"Each of us will be accompanied by our man-at-arms, and you will all be expected to mingle freely with the guests."

It was Snide who served the drinks. It turned out that, in addition to being Natania's chief apprentice in the art of magic, and head servant-chef-etc., he also personally attended to the serving of the Masters of the West and their bodyguards. For a few precious hours Tusci would be in a position to give orders to Snide, and though these would consist only of requests for food and drink, he intended to make the most of it. He ran through the scenario in his mind: Complaints about the food. Would you please freshen my drink? Could you fetch me some more fruit from the kitchen, Snide? Oh, sorry — you took so long I've lost my taste for it, why don't you take it back and bring me another drink instead?

But he knew it was no use. There was no way to irritate Snide. He would simply smirk and say something like, "I consider it my pleasure to serve you and thus obey the whim of my mistress." Or, "To serve is all I have ever asked."

Tusci sadly gave up the idea before it ever left his imagination, where, as he well knew, all such plans of getting back at Snide or Natania rightfully belonged.

The castle was lit with colored lights. But whatever the actual source of the lighting was, Tusci couldn't imagine. Here the air simply glowed a soft pale blue, there a lime green or purple. Natania, already in her party gown, wearing a strange tall conical hat, went around mumbling to herself, "No, no, not bright enough, lighter in hue, more

like that lake I saw last year," waving her hands, and somehow causing the light to dim and shift back and forth along the color spectrum until she got it just right. Last-minute touches.

"I don't understand; what's the source of the light?" Tusci asked her.

"Mind," she said. Then, "Well, aren't you going to ask it?"

"Ask what?"

"Oh, come on, my little ferret, see if you can come up with the pertinent question."

Tusci, who was a small, slender man, yet covered with a network of sinewy muscle, did not enjoy being called "my little ferret." He looked around to see if Snide was watching, but for once the sycophant was too busy to stand around and smirk at him.

"Oh, all right," he said. "What is the source of mind?"

"Light," Natania said, and flounced off to deal with the purple glow in the far corner. Her gown, which was the sky-blue of a mountain lake (to match her eyes) floated as she moved, billowing and curling around her figure as if it were alive or she were in a wind. It did this when she was still as well as when she walked about.

"Oh, I almost forgot," she shouted dramatically: "Let there be life."

For a moment or two Tusci couldn't figure out that one; then he caught sight of a small dark-green glow hopping toward him like a bouncing ball. He stared at it: a glowing frog? A flock of huge fluorescent red butterflies fluttered about the room and landed on him. A glowing blue bird of some sort flew over his head chirping happily.

How beautiful, he thought, looking up, when something wet and soft landed with a splat upon his upturned forehead. He pointed this out to Natania, who exclaimed, "Oh, by the Goddess, I forgot." Then clapped her hands, and shouted, "Sorry, my little ones, you'll just have to hold it till the party's over."

"You created them?" Tusci asked her in awe.

She frowned. "Of course not, I just called them here and made them glow. Why on earth would I go to the trouble of creating them? The world is full of them."

By the time Tusci had washed his hands and forehead, spent some time admiring his party attire in the mirror, and returned to the main room, the guests had begun to arrive.

And the first of them was Fermo, the Master of the Black Cloud. Dressed in black, all of his entourage dressed in black as well, they swept across the enormous room like shadows.

"Welcome to the party," Natania said, "how festive you all look in your splendid black outfits."

Yes, they really liven things up, Tusci thought to himself, staring at the brooding black-haired, black-bearded magician.

Natania held out her hand, and Fermo seized it and pressed his lips to it. "I lust after your slender perfect form," he said in a low deep voice.

"You'll never get it," Natania answered, still smiling. "Come, you must be thirsty. Snide. Snide," she shouted, clapped her hands, "the guests are arriving."

Tusci wondered if something had just gone wrong with his hearing: could that really have been what they said?

Now, here was Snide, bearing a tray of fancy, lethal-looking drinks in tall slender glasses. Some were steaming, some were sizzling, and they came in all colors of the rainbow.

"Mistress Natania's wish is my command," Snide said.

"Well, of course it is," Fermo barked, "What else would it be?" Then he examined the tray and said: "Don't you have any black drinks? You know I prefer black drinks."

"Oh, for heaven's sake," Natania said, and motioned at the tray, whereupon all the drinks turned black.

"Parlor tricks," Fermo said. "I could show you some real magic, turn everything in the whole place black." He smiled at this thought. "Cold, dead."

"Yes, you'll have to do that for us, Fermo, but please do wait until the rest of the guests arrive. I'm sure they wouldn't want to miss it."

Fermo snorted angrily and snatched a drink off the tray. Followed, one by one, by each of his retinue.

"I would like you to meet my new bodyguard, Tusci. Sometimes called the Ferret."

Fermo did not hold out his hand, but said, "My name is Fermo, Master of the Dark Cloud, but my friends call me Sardonicus."

Tusci nodded to him.

"I'm accustomed to men bowing before me," Fermo said matter-of-factly.

"So what?" said Tusci.

"Gentlemen, I will not have quarreling at my party," Natania said. Then: "Tusci, this is Fermo's bodyguard, Breaker."

Tusci, of course, had instantly known which one the bodyguard was. With Breaker, you couldn't help but know. The huge bear held out his paw for Tusci to clasp, and growled, "Pretty small for a bodyguard, i'nt he?"

Naturally he clamped down on Tusci's hand with all his strength. Tusci had expected that. He didn't try to squeeze back, but let his hand go limp. His left hand appeared at the side of Breaker's neck; a beautiful dagger was in it, pricking the skin.

"You squeeze, I'll push," Tusci said in his calm voice.

Breaker grunted, a drop of blood trickled down his neck. All at once, he let go of Tusci's hand.

"Well, well, it seems someone else among us knows magic," Fermo mused.

"Not magic," a new voice cut in. Tusci recognized it, smiled.

Tremmello the Ear, and his retainers, had arrived. His bodyguard, the man

Tusci knew only as Snake, all decked out in gleaming metallic tight-fitting blouse and trousers, had preceded them.

"Not magic at all, the man's just quick. Quicker than anyone I've ever seen. How goes it, Ferret?"

Ferret nodded to him and made a gesture with his left hand. The dagger disappeared back into whatever hidden part of his clothing it had come out of.

"Quick or not quick," Breaker said in a growl, "if I ever caught him without a blade . . ."

"Not at all likely, I'm afraid," Snake said, smiling.

"Greetings, Natania; Sardonicus, you old swine," a cheerful voice shouted. Four strong men carried a litter toward them bearing a huge fat bald man wearing only a simple white robe. This was apparently Snake's master, Tremmello the Inner Ear.

"Why must you always call me a swine?" Fermo pouted.

"Just instinct," Tremmello said, making an elaborate gesture of benediction with two fingers of his right hand; in his left, he held a long wooden staff. His servants lowered the litter to the floor and the man climbed down and moved toward them with slow, surprising gracefulness. Then he raised his right hand and made the gesture again.

"Bless you, all of you," he said. "You need it."

The clashing of cymbals and trilling of flutes drowned out conversation, as a group of people dressed in garish, brightly-colored costumes, each one totally different from all the others, approached. In their midst was a woman with a body as luscious as a ripe fruit. Her fingernails and toenails were painted bright glossy green, and her costume consisted of a gold anklet and a pair of ruby-red earrings. A leopard padded across the floor close beside her, and when she stopped before them the leopard purred and rubbed against her

legs. By all the gods, who wouldn't? She had come to the party nude.

"Shut your mouth, my little ferret, it's not dinner time yet. Chima, this is my new bodyguard, Tusci."

"He's lovely," Chima said sincerely, reaching out and touching him on the nose, just as Natania had earlier, and with the same results: immediately he felt dizzy, flushed.

Then she turned to Natania. "Greetings, dear sister, it's good to see you again. But first," she gestured at a glowing red sparrow flitting over their heads, "first all of these little ones, every living creature, must go back to whence they came. Now."

"Blast it," Natania said, "I'm not hurting them, I just want them to liven up my party."

"Every one of them, now," Chima said, voice growing angry. "No living creature may be interfered with in my presence." The leopard snarled.

Natania turned away from the naked woman, her fists clenched.

"I said, now."

Natania whirled back around and held her arms up over her head; her hands visibly glowed with a soft golden light.

"Go home!" she said. And for a moment Tusci thought she was speaking to the guests, but it must have been the birds, insects, frogs, and such, because they all disappeared at once, and now the two women were chatting happily as though nothing untoward had occurred.

Tremmello was laughing, a beautiful rich sound that made Tusci smile. "Oh, by the fearsome breath of Zimgogo, what an awful spell! 'Go home!' You're supposed to make it dramatic or rhyme it:

'Let every crawly creepy thing
And birds which flutter by the wing
Begone unharmed
By roll of drum
Back to where I called thee from.'

— That sort of thing, you know."

"By all the Gods, that's even worse than hers," Fermo said, laughing.

Now broken up into pairs, Natania with her arm around Chima's bare shoulders, and Tremmello chatting happily with the scowling Fermo, the four, followed by their retinues, drifted across the vast weirdly-lit room toward one of the tables at the far end.

For the first time Tusci turned his attention away from Fermo ("My friends call me Sardonicus" — what a lovely nickname!) and focused it on the tall, lithe blonde girl who he assumed was Chima's bodyguard. He arrived at this conclusion partly by a careful study of her slender, muscular body, and partly because of the weapon she openly wore to the party: a long sword in a scabbard which practically reached her ankles. Her size and musculature, combined with the feather-light weight of the metal from which they made their swords here, might make her a deadly opponent, he realized. More than the others, she looked like someone from his own world, almost familiar, as if he had known her a long time ago. Her long blonde hair was braided, and her skin was pale and clear. She was wearing a skimpy red silk tunic (almost the same shade of scarlet as his) and matching boots, with a lot of pale-skinned bare leg in between, but no make-up or jewelry of any kind. There was an astonishing air of self-confidence about her that manifested itself in the way she walked and moved. And she was, Tusci realized, quite beautiful.

Catching him staring at her, she walked over and held out her hand to be clasped, like a man, and smiled. Or perhaps she meant for him to kiss it?

"Nobody ever bothers to introduce me. I'm Bedelia. From what I hear, I'm from pretty much the same world you're from, only a few hundred years farther forward in time."

"Farther forward in time?" Tusci said. This was a new one.

"Yes, of course, didn't you know? These wizards not only have access to many worlds, but they can choose different points in time from which to enter them. Oh, not just any time they want, but there are certain areas where space and time weave together into a dense knot they can use as a tunnel." She shrugged, smiling. "That's the way they explain it to me, I don't understand it either. I'm from the north. The far north. Barbarian, probably, to you."

Tusci smiled. In all of the cities he had visited, anyone from someplace else was always labeled a barbarian.

"I'm a barbarian too," he said. Shaking her hand. Her touch didn't cause a magical allergic reaction like that of the two sorceresses, but still it was quite pleasant.

"Come on you two, stop flirting, it's time to feast," Natania shouted at them, sounding peeved.

Bedelia slung her arm casually around Tusci's shoulder and leaned down to whisper in his ear: "Let's go get some food, and get drunk, and maybe when the fancy four or whatever they call themselves get all involved in some long complicated conversation about sorcery or something our puny minds can't comprehend, we can sneak off and find a bed and . . ."

She whispered a detailed description of what they could do then, as she guided him toward the table.

I can't believe any of this, Tusci thought in bewilderment. *Can she really have said that?*

There were two tables: the long table was set for all of the bodyguards and servants; a separate smaller table some distance away had been set for the four.

"There are certain things that we may say or do or even think, that it would be quite harmful for you to hear," Natania had explained to Tusci earlier. "We are dangerous enough to mortals when we are sober and sepa-

rate, let alone together and tipsy. Believe me, it's for your own protection."

Just as well, Tusci thought, glaring in the direction of Fermo. Was it his imagination, or had Chima's shape altered for a moment? He had heard loud laughter, and suddenly the outline of her form had shifted and . . . He hastily looked away.

Music was playing now, but music from where? It seemed to be some incredibly complicated concerto for flutes, hundreds of flutes: he could discern no theme or direction to it, and it was from far away, yet near, as if the musicians were playing in an invisible closet here somewhere in this room, with the door shut. The laughter at the distant table grew louder, somehow more discordant, less human, high, shrill.

"Here, drink this, Tusci." Bedelia handed him a goblet of red smoking liquid of some kind. Her eyes were wide and bright green, and somehow filled with mischief. Was she trying to get him drunk? By the Gods — Tusci drank.

A few moments, and suddenly the room swam, then steadied again. The edges of things grew clearer.

"What was in that drink?" Tusci said.

"Here, have some more, come on. See, I'll have another." She snapped her fingers at one of the servants, but had lost the coordination with which to make a sound that way. "Oh, well," she said, and inserted her thumb and index finger in her mouth and produced a loud piercing whistle.

Across the table from Tusci, Breaker said: "Shut up, slut, you're upsetting my digestion."

"Quite right," Snake said, patting Breaker on the shoulders, from where he sat next to him. "The Breaker is a gourmet and a connoisseur of fine wines, from what I hear."

"Oh, is he?" Bedelia asked innocently. "I heard that he was a gourmet of the excrement of swine which he washes down with goblets of goat wine."

Breaker countered with: "Shut up, slut."

And Snake added: "As well as a master of the witty reply."

No, I'm not hearing any of this at all, Tusci thought, and glanced across to the far table where Bedelia's mistress dined in the nude — *Nor am I seeing it. It's all a dream.* Indeed, one of the strange effects of the potent red drink that Bedelia was plying him with was to add an extreme clarity to vision and hearing; colors glowed from within as if everything were composed out of light, and the edges of things grew darker, more sharply defined. A swallow or two more, and the geometry of angles and shapes took on meaning: he could almost read the relationships, as if they were a form of writing, understand what the glowing colors were trying to tell him. On the other hand, memory faded into a make-believe world, far away, even farther than the world of his dreams: it took a great effort to remember who he was, or where he was, or why he was here. In fact, why the Hell was he here? At first he thought he just couldn't find the memory, but then he realized the truth, that there wasn't any such memory. How he was here, he could, with effort, remember; but why he was here — there simply was no reason.

"Pardon me," he said to Bedelia, "but I'm like a leaf blown on a capricious wind, or a stone thrown randomly into a pond by an excited child."

"Me too," Bedelia said, smiling.

"And it seems to me — I know this will strike you as weird — but it seems to me that the arrangement of the chairs, tables, and other objects in the room is an attempt to tell me something, but I can't quite understand it, can you?"

Across the table, Snake choked on his mouthful of whatever he was drinking and Breaker said, "Oh, for God's sake."

But Bedelia held her left hand over her broad brow and peered intently around the room. "Means you've drunk too much," she said.

"Is that what it means?" said Tusci, genuinely astonished.

"That's it," Bedelia said, and slammed down her goblet on the table, spilling some of the red froth, which merged exquisitely into the yellow table-cloth.

"They're both drunk," Breaker said, disgustedly. Still smiling, Snake nodded.

"Have you drunk too much too?" Tusci asked Bedelia. He was going through a stage now where everything seemed astonishing.

Bedelia nodded, "Spilled my drink. Come on," and tugged at his arm. Then she rose up and knocked over her chair. "Whoops," she said, picking the chair back up. Then she staggered a few steps, turned back toward Tusci.

"Come on. You too drunk to walk?"

"What a complex and wonderful question," Tusci said. "How did you ever think of it? How could one ever answer it? It's not only a question, but a question and a test all at the same time. And the implications hidden in it. For instance, am I too drunk for you to walk? Is that why you knocked over your chair? Am I too drunk for anyone to walk? Am I . . . What was the question?"

"Oh, for God's sake," Breaker grunted again, holding his hand to his bullet-like head as if Tusci's words were giving him a headache. Snake was laughing again.

"Oh, the power of words," Tusci said in awe.

"I said, come on, or are you too drunk to walk?" Bedelia repeated. "Or at least I think that's what I said." Now she looked confused, swayed, and stumbled a little.

Tusci carefully pushed his chair out from the table, then suddenly sprang up out of it so that he landed standing on it. Everyone was silent. Even the four sorcerers at the far table were watching.

Suddenly Tusci sprang up from the chair, grabbed his knees, and spun backwards like a ball, over the backrest. At the same time he twisted around so that he was facing Bedelia when he landed perfectly balanced in a crouch; a dagger was in each hand.

Now he straightened up and smiled. Both daggers spun in his hands; and then, with a flourish, he put them back to wherever he'd got them from. Nobody could see quite where they came from or had gone to.

"No," he said, "I don't seem to be too drunk to walk. Lead on."

Still smiling, he followed Bedelia. Everything seemed funny now. And not only funny, but both funny and wonderful. It was miraculous to be here, living with magical people among the clouds. It was miraculous to be following this beautiful bold girl up this winding stairway. It was miraculous that her form was stumbling and slightly out of balance, yet as lithe and lovely as a cat's: her stumbling seemed coherent, as if part of a dance. It was miraculous to be himself. No — he had it now — miraculous to *be,* period. To be was a miracle, and he was living it now.

Around and around, up the never-ending stairway. Following Bedelia up and up. It seemed to be taking place somehow outside of time. Forever. He would never catch up with her.

And it was miraculous that she led him at last to his own room. "How could you know . . . ?" Then it dawned on him. "You screwed Arkand?" he said, totally amazed. Arkand was the giant blond swordsman who'd had this job and room before Tusci.

Bedelia dropped her sword belt and attempted to pull her party tunic over her head, but got it stuck halfway up and staggered across the room with it over her head like a hood; but luckily she was aimed the right direction and momentum carried her through to the large, slightly elevated platform bed in the far corner. She tripped and sprawled on the mattress, beautiful pale skin — nude, but no head.

"No," she said, voice muffled by tunic. "You could hardly call that screwing. Arkand was all sword and no . . ."

Tusci couldn't catch the word, but got the picture.

"Too drunk," she said, head finally popping out of the tunic. "Can't stand a man who drunks too much. Drinsh too much? You get the idea. Come here."

Tusci went there. And this was the most miraculous of all.

Later on, following Bedelia down the staircase, around and around, as if they were descending into eternity, suddenly his ears popped, and abruptly everything seemed normal again.

The drink's worn off just like that, he thought. But now his attention swept the room. Everyone was still seated around the tables drinking, perhaps eating fruit, nuts.

All that time, and they're still here, he thought. A sense of foreboding struck him. *It's as if they're all waiting for something to happen.*

As irrational as he knew this idea to be, he pushed past Bedelia and ran the rest of the way down the stairs.

Just as his feet touched floor, there was a loud sharp noise like a clap of thunder. Tusci would never know where it came from, but it was a loud mind-bending sound that assaulted the senses.

Two figures stood facing each other across the sorcerers' table, but though the lighting had not changed, it seemed difficult somehow for Tusci to make out who they were.

A black cloud of smoke seemed to issue from the hands of one of them and curl across the table to engulf the other. Now a blinding bright light began to glow inside of it. And there was another loud clap of sound. The smoke was gone. Tusci could clearly see his mistress Natania facing Fermo across the table.

"I say it isn't so," she said.

Fermo stood hunched over, but stiff, pointing one hand in her direction. He was convulsed with some kind of unfathomable effort, mumbling something Tusci couldn't hear.

And now again a cloud of black steam poured out of him toward Natania.

Strangely enough, throughout this attack the other two guests sat calmly at the table and watched: Chima with a content smile, and Tremmello of the Inner Ear with eyes half closed and a distant meditative expression.

Tusci sprinted across the floor toward their table, not knowing what he would do when he got there, and he sensed Bedelia running behind him.

Many things happened at once, so that later it would be impossible for Tusci to separate them out and put them in order, or to realize that all of this took place in such a brief space of time.

Bedelia's mistress, Chima, pointed toward Bedelia and shouted "Stay out of it." Bedelia stopped running.

As Tusci reached the table where the bodyguards and retainers were seated, the man called Snake was just springing up out of his chair. Fermo's bodyguard, Breaker, who held a short thick sword clenched in his right hand, perhaps hearing Chima shout at Bedelia, turned to face Tusci. His blunt brows were wrinkled in puzzlement.

Tusci shoved Snake back down in his chair with one hand and whipped the man's sword out of its scabbard with the other.

At the same time, two servants approached slowly and inexorably through the many-colored lighting, pushing an intricately embellished, wheeled cart with an enormous silver bowl on it.

Seeing Tusci now coming at him with Snake's sword, Breaker dropped down low and lunged at him with surprising speed and agility.

Tremmello pointed at Tusci, and nodded his head at Snake, who now jumped up out of his chair, and grasping the small blue metal tube that hung on a thong around his neck, aimed it at Tusci and put it to his mouth. Apparently it was already armed with a pellet of some kind of lethal or knockout gas, because his cheeks puffed out full of air, ready to blow.

He heard the rustling, whistling sound of sword coming out of scabbard fast, close behind him, and suddenly a long blade darted into the loop of thong between his neck and the blue tube he was holding.

"I have three choices here," Bedelia said, and she was still slurring her words. "I can separate the tube from your neck, or I can separate your head from your neck. Or both. If you move I will be forced to choose."

The man called Snake did not beg or threaten. He slowly opened his hand so that the tube of metal dropped from his mouth. He merely smiled.

Meanwhile, Tremmello was saying to Chima in a pouting tone of voice, "I thought you told her to stay out of it."

Chima laughed out loud, her bare breasts jiggling. "As usual, she disobeys."

Natania, the Mistress of the Shining Hands, whose upraised hands were indeed shining, was again merely a silhouette inside of a gathering cloud of smoke which seemed to be hissing out of Fermo's hands from across the table.

"I say no," she said, and the smoke was gone.

"I say yes," Fermo grunted, and this time the smoky substance rushed out, exploded out of his whole body, blossomed, thickened, and covered the whole table and everybody at it, an inky black flower so dark that you could not see anyone or anything in it at all. So dark that it seemed an opening into another world.

The two servants pushing the cart continued their inexorable approach, taking no notice of anything, as if indeed everything were so far above them, or perhaps even so far beneath them, that nothing really existed except the correct performance of their job.

Tusci, who had been surprised by Breaker's sudden lunge, nonetheless was too fast for it to have mattered, and had already twisted sideways around it and allowed the blade to slice through his red silk shirt but not quite brush his flesh, and still kept closing until suddenly he slammed his blade down hard up close to the hilt, on Breaker's blade up close to the hilt, and forced it on down, driving the handle of the big man's weapon through the weak point in his grip just between his thumb and forefinger. It was a wild move, but Tusci had done it before. It always worked best when the opponent was fully extended in a lunge and you were close enough to strike the blade very hard, right next to the hilt, which if you were not Tusci would probably occur never.

But it worked, as it always had for Tusci. Blasting the sword out of Breaker's hand, straight down. Tusci let it hit and shoveled it up on the first bounce and flipped it back over his shoulder in the general direction of Bedelia. And then, all in the same movement, delicately kissed Breaker's forehead with the point of his blade.

For a moment the big man just stood there looking at his empty sword hand, astonished, and Tusci waited, and suddenly a cut opened up across Breaker's forehead and blood welled out and poured down into his eyes: he howled in fear.

But it was a superficial cut. Tusci had merely wanted to be sure that if he continued to fight, he would have too much difficulty seeing what he was doing to be a problem.

Now Tusci jump-kicked him in the chest, driving him back and giving himself more room, and now took two running steps, hopped up into the air and jump-kicked him in the chest again, this time knocking the big man so far back that he toppled over and disappeared inside of that black cloud of smoke that was still spreading, and was now so dark that you could neither see nor hear anything inside of it, if indeed there was anything still inside of it.

The servants arrived wheeling the giant cart with the huge silver bowl.

Tusci approached the black cloud, peered into it. Backed off, turned, and there they were. Dropped his sword. Picked up the enormous bowl, which was icy cold to the touch, by the two handles. Stumbled and almost fell under the weight of it. Grunted, and making a supreme all-out effort, staggered with it to the edge of the cloud and hurled the contents into where he had last seen Fermo.

Instantly the black cloud was gone, so completely that it was difficult to believe it had ever existed, and a grotesque scene was revealed.

Everyone except Natania, who had been standing at the far end of the table, was covered with a bright green creamy substance that looked to Tusci rather like snow. Tremmello was trembling and frantically brushing it off his chubby form with his hands. Chima was shivering but smiling, even laughing a little. She actually scooped a handful from between her luscious bare breasts and put it in her mouth. Had she really said "Delicious" in that throaty voice of hers?

But Fermo was the one whom Tusci had thrown it at, and Fermo was the one whom Tusci had hit.

The tall saturnine magician was a pathetic figure, practically buried in an avalanche of whatever it was. Dripping, shivering, arms wrapped around his own shoulders. On the one hand, he was freezing; and on the other, he was practically smoking with rage. You couldn't tell which he was shivering from. Even his coal-black hair was bright, wet, frothy green.

One of the servants, who perhaps had a sense of humor after all, said, "Ice cream is served, My Lady."

Still chuckling, Chima said, "Pistachio."

"What's ice cream?" Tusci said.

Meanwhile, quite slowly and unobtrusively, Bedelia removed her blade from Snake's neck and sheathed it.

Now Breaker, whose legs were sticking out from under the table, sat up suddenly, bashing his head and knocking over whatever goblets or bottles or bowls were still standing.

Then he emerged, squirming out right next to Tremmello's chair, holding his head in his hands and moaning and groaning, mumbling something like "Wait till I . . ."

Biting off the words sharply, Fermo said: "Shut up. Do not speak. Do not move. Do not even remind me that you exist."

Natania sad, "Don't you kill him, Fermo. Not at my party. Don't you kill Tusci either."

"Kill your servant?" Fermo said, his speech getting sharper and meaner with each word. "Kill your groveling lackey? Me? Fermo the Magnificent? Sardonicus the Great? Kill your servant?

"Oh no, no, no, no," he hissed. "Why would I kill? Just because I was performing a parlor trick at your request? At all your requests? Just because I was playing a festive party game of Black Cloud with Natania when your lowly worm of a servant humiliated me by drowning me in dessert? Green, freezing dessert imported from some faraway place in time and space especially for the occasion? Which is, by the way, far too sweet. Cloyingly, ridiculously, enormously too sweet. Just because of that, I should stoop to killing your servants for you? Oh no. No. No. Not I. Not Fermo of the Black Cloud."

Tusci, backing away from the table, as were Bedelia and Snake behind him, noticed that now Natania was getting angry.

"Well, I'm not going to kill him for you," she said. "Besides, I would have won the game anyway."

"I will not forget." Fermo grunted the words. Then whirled, spraying everyone near with ice cream, and stalked toward the far door, Breaker stumbling after him. But the funny thing was that, in the midst of all this, Tusci noticed Snide standing off to the side, holding a tray of drinks, looking into his eyes. The really funny thing was that Snide was smiling.

Part Two: The Journey

Tusci was bored. Only a few days had passed since Tusci's terrible judgment had resulted in the calamitous ruin of Natania's party, and already he was bored.

"What will Fermo do?" he asked Natania.

"Oh, he might forget about it. Yes, I know he said he wouldn't, but he is, among other things, a liar. Or he might come back here and tear my heart out and eat it, and change you into a worm and make Breaker eat you.

"And then again, he might try to do that, but fail, in which case I might subjugate him and then tear your heart out and eat it, and train Fermo to take your place. At least I wouldn't have to worry about his ability to discipline my spiders." She shook her head, smiling. "That man could discipline furniture. A couple of hours and he'd probably have those spiders dressed up in servants' clothes, serving dinner. Not nearly so flamboyantly as you served it, however, my poor little ferret."

A few more days uneventfully struggled by.

"The Mistress of the Shining Hands has retired to her room to practice a complex and dangerous form of travel. She must never be disturbed at this hour," Snide had informed Tusci, one day when he had gone looking for Natania.

Every day. Same time. And Tusci was bored. So here he was, hiding underneath her bed, in her room, waiting. *You're quite insane,* he told himself, and knew it was so — but . . .

A few moments later, moments which creaked and crawled and barely moved along, and Natania entered the room.

She wasted no time, but went directly over to a low table with a round ball of some kind of colored crystal on it, raised her arms dramatically and shouted "Ortum natar lilalami dantas." Turned the crystal one complete turn on the table, and marched directly over and opened the door to her clothes closet and went in and shut the door and there remained. Tusci knew it was her clothes closet, because he had peeked in it earlier when he had first come in here. It had been filled with gowns on glass hangers hanging on a rod. Shoes, boots, sandals — no more, no less.

But that was where she had gone, and that was where she stayed, until about an hour later she had come back out, marched over to the table, and again repeated the phrase "Ortum natar lilalami dantas." Turned the crystal ball back to its original position, and left the room.

For a while Tusci lay there underneath the bed whispering the words over and over again so that he would not forget them. Somehow he felt that it was deadly important that he remember them, so he lay there, eyes closed, concentrating for all he was worth. And it seemed to him that after a while, a strange thing happened. That the words began to stretch out and run together in his mind into one huge liquid river of a word. Then it began to repeat itself over and over, of its own accord. He knew he would never forget it, that for the rest of his life, till the day he died, it would be there somewhere deep inside his head slithering around like a snake, of its own accord.

He crawled out from under the bed, went directly over to the table, said the words and turned the crystal a complete turn, then entered Natania's clothes closet and shut the door behind him.

Except it wasn't a clothes closet. Tusci could think of a lot of words to describe it, but "clothes closet" wasn't one of them.

It was swirling mists, it was dancing light, it was changing colors, it was vast expanses of something that was always just now starting to take shape, it was living void, but it was not shoes and gowns.

Without shifting his gaze from the maelstrom, Tusci moved his left arm behind his back and gingerly explored with his fingers: the doorknob was still there. He couldn't see it when he turned and looked, but he could still feel it. It seemed to be invisible, right in the middle of nowhere. Tusci thought, *I ought to mark it in my mind so I can find it again, let's see — a little to the left in unfathomable field of just-now-forming reality. Great. How can I miss?*

Of course the only thing to do was to open the door right now, while he still had hold of it, and go back out. But then, why, why, oh why did he let go of it and walk forward into . . . into . . . ?

It was different things at different times, rising through a changing series of geometric planes, rushing into a vortex, watching light and shadow shift and play and shift and play.

Just nothing. But no, now it was a deepening darkening flood of reddish light. Shifting to yellow. Bright yellow, brighter, brighter, too bright to endure, glaring, gleaming, screaming yellow, hurting yellow.

Cool green. Shifting myriad shades of green, and now blues, dark, brighter, brighter, and now . . . stop — freeze.

A blue monkey, with lovely soft fur and bright blue eyes, reaching for a piece of gleaming yellow fruit, frozen in time and space. The ocean of green from which he emerged broke up into leaves.

Suddenly everything was moving, fluttering in a warm summer breeze. The breeze rustling the leaves, playfully ruffling the monkey's blue fur. It was alive. It was real.

It was not that Tusci could not remember who or what he was or where he had come from, it was that it never entered his mind to do so. This was it!

The monkey gestured to him, a slow, liquid movement conveying all the authority and dignity of a prince, then turned away and disappeared into the foliage.

Tusci followed, then noticed darting furry blue figures all around him, and tuned in to the chattering, screaming calls of the pack of blue monkeys.

Why was he so slow, so awkward? He could not keep up with them. The leader, Cho Cho, paused and gestured to him again, then darted off.

Tusci felt himself changing, but did not understand what he was feeling. Only the rage at being slow, awkward, left behind — he would not accept it. Never. He was always the fastest, the most nimble, and he always would be. This he demanded with all his consciousness, one-pointedly. Totally. He felt the act of will changing and reforming his body, the ecstasy, the pain. But nothing broke his concentrated furious will, until at last he moved through the trees in the form of a blue monkey, faster and freer than the rest of the tribe.

Screaming and eating fruit. The rich glowing fruit that hung from the trees and bushes in the magical forest glistening with life force. When you ate of them you felt as if you were being charged with sizzling energy, waking up and up.

Tusci was the fastest, the nimblest, the most mischievous and careless of them all. But Cho Cho was the best of them. The smartest, the sweetest, the leader. It was always Cho Cho who warned them, "Beware, a snake lurks there. Don't go out in the open. Shh, I hear a cat somewhere nearby. Don't eat that fruit, it's poison." Cho Cho was the smartest and so he cared for the rest of them, but was it because he cared that he had become so intelligent, through his selfless act of will, for the benefit of the tribe?

Yes, it was that. And Tusci knew it, but did not bother to look at it. Knew that the same act of will that through concentration had transformed him into the most swift, the most agile, had transformed Cho Cho into the caring leader of them all.

Tusci did not care. All he wanted was what he wanted. No more. No less.

They did not need to sleep here. Ceaselessly they roamed the jungle and ate of the fruit and woke up and up. Time did not pass, an instant was forever. Everything went on and on, but all encased in one single moment like a bubble. There was nothing else but now.

Once they had wandered to the edge of a clearing and Tusci saw, for the first time, through the foliage, a glimpse of something different. What was it? Vaguely he dredged up the memory from his distant past. A house.

A small cottage with a thatched roof and flowered vines growing all over it. More like a bush with a door, than a house.

Somehow it seemed to be hidden in shadows, though as far as Tusci could tell, the shadows originated from it like purple smoke seeping through the walls and roofs, vines and flowers. Something about it Tusci could not quite identify, some sensation, throbbing, sharply edged. Then suddenly he had it: fear.

Cho Cho was pulling at his arm. "Away, away," he said. "Bad place, fire witch. Away." Screaming blue figures darted through the rustling foliage like shadows of birds.

And so it went, one moment spreading without moving through time: encased in a bubble, but a bubble growing.

"No," Cho Cho shouted for the thousandth time. Tusci knew not to leave the safety of the trees and go for the berries that grew in the bushes alongside the gurgling, bubbling river. Knew it was dangerous for a monkey there. Knew he had all the fruit he could eat hanging from the heavy-laden branches of the trees. But Tusci was Tusci. What he couldn't have, he wanted most.

So now, once again ignoring the warning cries of Cho Cho, he ran (awkwardly in his blue monkey form) through the tall grass along the river's edge, ignoring the chorus from the trees, for the tribe had taken up Cho Cho's warning cry, and a steady chant of "No, no, no, no" permeated the warm, wet air.

Eating the forbidden berries, Tusci listened to the mystical chanting and coughing of the river. It reminded him of something long ago and far away. Something soft and quiet. For the first time in this eternity of jungle, his eyes closed, thoughts drifted. The river sang, babbled, and lulled, more seductive than ever. All sensations fell away.

All at once something brought Tusci out of it. Whether it was the shifting of the chorus of monkey cries from scolding to screeches of terror, or whether it was the loud droning from far away drawing nearer and louder, Tusci did not know.

The noise in the sky became a roar, and now even the earth trembled. Transfixed, Tusci sat rooted by the river and watched the frantic tribe of monkeys disappear into the green foliage like blue sparks, flaring and sizzling out. Nothing was left but the trembling of leaves. And the roar grew louder; something seemed to be brightening the edge of the sky over the trees.

And now Tusci noticed that not all of them had run away; one of the tribe had dropped from the trees and was scrambling toward him through the grass, screaming something he could not make out over the deafening roar. Then he had it. "Firebird," Cho Cho was screaming,

"Firebird. Run, run for the trees."

Then everything was obscured within light, blinding light, paralyzing light accompanied by searing heat, as the firebird fell from the skies and struck Cho Cho, and then both were gone.

For a moment Tusci was blinded, and scrambled around and around in circles in the grass, the afterimage of a giant blazing birdlike form with Cho Cho flaming in its clutches burning in his mind's eye. Then gradually his vision came back. Cho Cho, the best of them, was gone.

"You must lead the tribe now," they told him. But Tusci was not wise enough to lead, and soon he had guided them to the last place in this world they wanted to go. Screaming, they had left him all alone, as he dropped down from the trees and approached the bungalow in the clearing.

Working up his courage, he had raged up and down before the house, shouting, "Cho Cho, Cho Cho" and throwing stones and sticks which he found in the grassy clearing at the door.

Seemingly of its own accord, the door creaked open. "Welcome," a high-pitched old woman's voice said. "Do come in." Then broke into laughter which sounded a little like the cackling of a crow.

Tusci crept up to the doorway.

"Why be afraid? I've eaten. Surely you know that. You watched me. You aggressive little fool, why should you be afraid? Surely you can't expect to live long with *your* personality, can you? No, come in, come in."

Suddenly the tone changed, the voice thickened, grew more forceful, commanding. "I said, come in."

Against his will, Tusci felt himself stumble out of the light and through the doorway.

Inside, the furniture was sparse, functional: a couple of rickety chairs, an old wooden table with a sword and some candles on it. A many-colored cloak of feathers hung from a hook on one wall.

"Yes, that's it. My firebird cloak. Your instincts are quite sharp for a foolish little blue monkey. Wait a minute, what's this? A shapeshifter who doesn't even know it? Yes, I see it clearly. And I can smell it. Smell my old nemesis from the other world on you. You reek of her. Ainatan the Sorceress, or, as she calls herself out there where everything is backwards, Natania. What? You've forgotten the name? Oh, you are a foolish little blue monkey, aren't you? Here, let me help you."

The old woman held out her hand and closed her eyes and mumbled something unintelligible. Tusci felt his form stretching, twisting, popping, so suddenly that he screamed, but whether it was in pain or pleasure he did not know. Now he stood before the old woman as a man. A small, wonderfully elegant figure of a man.

"Oh, not so very different from a foolish monkey after all, are you?"

Suddenly the features of the old crone wavered like smoke or water, and for one moment the wrinkles were gone and it was the face of a young woman with clear skin and clear dark blue eyes, cold and lovely as a precious jewel. Then the features wavered and wrinkles grew like delicate spiderwebs, and the eyes seemed to shrink back into their sockets, while the nose and ears grew. She was old, oh so old, again.

Tusci blinked. "You were young and beautiful for a moment," he said.

"As are we all young and beautiful for a moment. But it is only for a moment, and then we grow old forever. I think we make far too much of it." Again she cackled like a crow.

"Cho Cho is gone," she said, rising up from the wooden chair where she had been seated. "He is part of me now. Just as you use the fruit for energy in this jungle, so have I used Cho Cho. He was the best of you. But he is gone.

"And you too will be gone soon. Won't you? Oh, you foolish monkey, why did you come here? Surely not just to offer yourself as my next meal? There must be a reason for it. No?

"Hush, let me think. He's a shapeshifter but he doesn't know it. Oh, he has many powers of which he is not yet aware. He sleeps. He dreams. A dreamy blue monkey.

"But there must be a reason for it. In the past? Let me see."

Tusci felt a strange churning sensation as if someone were stirring his thoughts in a cauldron.

"No, nothing in the past. Certainly not Cho Cho's death. Then it must be in the future. Something you know but don't know you know. Do you see?" Another loud long cackle.

"Of course you don't. But so it must be. Shall we keep it a secret, from both of us? I like that. Too little humor in the world." Another wild cackle.

"But do you know the funniest part of it all? No? Let me tell you. The funniest part is that none of it will matter at all to you if you do not live to see the future. Do you see? No? Of course not.

"Well, let me put it this way. I have eaten. Cho Cho was good. I am satiated. But I will grow hungry soon, and then I will don my cloak of fire and roam the skies in search of food.

"I have your scent, and I will not forget it. It will lead me to you wherever you are in my jungle, and I do not see how you can find your way out of it. You can't remember anything. And do you know why you can't remember anything? Because you don't concentrate enough on it while it's occurring. Do you see? Now get out of here. Run for it. I begin to hunger already. You have only a short time to live — Why don't you spend it fleeing in terror?"

Suddenly whatever power was holding him there (the old woman's concentration?) released him.

He raced out the door and into the jungle, crashing through the foliage. But it was too thick. Frantically he pulled himself up on some lower branches and began to make his way from tree to tree, not even noticing when his form shifted back into the shape of a monkey.

Once he saw his tribe; but screaming, they fled from him, as if somehow they could sense that now the firebird had his scent and he was doomed.

Once, in the midst of his wild flight, he paused for a moment; somewhere in the deepest part of his mind, something was moving, repeating itself. A word of some kind. It seemed to him that it was somehow the key to a door. The key to concentration. The key to remembering. But remembering what? Then fear rushed in and chased the word deeper. Screaming, he fled.

Screaming because the sky had begun to brighten. Because a distant drone was in the air. Because he knew instinctively that now that she had his scent, none of the shrubbery or foliage would hide him.

And now, scrambling, leaping, smashing through leaves, branches, springing from tree to tree, the sky suddenly blazed with light and heat and it was as if a flaming meteor rushed across the sky, homing in on him, to where, paralyzed with fear, he clung to a delicate network of swaying slender branches. And it was falling, falling, the deafening roar like thunder in his ears, when suddenly something plucked him up and away; he heard the firebird smashing through the trees and brush behind him, while whatever clutched him in its talons rushed away from it.

"Silence." It was Natania's voice. Then was only that silent desperate flight. Tusci could see the light gaining on them, hear the drone getting louder again, and at one point even feel the rush of heat as the firebird drew closer and closer, shrieking, and gained even more, and then finally fell behind.

And later, in the land that was no land, of constantly shifting planes and angles, where they changed back into their human forms, he from that of a monkey and Natania from the form of a giant fierce eagle with coal-black shining feathers, still Natania held her fingers to her lips, as if to say, "Quiet, we're not out of this yet, you oaf." Then she opened up the door in empty space, and the two of them walked through it into her bedroom, just like that.

Smiling sweetly she turned to him. "Oh, you are such a fool," she said. And moved her hands and lips as though struggling to say something else but not quite able to come up with it. Then she walked back and forth in front of Tusci, pacing from wall to wall like a cat, while Tusci, uncertain of what to do, just stood and watched.

Finally, she stopped her pacing and pulled up in front of him. "Such an incredible fool," she said, this time with a tinge of sorrow, or so it seemed to Tusci. Shook her head and walked out of the room. Her room! Leaving him there alone. Tusci remembered to re-turn the crystal on the table and to speak the magic words before he too went out and closed the door.

Part Three: A Different Kind of Party

A few days later and things had gone back to normal. Well — as normal as you could expect if you were living on a cloud and training spiders.

Natania had not forbidden Tusci to enter the magic closet; but on the other hand, she had also not forbidden Tusci to jump off the cloud they lived upon and see how it would feel to impact the earth, and he was as likely to do one as he was the other, which is to say, not very.

She had, however, demanded a full account of his experiences in the magical forest, which she had alluded to as "that other plane of existence." When Tusci had mentioned memorizing the magic words but forgetting them later in the forest when he was fleeing for his life, she had smiled.

"How did you memorize them?" she had asked him.

"I concentrated on them until I remembered."

Natania had smiled again, and shook her head.

"Wrong! You concentrated on them until you almost remembered."

"They were magic words, weren't they?" Tusci was irritated, because it seemed to him that she never told him anything.

"It depends upon the degree you concentrate on them," Natania said. "Magic is concentration."

Tusci looked puzzled. And now Natania actually laughed. A lovely light pure high sound, like bubbles from that river. "You've never concentrated that much, is all."

So Tusci stayed away from the sorceress's closet and worked with the spiders. And somehow, his journey onto "that other plane" had affected him, because he definitely had more control over the spiders. He was not aware of doing anything differently; he still gave them orders out loud, and certainly wasn't aware of doing anything "telepathic." But the spiders obeyed, to some rudimentary degree. They came when he called. They stayed when he told them to.

Natania had said to him in a very exasperated tone of voice, "By the Goddess, what an incredible fool you are. I told you that the spiders could only be controlled by telepathy. You are gaining control of them. I would think that even you could deduce what that means."

"But I don't . . ."

"That's how you tell, Tusci."

Now, in the farthest part of the garden, near the edge of the cloud, Tusci called out, "Come here, Mimi" to his favorite spider. Mimi bounced up and down like a huge hairy ball and let out a high-pitched squeaking noise, then darted at Tusci in what appeared to be a threatening manner. All of the other spiders followed, except for the biggest one of all, the one Tusci had named Timba. Timba had never yet paid any attention to anything Tusci had said.

The rush of leaping hairy creatures had frightened Tusci at first, and now it only frightened him slightly less. But they stopped just short of pouncing on him. They always did. And now they hopped up and down before him, squealing excitedly.

The thing about Mimi was that Tusci felt, or imagined he felt, something emanating from her. Something warm and pleasant. Affection? Was this telepathy? *Go away,* he thought. But the spiders, including Mimi, did not go away from him. "Go away," he said out loud. They all hopped and scrambled away until he shouted "Stop."

Were the words an aid to his concentration? he wondered. He was so absorbed in his "work" that he did not even notice when they came, or how they came. The sky had darkened, but that was not unusual here.

Suddenly he was aware of applause, and he looked over to see two figures dressed in black, seated on the low wall that marked the edges of the cloud. It was Breaker and someone else, a thin man holding a strange device of some sort. Beside them, three more shadows appeared on the white stone surface of the wall, rapidly darkening and gathering density, somehow taking on human form. And then one of the shadows moved, and Tusci could see now that it wasn't really a shadow at all: it was Fermo, the magician.

"Well, well, just the man I wanted to see," Fermo said, but he didn't sound all that pleased.

It's an invasion, Tusci realized, and turned toward Natania's castle.

"Oh, don't move," Fermo said. "Freeze. Like stone. Like ice. Now."

Tusci found that he could not move.

"Let me have him, please." That was Breaker's voice. "Let me have him without his weapons."

"But of course," Fermo said, "I wouldn't soil my hands on him. But don't waste too much time playing with him. Just torture him a little and get inside the castle; I may have need of you, though I doubt it. You and Jacques stay here, and I suggest you let Jacques cripple him first — no point in taking any chances, am I not right? Filmore, Gartch, you two come with me."

Tusci felt his sword being drawn out of its sheath, hands patting him down, finding one dagger, another, and finally even a third.

"Zounds, this guy's a veritable arsenal," yet another voice said. And now Fermo and two more men walked past him, one of them carrying his daggers, and headed toward the castle. Fermo stopped and waved his hand. "I almost forgot — you may move now." And then they walked on casually.

And it was true, he could move. Tusci turned toward the two men seated on the wall. But one of them was standing facing him, the one holding the contraption.

"Know what that is?" Breaker said.

Tusci could see that it was some kind of automatic bow and arrow, probably invented in a later time period than his own.

"It's a crossbow. Show him how it works, Jacques."

Jacques smiled an evil smile and aimed the device and squeezed a trigger. There was a loud sharp clicking noise and Tusci tracked the bolt, which sped through the air almost too fast to see and buried itself in Mimi's furry black body. And now, for the first time, Tusci experienced, without a doubt, telepathy — the pain, the fear, the falling away into nothing. It was more like feeling than thinking, he realized.

And now the thought-feeling surged out of him, *Run away.* And the rest of the spiders ran for it, without him having to say anything out loud. Even Timba obeyed him. *It's such a hard way to learn,* he realized. He was aware his cheeks were wet. Over a damn spider.

"Hey isn't that cute, Jacques, I swear he's crying. Scared to death, my little ferret? That's what she calls him. Oh oh, here he comes — watch out, Jacques. Snake tells me he's so-o-o fast. Maybe he's faster than a crossbow bolt. Shall we see? Yes, why don't we?"

"You just killed my favorite spider," Tusci said, walking calmly toward the man who was holding the crossbow. "And now you're going to pay for it."

Breaker taunted, "Oh really? What's a spider worth these days? I hope we can afford it."

"Both your lives," Tusci said. Still calmly advancing.

"Don't let him get too close," Breaker said, sounding a little worried for the first time.

Tusci smiled, concentrating on the bolt with everything now. He stopped and held his right hand out to the side, as if in greeting, and waited.

"Shoot," Breaker said, and at the same time, Jacques released the bolt, which streaked through the air, drawing a straight line from Jacques' shoulder to Tusci's heart, too fast to see, wasn't it? Surely too fast for any man to do anything about.

Tusci plucked the bolt out of the air. Breaker shouted. Jacques cursed, or started to, and was frantically scrambling to draw back the bowstring, when Tusci, who seemed to Jacques to be moving so fast that he was flying, was suddenly right there striking the crossbow up and out of the way and slamming something into Jacques' chest, and suddenly he needed air so badly, but couldn't breathe and his chest was on fire, and everything whirled and he fell, and as he was falling he realized what it was, that Tusci had jammed his own crossbow bolt into his chest, and he wasn't going to live through this one. Then he was down, and Tusci was hopping over him to get to Breaker. And it was now that Jacques did the greatest thing that he had ever done in his whole life. Now, when it was too late — or was it? He could have just died, should have just dissolved into that sea of pain like a piece of dirt thrown into the ocean. Should have; after all, he only had a few seconds left, and what did he owe Breaker? Or that evil bastard Fermo? Nothing; he had worked with them and for them, out of fear. What a waste. His whole life had been a waste, until now. And strangely, magically even, he realized all of this in one blindingly clear instant. The last instant. And he also realized that he had only one moment left to do something not out of fear, but something of his own. And so, with this last surge of strength, in the fading of the light, he grabbed hold of Tusci's ankles as the man went over him, and jerked up and sideways with such intensity that he brought Tusci down, because, damn it, he was in a fight, and he intended to fight to the very end.

And then, falling through the air, in that fading light, which was to be the last thing Jacques would ever see, Tusci twisted around, freeing one foot; and kicking out with infernal accuracy and speed, drove the crossbow spike the rest of the way into Jacques' chest and rolled the rest of the way over to land on his hands and knees. And Jacques would never know that, at least, what he had done with his last moment had slowed Tusci down just enough for Breaker to get hold of him. And now it was up to the Bone Breaker to make good his boast.

Inside the castle, Fermo, flanked by his two henchmen, stood staring into the eyes of Natania of the Shining Hands, whose servants huddled in a frightened group behind her. Scarcely the length of two tall men's bodies lay between the two sorcerers, and they

stood in the center of an immense room. The same one, in fact, where they had dined, drunk, and quarreled, such a short time ago. The room was not so festively decorated now, however, and anyone could quite easily sense that this was to be something entirely different from any form of celebration.

"I still don't understand what it is that you want. Alas, I fear your magic has driven you insane, Fermo. — All too common an occurrence," she added.

Fermo snapped: "Why, let me tell you what I want. It's all so simple. I want you dead. All of your servants dead. All of your friends dead. Anyone you have ever known dead. Your castle smashed into ruins. The ruins obscured by a black cloud, and the cloud removed from my consciousness, and then whatever memories I have of you and everything related to your existence blotted out forever. Rejoice! I have the means at my disposal to accomplish this."

"But you are insane, Fermo. Totally gone over, like bad cheese. Can't you see that? You have nothing to gain here. You're quite mad."

"Mad," Fermo muttered, obviously astonished. "Why, you silly twit, of course I'm mad. Are you just now realizing that? By the Goddess of Darkness, I'm mad, mad, and even more mad than mad. That's why I'm stronger than the rest of you. Logic has no grip on me. Nor am I a slave to the consequences of my actions; I shall probably feel terrible once this is over, but who cares? My very madness is my magic. And nothing can interfere with it. Surely you see that? After all, that's why the rest of you put up with me, it was hardly my great charm and wit."

"Yes," Natania said in a sad low tone of voice, "of course that's it. We're all to blame. We should have seen it coming. But we used you, and now . . ."

"And now the time for talk is over."

Fermo began to concentrate; you could see it: the straining muscles in his face, the mouth moving, mumbling but saying nothing, the vacant stare. Tendrils of black smoke poured out of him and crawled across the space which separated the two.

Both groups of servants backed off to opposite sides of the room, flattened up against the walls, to await the outcome. No one among them harbored the notion of attacking a sorcerer in the act of performing his or her art, and they understood that there was little to be gained from attacking each other; this would all be settled, forever, soon enough.

While outside, in the garden, the man called Breaker wandered aimlessly about, hugging in his massive arms, like a lover, the inert body of Tusci. And like a lover, all the time he was whispering sweet nothings in Tusci's ear. Nothings like: "How do you like being mangled, crushed, smashed to bits by the mighty grip of the Breaker, eh, little one?"

Or: "When I am finished with you I will twist off your head — ah yes, I can do it, little one, I've done it before. And throw it from the clouds. Who knows, maybe it will fall from the skies and bash someone's brains out down below. Ah, yes, I would like that. 'Look out! It's raining heads,' they would cry out."

Even after Jacques had tripped Tusci up, Breaker had only barely managed to catch hold of one of Tusci's ankles, had almost missed him completely; but no, he'd just snagged it. True, the little ferret, or swine, or whatever they called him, had managed to twist around somehow and kick Breaker flush in the face. In fact, his nose was broken from that kick. Hard to believe one so small could kick so hard, it must have a lot to do with speed, more than he'd have thought.

Still, what was a broken nose to Breaker? Nothing much. And he'd hung on and dragged Tusci in, and fallen on him and clamped his arms around him, and now he had him in his famous bear hug and he was slowly and happily crushing him to death.

"Feeling sad, little one? It's almost over now, I'm going to crush you until your chest and ribs cave in and mangle your heart and lungs. Then I'm going to crush you some more. Then I'm going to . . ."

What was the little guy doing, anyhow? Had he given in, or was it a trick? He knew Tusci wasn't unconscious, yet the man wasn't struggling at all. Just lying there limp in Breaker's big arms, eyes tightly shut. Looked like he was dead, or passed out, or . . . concentrating?

Suddenly Breaker felt a sharp severe pain in his right shoulder, and he twisted his head around to see a terrifying sight. A hairy black spider the size of a dog had jumped up and was biting him on the shoulder.

And at that moment he must have slackened his hold, because suddenly the limp body of Tusci had come alive and somehow slipped out of his grip. He slapped frantically at the spider, which jumped off and ran away.

"The poison," he whispered, voice hoarse with fear.

"It'll take a few minutes," Tusci said. "But don't worry, you won't live to feel it."

And Breaker was thinking, *I've still got him, I've crushed him half to death, he's still weak, if I can just get to him and get ahold of him again in time. Just not let him get away.*

But to his final amazement Tusci did not try to get away, but rushed straight at him, and suddenly he was caught in a whirlwind of punches and kicks coming at him from impossible weird angles, and striking him so hard and crisply and often that it was like being struck with rocks; yes, like being stoned by a mob of do-gooders for all your sins. You held up your arms and tried to block, but the stones kept slipping in and catching you and dazing you; and then, reaching out

his arm trying to grab something, anything, Breaker felt rather than saw the slender shadow sliding along his outstretched arm and disappearing from his view.

Felt the choke hold clamp shut like some kind of metal collar or chain around his neck, and heard the voice behind his left shoulder whispering in his ear:

"Now who's going to crush who?"

A few moments later, and Breaker lay dead. And Tusci, snatching up a dagger which had fallen out of Breaker's belt, was running for the castle.

When Tusci rushed into the main room, he had to stop for a moment to try to comprehend just what he was seeing here. Natania was lying flat on the floor, encased in some kind of bubble of light. She appeared to be limp and unconscious, but apparently was not, because the bubble of light seemed to be protecting her from a cloud of some kind of black force emanating from the gaunt figure of Fermo, which seemed to be slowly but systematically eating away at the light.

The servants and retainers were all lined up on opposite sides of the room, watching. Except, seeing Tusci entering the scene had evidently inspired one of them to action, for one of the two men who had accompanied Fermo and left Tusci to his fate with Breaker and Jacques, a tall slender devilish-looking man with a nasty thin moustache, sprinted across the room and grabbed Snide and held a knife to his throat. "Make a move and I'll kill Snide," the man shouted. Snide snorted, and managed to look a trifle indignant.

"Go ahead," Tusci said, and ignoring them, rushed across the room and without hesitation buried his dagger in Fermo's chest.

The magician made no effort to avoid or block the blow, but now the steady stream of black smoke pouring out of his hands toward Natania lessened, and then stopped altogether. He turned his head slowly and looked down at the dagger jutting from his chest, and then up into Tusci's eyes. Then he did something that caused Tusci's skin to crawl: he smiled. Actually smiled. In fact, it was the happiest Tusci had ever seen him.

"What?" he said. "You've managed to kill Jacques and Breaker? Ah well, there's more where they came from. That's nothing. But do you actually dare to attack me? You do! With a dagger? A mere dagger? Tell me, my little ferret, what does it feel like to stab a magician?"

And now Tusci was aware of it. It was subtle at first, a cold sensation pouring through the handle of the knife and into his right hand and wrist, subtle, but growing stronger, biting cold, but not a cold of this world, or any other, a cold from beyond. He tried to let loose of it.

"Oh, no," Fermo said, "You can't let go of it. It's yours forever."

Frantically Tusci jerked it free of Fermo's chest and tried to throw it from him, but could not let go, and the cold kept pouring through it, seeping in from some unseen dimension faster and faster.

He began to shake, wrapping his arms around himself; now bits and pieces of black empty nothingness flashed briefly into his thought stream, causing him to sway and close his eyes.

"Oh, yes," Fermo said. "It will keep pouring into you, you can't stop it, you can't get rid of it. In a short while you will go mad, like me; only unlike me, you will die. You see, *I* visited *it,* whereas *it* is visiting *you.*

"But enough of that, where was I?"

He turned back to Natania, who now was standing up.

"No," she said, "I do not like it like this." She took up a stance rather like that of a gypsy dancer, with hands over her head, fingers spread. "It shall be thus."

And now the black cloud of force simply disappeared, and strangely enough the lighting in the room had changed to many different-colored sourceless glowing areas, as it had been the night of the party. She had not only dispersed the black cloud, Tusci realized, but had redecorated the room. *Women!* he thought, shivering, irritated for some unknown reason.

"Women!" Fermo snorted sarcastically. "Now I shall just have to start over again. But don't worry, I'll get the job done."

Shaking and stumbling, still twitching spasmodically in an effort to throw away the knife, Tusci searched for and with great effort spotted the door out of the room. So far away. But then, everything was so cold and far away. The door seemed to be at the far end of a long, dark tunnel. Tusci headed for it.

"I warn you, I'll kill Snide if you move," the man holding Snide shouted.

"Stop talking about it and do it, will you?" Tusci grumbled as he ran out of the room, if you could call that staggering gait running, and slammed the door behind him.

Out of the room and down the hall and down the stairs, as if in a dream, a cold, distant dream. *Where am I going?* he wondered. Blanking out, flashing in, until he found himself in Natania's room. Somehow he managed to turn the crystal ball, chant the magic mantram, and stumble into the closet that wasn't a closet.

Through the rich green of the shrubbery, a patch of bright clear sweet blue. He must be lying on his back, looking up, because . . . But how could this be? A white horse, wading through the blue sky, hooves splashing it up like water, waves of air in its wake, bubbling white frothy foam churned up by its hooves. Tusci closed his eyes and once again descended into the icy cold darkness. Then snapped his eyes open. *I'm dying,* he realized. *In fact, I'm almost dead. I've got to fight it. But why? Why should I fight it?*

"Because fighting is what you are," a clear, sweet, familiar voice said. Cho Cho's lovely blue-furred face floated down to him. He felt the cool touch of lips to his cheeks.

"You're the best of us," Tusci mumbled.

Cho Cho chuckled, a bubbling sound. "Yes," he said. "But you're the best and the worst of us, Tusci. Both at once. Do you see?"

"But Cho Cho, you're dead. Aren't you dead?"

"Like all of us, Tusci, sometimes alive and sometimes dead. Over and over like sparks from a fire, or a constantly recurring idea.

"But you must wake up, Tusci. And fight it. Hold it off. Don't rush things. Whenever you die, it will always be too soon."

Tusci had a vague awareness of being helped to struggle up on the back of a white stallion, a creature so blazing with the force of life that all of the time it snorted and pranced and could not bear to stand still, even for an instant. Some of this force must have seeped through into Tusci's consciousness, because suddenly he woke up a notch, to find himself clinging automatically to the horse's back with his knees, Cho Cho struggling to hold him from behind, while the horse crashed through shrubbery and then green trembling leaves and the branches of trees, until they were pounding into the pure clear sky, cutting straight through and dropping down into the clearing.

"Now it's up to you," Cho Cho said, pushing him toward the door of the little bungalow.

"What should I do?" Tusci asked him. "Why am I here?"

"I don't know," Cho Cho said. "Remember, I'm dead." And faded and disappeared.

The white horse screamed and turned and smashed back into the shrubbery, and it too was gone. And since Tusci did not know what to do, he opened the door and with the last of his strength went through it.

"Well, well, well," the old woman cackled, "company. You fool, why did you come back? You are doomed now. What is it you want?"

Tusci raised his hand with the knife in it and moaned.

"Are you mad? You must be mad. You dare to threaten me with a dagger? Throw it down. I command you to throw it down!"

Tusci tried to throw the knife on the floor of the hut, but could not. "No," he mumbled.

"What?" she shouted. "You dare defy me? Give me that knife — now. Put it in my hand."

She held out her withered old clawlike hand. Tusci tried to put the cursed dagger in it, but he could not let go of it.

"What is this?" the witch shouted in fury. "You resist my will? Put that knife here in my hand. I command you, by my all-powerful will. Now let go of it."

"No."

"Let go."

"No."

Her eyes closed, jaw muscles clenched with effort. "You will let go. Now."

Tusci felt his hand ripped open by some invisible force and the knife fall out of it into her withered claw, which snapped closed around it. She cackled hideously in glee. "Told you."

The relief was immediate. Although his body was still weak, and spasmodically wracked with shivering, his vision cleared up and his thoughts became instantly more coherent. He even managed a faint smile.

"Now that you've got it," he said, "how do you like it?"

One of her huge blue-black eyes widened like an owl's; the other remained a mere slit.

"What?" she hissed. "What is this?"

127

She tried to throw the dagger away, but couldn't.

Now it was Tusci who laughed.

"A magic spell," she whispered, more to herself than to Tusci. "A primitive one, but strong. Is this Natania's work?"

Suddenly she moaned and shivered.

"What's the matter?" Tusci taunted her. "Too cold in here for your old blood?"

"You silly, silly fool. There isn't any magic spell the old one can't break. This isn't anything more to me than a mere nuisance. A few moments more and I'll break free of it, and when I do, I'll . . . I'll . . ." Abruptly she clamped her thin lips together and shut up.

"You'll go over to the wall, put on your magic cloak, change into the firebird, and come after me." Tusci finished the thought for her, then he staggered over to the wall and took down the feathered cloak. It shivered in his hands like a living creature.

"No," she croaked, as he settled it over his shoulders and tied it on. There was a moment's delay, and then all at once a surge of power flooded through him, and his vision cleared and cleared beyond the point of clear, penetrated the walls of the little bungalow, spreading out and rushing to encompass everything everywhere.

Tusci screamed and closed his eyes, no difference.

"I'm burning up," he groaned.

"You fool, no mortal body can contain such forces without being destroyed. You will be dead in a few moments. Your only hope is to wait here for me to . . ."

Tusci smashed through the wall and flashed across the sky, screaming "Aah, I'm burning up, I'm burning up. The awful dizzy heights — aah."

Everything was rushing at him, other worlds, other planes, the living, the dead, the void, the formation and destruction of each moment. He simply could not stand it all at once, and he could not do anything about it.

And he had no idea what pinpoint in all this mishmash of eternity he was rushing to. There were too many possibilities, too many dreams, stars, worlds, planes of existence: he was lost.

But down deep inside him, something moved. Had always been moving. A word. Gradually, more and more, he was learning to reach for it. He shouted it aloud.

"Ortum natar lilalami dantas."

Then he shouted it again. And again. He began to zero in on the one point in time and space he needed to be. He shouted it again.

And now he was chanting it steadily, mumbling it to himself, as he rushed down the hallway, up the stairs, and flashed across the big room toward the two figures locked in a death struggle in the center. Magicians, both of them. Not ordinary mortals, these. Magicians. Magical people. Wielders of terrifying forces. But then, so was he.

Fermo looked up just in time to see the room light up and that source of light and heat flashing directly toward him like a blazing destructive comet.

Then Tusci was upon him and unimaginable forces sizzled through his brain and body, causing him to twitch spasmodically, like a frog with a pin stuck in it. The black cloud was simply eaten up by light and absorbed and gone. But there was even more light. More and more. Fermo tried to fight it. But why fight it? Wasn't this what he had always wanted? Yes! This was it! And Fermo opened, screaming, into the light, and flashed away.

Tusci was distantly aware that someone had removed the cloak. Everything was distant now. He strained to see who it was. Natania, of course, it would have to be Natania. And Fermo? Yes, the empty husk lay at his feet. He swayed, started to collapse.

"Not yet," Natania said. "Tusci, wake up!" She slapped him viciously.

"Can't," Tusci groaned.

"You have to." She slapped him again. "What is it?"

"Before you pass out, you have to save Snide."

"What?" Tusci groaned. "You save Snide."

"I can't. My magical energy is all used up. I can't direct it. I might harm everyone in the room. It has to be you."

"Damn it, woman, I can't even see him. Where is he? Snide, you groveling lackey, where are you?" Everything blurred and swayed.

"I warn you, one move from anyone and I'll cut his throat," a voice called out of the fog.

Tusci remembered. He peered at the twin fuzzy figures: man with knife at Snide's throat.

"Knife," he mumbled.

Natania pressed a blade into his hand.

"Blast it — dagger, not kitchen knife."

"It's all I can find," Natania said.

He took the awkward blade of the carving knife between thumb and fingers of right hand and raised it over his shoulder, turned sideways, pointing his left hand toward the two fuzzy figures — which was which?

"I warn you, one move and I'll slice his throat."

"What?" Tusci shouted.

The fool repeated his threat, and Tusci pointed at one of the fuzzy figures, the one which had just spoken. Then suddenly Tusci's loose upper body snapped forward and the knife arced through the air, whirling end over end.

"I doubt that," Tusci mumbled.

One of the figures stumbled backwards and went down, with a knife handle and part of a blade protruding from its eye socket.

"Usually you get a blade into their brain and their arms and legs fly wide open, instead of . . . instead of . . ." Tusci passed out.

Dreamed troubled dreams. Once he woke back in his own bed to see a furry black ball purring like a cat, at his feet. Timba? Or was that a dream too?

"Well, finally you're awake. We all thought surely you were going to die, which is why I had you save Snide first. What would I have done without both you and Snide at the same time? Right, Snide?"

"As always, My Lady."

Tusci groaned. "Are you sure I'm not dead?"

"By all the Gods and Goddesses you should be, or at least mad. Surely no human nervous system could endure that overload without . . . Well, are you crazy?"

"Of course! Everyone I know is crazy except one. And he's only a little blue monkey. A dead little blue monkey."

And when she had left, and Snide had stayed behind to "tidy up," Tusci had said to him, "I saved your miserable life, right, Snide?"

"I suppose so," Snide said down his long slender nose.

"You owe me a favor, isn't that right?"

"How nice of you to remind me."

"Tell me, Snide, do you know what the words 'Ortum natar lilalami dantas' mean?"

"Of course. This language is the mystical tongue of the ancient ones. The language of power and enlightenment. Spoken long before this world was even formed. In fact, some say . . ."

"Snide," Tusci cut in, "what does it mean?"

"Let me see, it means: 'What is that jackass doing hiding under my bed?' or something very like that." Snide smiled smugly and went out, and closed the door. Ω

The Classic Horrors: It, drawn by Allen Koszowski "It walked in the woods.
"It was never born. It existed. Under the pine needles the fires burn, deep and smokeless in the mold. In heat and darkness and decay there is growth. . . . It grew, but it was not alive."
— Theodore Sturgeon's "It."

130

www.ingramcontent.com/pod-product-compliance
Lightning Source LLC
Chambersburg PA
CBHW070602180626
46817CB00005B/1949